THE REDEEMING AFFAIR

A novel by C.B. Lane

Acknowledgements

I am indebted to the following people for their help and support:

To my husband, Lewis, thank you for tolerating my obsession over this, supporting me throughout it all and helping me with the editing.

To everyone at Publishing Push, including Alex, Patrick and Christine, thank you all for making my dream a reality.

And last but definitely not least, thank you to my mum, for always being my rock andmy support and helping me believe that I can do anything if I put my mind to it.

Contents

Chapter One

I stand in a dark alleyway and check my wristwatch; just past midnight, all is quiet in New York City. I rub my hands together in an attempt to keep warm against the bitter cold. I walk out of the alleyway, my feet splashing in a few puddles as I cross the recently rain-drenched street. I can smell the steam evaporating from the nearby manholes as I reach the opposite sidewalk and stand outside Preston's Jewelers. This is the place that my boss, Tobias, wants me to break into and wipe clean. I don't want to do this, but it's the only way I can escape from this life. I've never broken into anything before. Tobias has always kept me in the background of his crimes, so I have no idea what I'm doing or how to get in. I case the building closely while pulling my leather gloves from my pocket and slipping them on. Smashing the window is definitely a no-go. I examine the door. It looks like I could pick the lock. I stoop down, remove the satchel from my back and take a look inside. *Damn. No tools. Why didn't he pack any?* I sit on the wet ground and raise my face up to the cloudy night sky. *Who am I kidding? I can't do this.* Losing all faith in Tobias, I stand, leave the empty satchel on the ground and begin to walk away. I turn to take one last look at the store. I know that my mind is made up. I won't do it. Tobias may

1

come after me, knowing I haven't fulfilled my end of the bargain. I have no ties in this city, so I could run far away from here, where Tobias will never find me. I want to get as far away from my unwanted criminal life as I can, but I have no clue how. All of a sudden, I'm stopped in my tracks, deafened by the sound of police sirens closing in around me. I panic, my pulse racing. I need to decide what I should do. *Run or stay?* Before I can decide, police cars surround me; officers emerge from their vehicles swiftly and draw their weapons at me.

"Freeze! Hands behind your head," one officer orders.

I nervously comply, slowly raising my hands and placing them on the back of my head. A female officer who is tall, lean and slim steps forward. She holsters her gun and grabs me firmly by the upper arm. She slams me against the hood of her police car with a loud bang, incapacitating me.

"You're under arrest," she barks.

She pulls my hands down to my back and snaps the handcuffs tightly around my wrists.

"On what charge?" I ask, my voice muffled.

I attempt to look up at her, but she has the right side of my face firmly pinned against the car.

"We had a tip off that this store was going to be hit by a 6ft male in his late twenties with long brown hair. Seems to fit your appearance," she snaps.

I chance another look at her, still to no avail. *Who tipped off the police?* I have only been in New York for a couple of months and I don't know a soul in this city, apart from - *Tobias...* He set me up. *Why would he do that?*

"Move," the female cop demands, interrupting my thoughts as she stands me back up.

She begins reading me my rights as I am loaded into the back of her car.

I wake up late on Saturday morning. Yesterday, I was thrown in here. I've been processed, fingerprinted and photographed. Now, I await my trial hearing. I sit up, my head and neck still throbbing from the firm hand of that hot-headed policewoman. I look around my cell; three cold grey walls, eroded from the leaking pipes above, and a façade of steel bars surround me. It's cold, wet and bleak and it smells of rot. The noise of the neighboring prisoners and the prison guards shouting back at one another unsettles me further. I rub my face vigorously and rake my fingers through my scruffy hair. I get up from my hard mattress, walk over to the opposite wall of my cell and scribble another number onto the tally. Day two, not very long, but God knows how long I'm going to be here. I make my way back to the bed and sit on the edge. I sigh deeply and flop back onto the uncomfortable mattress. Feeling more alone than I've ever felt, I close my eyes and drift back to where my life went so wrong.

I play with my old train set on the smelly, dirty living room floor. Dad is doing what he always does, sitting at the dining room table, smoking something that smells horrible and ignoring me completely. Mom is sitting on the couch, staring blindly at the wall. I get up from the dusty floor and sit beside her.

"Come and play with me," I beg.

"Not now, runt," Mom replies glumly.

She brushes me off and lies back on the couch, forcing me to jump back to my feet. I look at her, worried and desperate to help.

"What's wrong, Mom?" I ask gently.

She says nothing as she folds her forearm over her eyes and continues to lie still.

"Leave her alone!" Dad shouts, startling both me and Mom.

He jumps to his feet and storms towards me, looking furious.

"Please... not again," Mom pleads.

"Shut up," Dad barks.

Grabbing my arm painfully, he forcefully drags me into my bedroom.

"Now stay in here out of the way."

He tosses me towards the bed.

"Stupid kid," he mutters.

He slams the door shut, rattling the furniture. I stare at the closed door and start trembling, feeling cold, afraid and alone. I wrap my arms around myself protectively as I walk slowly to the corner of my room and sit, weeping to myself softly.

I'm startled awake by a loud clanging noise coming from the bars. I turn over on the bed and see a burly prison guard with a baton in his hand staring angrily at me.

"Exercise in ten minutes, Flint," he barks at me.

I hate when I'm called by my surname; it reminds me too much of my parents.

"Why can't you call me Mark? That is my name, isn't it?" I growl back.

The guard sneers at me through the bars.

"Exercise in ten minutes, *Flint*," he repeats, emphasizing my last name before he walks away without a backward glance.

Christ. What a dick. I pace my cell, trying to calm myself down, but fail miserably. I pull at my hair with frustration and grumble angrily, falling short of screaming. I slam my hands onto the rim of the scabby sink and grip it tightly, my head lowered as I breathe deeply, further restraining my temper. I glance up slowly to face the cracked mirror and scowl at the dirty, unkempt man looking back at me. He has light brown hair, unwashed and uncut, so it flops over his eyes, muzzle unshaven and dirty blue eyes, dark circles under them through lack of sleep, staring angrily back at me. I try to push the greasy forelock of hair off my forehead so it doesn't obscure my vision before I hear my prison door slide open. I look over my shoulder and watch the burly prison guard who berated me earlier step into my cell, brandishing a pair of handcuffs.

"Exercise time," he states gruffly.

I fold my arms like an angry teenager as we glower at each other.

"I'm not in the mood," I protest.

His brow knits together as his dark brown eyes blaze into me.

"You're coming with me," he demands.

Stepping forward, he grabs my arms firmly. I attempt to shrug him off, but he grips me tighter and snaps the cuffs around my wrists. Tugging my arm sharply, I am forcibly led out of my cell and down the corridor, past the other cells.

"You're a *friendly* guy," I quip.

He shoots me a furious look.

"Shut up, Flint!" he booms.

Though I am shaken by his loud voice, I smile briefly, for the first time in months, satisfied with my little joke. We approach what looks like a large cage. Mr. 'Burly Guard' unlocks the door and leads me into a dreary indoor gym, releases me from my cuffs and shoves me forward.

"I'll be back in thirty minutes," he informs me before turning to leave, slamming the door shut.

I walk around the gym alone. I'm not in the mood to exercise or to risk going near the other prisoners, so I sit on the bench in the corner, isolating myself as I continue to reminisce.

I wake in the middle of the night, feeling suddenly unsettled.

"Mom," I call out, but there is no reply.

"Mom!" I try again, louder this time, but still no response.

I climb out of bed and make my way to Mom and Dad's bedroom, pushing the door open. *They're not in here.* I look in every room of the apartment, but no one is home and I'm terrified. *What's happened to them? When will they be back? Will they ever come back? What will happen to me?* I sit on the couch, hunch myself into a ball and start wailing. My parents have left me. Dad always said he didn't want me and he would leave one day with Mom. He was right, and they have left. They're gone. I stay curled up on the couch, tears pouring down my face as I wait, hoping that they might come back.

The sun is starting to rise and I'm still alone, though my tears are starting to subside. I hear a jingle of keys and the door handle being turned. I leap up expectantly. They're back; I knew they would be. The front door swings open, but it's not my parents at all. Grandma walks in, followed closely by a police officer. I look at the policeman nervously and hunch back onto the couch. Grandma steps closer and holds out her arms to me.

"Mark, what are you doing here all alone? My poor little man. Come home with me." She offers her hand which I take hesitantly as I look up at her warm, gentle face.

I look towards the police officer who continues to watch me closely.

"Grandma, where's my mom and dad?" I whisper.

Grandma looks solemn and turns to the officer who copies her expression.

"They've gone away for a while, son. Your grandma will take care of you now," he says softly with a slightly reassuring smile.

Grandma cuddles me in her warm embrace and I snuggle in close.

"Let's go home," she says quietly.

She places her arm around my shoulders and slowly leads me outside into the balmy mid-morning air, towards her car.

I never put any thought into just how much that day hurt. I still have so many unanswered questions from my childhood. *Where did my parents go? Why did they leave their six-year-old son alone? Why didn't they care about me?* I always tried to ask Grandma these questions, but whenever my parents were brought up, she would always change the subject. I'm sure she was just trying to spare me the pain of the truth. She always went out of her way to keep me happy and give me the best future possible. *Boy. I blew that to hell.* I wipe my eyes, trying to erase my memory of the pain that is my childhood. I get up from the bench and walk around the gym, but my thoughts continue to gnaw at me painfully. I know in myself that my parents are dead, either through suicide or something to do with Dad's drug or gambling debts. I shake my head, desperate to clear these dark thoughts and look up at the over-large florescent lights, constantly flickering above me, and then divert my gaze to the prison guards patrolling the perimeter, watching us all attentively. My mood continues to take a nose dive, as bleak and dark as my confines. Grandma always thought I would grow up to be a good man; she did her best, but I've failed her.

"Time's up," a guard shouts from outside the cage.

Prison guards start filing in to collect all the inmates. As before, the jerk guard approaches me while unstrapping the handcuffs from his belt. Not feeling in the mood to annoy him any further, I turn my back to him and let him snap the cuffs back on, then he leads me back to my dark and miserable cell.

I lie on my uncomfortable bed, staring up at the ceiling for what feels like hours. I'm paranoid by the slightest sound; rats are scrambling around in the darkness underneath me. I hold on tightly to the thin, smelly blanket and try to get some sleep, not wanting my day to last any longer.

I've just turned seventeen. It's been a week since Grandma passed away, I've been lost without her. I find myself homeless, sitting and sleeping in the doorway of Chicago

Union Station and stealing food from the local market. I can't help remembering what Grandma said to me when I got in trouble at school for stealing from the cafeteria.

"Be careful how you choose to live your life, Mark. One day, your bad deeds will catch up with you."

I'm trying to be a good person. She wouldn't want me to go down the same bad path as my father, her son, but right now, I have no choice but to steal to survive. I have been begging passers-by for spare change for the last couple of hours, taking a break from thievery, but they walk by, ignoring me. In the distance, I notice a man who is tall and stocky with a broad face, piercing green eyes and black slicked-back hair, wearing a finely tailored pinstripe suit walking towards me. He stops in front of me and grins down.

"Spare change?" I ask, holding out my hand hopefully.

His grin broadens.

"You want some money, kid? Follow me."

I stare at him, stunned by his offer. I scramble to my feet, intrigued.

"Who are you?" I ask.

The stranger says nothing, he just continues grinning. He turns on his heel and strides casually away from me. I stand frozen to the spot, suspicious and confused, but my desperation and intrigue gets the better of me and I race after him. I follow through the station, barging my way through the bustling crowds of businessmen and tourists, struggling to match his pace, but I finally catch up and stand beside him on the busy train platform. He turns to face me suddenly and I stare back. He nods, seemingly satisfied at me.

"Who are you?" I try again.

"All in good time."

A train rumbles to a halt and people start to pile in and out of the carriages.

"After you," he gestures politely with his hand.

I look around and take a cautious step forward before pausing.

"It's okay," the stranger says reassuringly.

I climb onto the train, followed closely by him. The doors slide shut and the train pulls away from the platform. We take a seat in the first booth that we find, sitting opposite each other. The stranger stares out the window as we both ride the rest of the journey in an uncomfortable silence. I feel increasingly uneasy around this man, which is further aggravated by the long journey. *Why are you following this man, Mark? Grandma taught you better than this.*

After a train transfer and a bus ride, we have now arrived in a neighborhood called Riverdale. It is close to eleven at night and I'm freezing. We walk down the quiet streets as he continues to remain silent. I contemplate running from this strange man, but we arrive at an old dilapidated house. It's a large red brick building with a couple of cars parked on the driveway.

"This way," he prompts, finally turning to look at me.

I look into his green eyes and follow him inside. We walk down a long, narrow corridor which is drab and very cold, then he suddenly turns left and opens another door.

"Through here, kid." He holds the door open for me.

I step in through the door. I widen my eyes in surprise at the surroundings, contrasting what the exterior of the household suggested. This once would have been a much-loved family home. It's warm with a welcome, fully-lit fireplace, a well-stocked bar and two green leather couches. There are several other young men sitting around the fireplace, who all look up and smile at us both. The stranger walks away from me, shrugs out of his pinstripe jacket and tosses it onto one of the couches before he greets the other men warmly.

"Excuse me, who are you?" I attempt once more, interrupting his conversation with another man.

I am feeling more afraid of him, because he refuses to introduce himself. He turns and produces a warm smile.

"Take a seat, kid."

He kicks a chair towards me. I grab it hastily and take a seat next to the welcoming fireplace beside the stranger.

"Forgive me for not answering your question sooner. My name is Mr. O'Malley, and these are my friends."

He gestures with his hand at the others who continue to smile and greet me.

"Now, may I ask who you are?"

He leans in, closer to me and I swallow nervously.

"My name is Mark Flint."

Mr. O'Malley smiles again, his eyes crinkling in the corners.

"Pleased to meet you, Mark Flint."

He offers his outstretched hand and I shake it.

"What is a kid of your age doing out on the streets all alone? Where are your parents?" he asks.

"My parents abandoned me a long time ago. I used to live with my grandma, but she passed away last week."

Mr. O'Malley's smile fades.

"Oh. I'm so sorry to hear that. Do you know when the funeral is?"

"It was yesterday. I didn't go," I choke, holding back tears.

Mr. O'Malley cocks his head to one side and looks momentarily confused.

"My grandma was born in Wisconsin. Her final wish was to be buried back up there with her late husband, my grandpa. I had no way of getting up that far."

He nods, seeming to understand.

"Don't worry, Mark. You will be safe with me. My boys and I will take care of you from now on."

For the first time since my grandma died, I feel safe, and at home.

"Thank you, Mr. O'Malley."

He smiles warmly.

"Please. Call me Tobias."

I'm abruptly woken by the sound of my cell door opening.

"Time for your interview, Mark," a female voice states calmly. There's a familiar ring to her voice.

She referred to me by my first name. Strange. I sit up in bed and see a young, fair-skinned police officer standing in the doorway. *Is this the same officer that arrested me?* I squint at the policewoman's name tag under her badge. It reads: *Clarke*. I look directly at her.

"You arrested me?" I ask, but feel utterly ridiculous. *What a stupid question!*

"Yes, I did," Officer Clarke states proudly, chuckling slightly.

"Good memory," she continues as she smiles at me.

This is the first time I have seen her properly without the flashes of blue and red from the police cars obscuring my view, and I can't help myself. I'm staring at her, in awe of how pretty she is and how infectious her chuckle sounds, despite how firm-handed she was with me on the day of my arrest.

She has a kind face with a slender jawline, full lips and a straight nose. She has warm hazel eyes that bore into me and mahogany hair which glints in the light above us. It is tied tightly in a bun with a couple of loose tendrils hanging loose down either side of her face. No one has smiled at me like that in a long time. I can see kindness and sympathy in her eyes and I warm to her immediately, totally forgetting about our first encounter. She continues to regard me, but then her smile slowly melts away and is replaced with a more focused expression etched on her lovely face.

"Are you coming?"

I jump off the bed and step towards her a bit too eagerly.

"Y-Yes, of course, Officer Clarke- I mean, ma'am- I mean- I'm sorry. I don't mean to stare."

Her smile returns as she walks around me and snaps the cuffs gently on my wrists.

"Let's go," she says.

She pulls my arm lightly and leads me out of my cell.

Officer Clarke and I enter an interview room where another officer is already sitting at the solitary metal table. He's lean and tall and appears to be in his late thirties. I look at his name tag: *Benson.*

"Thank you, Rachael. Take a seat, Mr. Flint," Benson says calmly.

Rachael. A beautiful name, for a beautiful woman. I shake my head to clear my abrupt inappropriate thoughts and sit in the lone metal chair while Benson and Rachael sit opposite me. Rachael sets up the voice recorder quickly, then presses the record button.

"Interview commencing on November 6th 2016 at 8:25 am. Interviewee is Mark Flint. The interview is being conducted by Officer Rachael Clarke and Detective Greg Benson of the 17th precinct," Rachael states clearly into the recorder.

She lifts her delicate head and turns her gaze at me. For the first time since I was arrested, I feel nervous around her.

"Can you tell me what you were doing outside Preston's Jewelers on November 4th 2016 at ten past midnight, Mr. Flint?" Detective Benson asks the first question.

I swallow, unsure how to respond, but decide wisely to opt for honesty.

"I was on a job for my boss," I state simply.

Rachael and Benson stare at each other, then she looks back at me.

"Could you tell us about your boss, Mr. Flint?" Rachael asks sternly.

"I can't say," I lie, with a slight shrug.

"Mr. Flint, we know who your boss is. If you don't divulge any further information about him, we will charge you further, as an accessory to his crimes," Rachael threatens, in an authoritative manner, her perfect brow narrowing.

Shit. They know. She knows, but how? I look down at my orange jumpsuit and pick at an invisible piece of lint on my knee.

"You were wearing a dark suit, similar to what your boss normally wears and if that wasn't enough proof, you also had a red carnation pinned to your chest, like the other members of his organization."

Rachael answers my unspoken question and continues to press me for an answer.

She is being *very* intense, her hazel eyes wide with determination. I suck in a breath and turn to look at Benson, who is also glaring at me, his fingers steepled in front of his mouth. I face Rachael.

"Tobias O'Malley. He sent me to the jewelers."

I take a large exhale, relieved to finally have it out.

"Tobias O'Malley," Detective Benson reiterates.

"He is on the most wanted list across eight states with the FBI, DEA and CIA all after him. He's wanted for a number of serious crimes including kidnapping, extortion, racketeering, forgery, battery, rape, trafficking and murder," he continues, raising his fingers after each felony that he recites, all the while, staring at me sharply.

Wow. This is new. I never realized just how dangerous and sought-after Tobias was when I worked for him. I saw him kill a man a few weeks ago, but I never thought he committed all these other felonies.

"I didn't know," I admit, hanging my head and feeling utterly ashamed of myself.

Rachael leans across the table, closer to me, her badge catching the light.

"You didn't know? You were part of a very dangerous gang. How did you *not* know?"

She is furious now.

"I was never part of the criminal activities. I wasn't even aware of them until a few years ago. I was always kept on the sidelines," I attempt desperately.

She sits back in her chair, resting her forehead against the index and middle fingers on her right hand. She looks back at me after a couple of seconds.

"You're lying," she scorns.

I'm astonished at her menacing tone.

"I'm not. I swear."

Rachael takes a deep breath and looks towards Benson.

"Where is he hiding?" Benson asks.

I think hard but know I can't give them a definitive answer.

"I'm not sure. He moves location all the time, but I last saw him in the Bronx, where he gave me the job assignment."

I'm nervously clutching onto the side of the table.

"Where in the Bronx did you meet him?" Benson continues.

"It was in a park. Let me think, um, Barretto Point Park, I think?" I stammer.

Rachael lets out another long sigh as Detective Benson strokes his chin, seemingly deep in thought.

"We'll check it out," Rachael says to Benson.

"Thank you, Mr. Flint. That is all we have for now, so we will end the interview. Time is now 8:40 am," Benson states.

Rachael leans over and presses the stop button on the recorder.

"I'll take him back," Rachael says.

She stands and walks around the table towards me.

"On your feet, Mr. Flint."

She pulls me up and leads me out of the room.

"What happens next?" I ask, testing her bad mood.

"Not sure yet. We will have to see what the court chooses to do. What you have told us is very serious. You had better hope you don't get charged as an accessory to O'Malley's crimes."

I feel more nervous than ever.

"I didn't know the extent of Tobias' crimes. I didn't even perform any of his dirty jobs. I was just his bar boy."

Rachael holds her hand up to silence me.

"Just - save your words for tomorrow," she says, exasperated.

"Tomorrow?"

"Yes. You will be taken to court tomorrow morning at 10 am by myself and my colleague, Officer Bailey."

She opens the door to my cell, removes the cuffs and pushes me in, slamming the door shut behind me. I turn and run quickly to the bars just as she starts to walk away.

"Wait, Rachael," I call.

She turns slowly and glares at me.

"*Officer Clarke*," she corrects angrily.

"Sorry. Officer Clarke, please. You have to believe me."

Her expression softens and she blinks a couple of times; she looks lost in thought momentarily. After a few seconds, which feels more like minutes, she finally replies,

"I believe you."

Then she turns and walks away, leaving me alone with my thoughts. *She believes me.*

Chapter Two

I have no idea what the time is, but it's pitch black in here. I have been tossing and turning for hours. I don't know what's wrong with me. I can't stop thinking about... *Rachael Clarke.* Her bright hazel eyes draw me in every time. She really is *very* pretty. I may even say... beautiful. She was stern towards me during the interview, but I can tell she has warmth and kindness in her too. I consider the thought that maybe we could... *No, that's crazy. You're clutching at straws, Mark. We come from two different backgrounds; I'm a criminal and she's part of the police force. It just wouldn't work.* I sit upright, still deep in thought. Maybe if I could *convince* Rachael that I'm a changed man, that I'm no longer a criminal. When I'm released or *if* I'm released, I will change my life around for the better and attempt to get close to her. I may not strike her as the honest type, especially after that disastrous interview earlier, but afterwards, she said she believed me. Maybe it was just to shut me up. I don't know. One thing I am sure of is that I have always wanted to lead a good, honest life. I won't be a failure like my parents were. I finally drift off to sleep, hoping that my plans of redemption will come to pass.

I'm in the darkness; there is no light and I can't move. I'm trapped, shackled to a wall. I try to scream for help, but no one hears me. I can't even hear my own pleas, which terrifies me as I struggle harder. The walls are closing in around me and the darkness is getting denser. In the distance, I hear a sinister, disturbing laugh. I hear footsteps, but I see no one, until I'm blinded by a flash of lightning and I see *him* for a split second. Tobias stands in front of me, grinning wickedly and I screw my eyes shut, angered and terrified of him. He grabs my face in his firm grip.

"Well. In trouble again," he sneers arrogantly in the darkness as his fingers dig into my skin painfully.

"*No...*" I try to scream.

He merely laughs wickedly again, his foul smell invading my senses. Suddenly, he vanishes. I can no longer see or hear him; his sharp fingernails are no longer cutting into me. I open my eyes to look around desperately and in the outer periphery of my vision, I see an angelic beam of light. The shackles disappear from my wrists and I make my way towards the light. A woman walks forward. It's Rachael. She stands in front of me, smiling and dressed in white. She reaches out and deftly strokes my cheek with her smooth palm, soothing my earlier terror, her eyes shining into mine with affection. Rachael is my light and she's going to pull me out of the darkness.

"Mark," she says softly, as she places her delicate hand in mine.

I try to answer, but I still have no words.

"Mark," she repeats, sounding more desperate, replacing her warm gaze with a more haunted expression.

I wake suddenly, drenched in sweat. *What the hell was that about? My dreams are getting out of hand.* I look over, and there she stands in the doorway of my cell - Rachael.

"Finally. I've been calling you for the last few minutes. You were really out cold."

She stares at me, bewildered. I sit up in bed, embarrassed to have kept her waiting.

"Sorry. What time is it?"

I rub my eyes as the dream melts away into memory. She looks down at her wristwatch.

"It's 9:15. We need to leave for court soon."

She has my dark charcoal suit draped over her arm which she rests at the foot of my bed.

"I'll leave it here. Hurry up, get changed. I'll be back to collect you in ten minutes."

I nod gently at her as she makes her exit.

"Thank you," I call.

She glances over her shoulder and nods back at me. I pick up the suit and without any more thought, I hurriedly get changed, with a little ray of hope. Today, I may be free.

I'm ready to go, dressed in my suit and hair combed away from my face. I pace my cell impatiently, wondering what my life will be like if I am set free today. *What will I do with myself? Where will I go? Will it be with her?* I shake off the unbidden thought once again. I don't have a shot with her, we live very different lives. I sit in the corner and place my head in my hands at this depressing thought. I hear footsteps striding towards me and I peek up expectantly. I hear a jingle of keys, then Rachael appears in my view. She unlocks the door and breezes in.

"Time to go," she announces nonchalantly.

I scramble to my feet as she steps closer. She takes my arm firmly, escorts me through the jail before emerging outside and leading me towards her patrol car. The air is cold and bitter, not unusual for mid-fall. The leaves on the trees have turned orange and red, but only a few remain. I am loaded into the back of the police car and notice another female officer. She appears to be African American with long black hair, which is also tied up, similar to Rachael's. She is sitting in the driver's seat, drumming the steering wheel with her long, thin fingers impatiently. This must be Officer Bailey. I vaguely recall seeing her on the day I was arrested. Rachael climbs into the front passenger seat and catches me staring at Officer Bailey. I look at my rough, chapped hands, embarrassed.

"This is my friend and colleague, Officer Bailey. I believe I mentioned her to you yesterday," she explains kindly.

I look up quickly, smiling at Rachael first, before drawing my attention to Officer Bailey.

"Morning," I try to greet her warmly.

She glances at me in the rear-view mirror, nods once and grunts her greeting, her dark brown eyes focusing shrewdly on me. She starts the engine and pulls out into the busy mid-morning New York traffic. I ride in the back of the police car in silence. Officer Bailey gives me the occasional glance, but Rachael continues to stare ahead throughout the journey.

We arrive at the New York State Supreme Court. Officer Bailey parks up before Rachael steps out and opens the back door wide to help me climb out. I look at the building; it has stone pillars at the top of a wide flight of stairs, and above the pillars, it reads: *The true administration of justice is the firmest pillar of good government.* I feel sick to the bottom of my stomach, but I am distracted by Rachael taking my left arm and Bailey taking my right, as they both lead me up the stairs and past the pillars. There's a revolving door at the entrance, but we avoid it. Instead, they take me through the door on the right. We are now inside; a security guard who sits at a desk, reading a newspaper, glances up. He smiles warmly towards the officers but shoots me a disapproving look. He discards his newspaper and stands up.

"Name, please," he asks.

"Mark Flint," Rachael announces.

He checks his computer screen quickly, then looks at us again.

"You're just down the hall. On the left," he instructs.

Rachael and Bailey lead me a little further, then let me go.

"You need to walk through the magnetometer," the guard orders to me.

I step through slowly as the two officers skirt around it and wait for me on the other side. I'm not surprised to know the magnet-o-'whatever' remains silent. Rachael and Bailey get hold of me again and proceed to escort me along the marble corridor. Our footsteps click and echo off the immaculate marble pillars that stand around us. I glance at Rachael, but she doesn't look back at me; she remains stone-faced and stares ahead. I am led through another door on the left and find myself in a small courtroom. I look at the clock that hangs neatly on the wall behind the judge's bench.

It reads 9:50; we are ten minutes early. Rachael and Officer Bailey put me into a wooden chair behind a small table at the front of the room, then they retreat and stand in the corner, watching me closely. I nervously try to comb my scruffy hair with my fingers so that it looks more presentable, but I fail miserably and give up. My stomach continues to twist painfully with nerves, so I distract myself by looking around the courtroom. I observe the old paintings on the wood-paneled walls, and the American flag hoisted proudly in the corner. The courtroom starts to fill with a few members of the public. It's daunting and irritates me slightly. *Couldn't this have been a bit more private?*

A bailiff strides in and announces, "All rise for Justice Miller."

The audience stands promptly and I quickly get to my feet. Justice Miller emerges from a door on the left side of the room and makes his way to the bench. He appears to be in his early sixties, with short grey hair and wearing glasses, outfitted in black judge's robes and carrying a folder, which, I assume, holds my records. Justice Miller takes his seat, looks directly at me, then looks ahead towards the audience.

"You may all be seated," Justice Miller announces.

Everyone sits back down, including myself. Justice Miller redirects his stern, no-nonsense stare back to me.

"Mr. Flint, you are here today on the accusation of attempted robbery of Preston's Jewelers on November 4th 2016. How do you plead?" Justice Miller asks sternly.

I stand up and look directly at him.

"Your Honor, I plead not guilty. I was set up," I state clearly, trying to remain calm.

I hear gasps, a few chuckles and hushed, incoherent murmurs behind me. Justice Miller removes his glasses and rubs his forehead in apparent frustration, then places his glasses back on and looks me squarely in the eye.

"Set up? By whom, may I ask, Mr. Flint?"

I swallow nervously as he continues to scrutinize me.

"Tobias O'Malley," I answer.

The murmurs behind me get louder, still incoherent, albeit more alert than amused.

"Order," Justice Miller bellows to the audience, slamming his gavel against the wooden block to silence them, before turning his attention back to me.

"Tobias O'Malley?" he repeats.

"He is one of the most wanted men in the United States of America. *He* sent you?"

I square my shoulders to appear more confident.

"Yes, Your Honor. Before he gave me the job, I told him that I wanted out, that I'd had enough. That's why I believe he betrayed me," I state calmly.

Justice Miller regards me carefully. After taking a quick sip of my water, I continue.

"I started to hate the man he was becoming. He used to be a good man when he first took me in at the age of seventeen, but he became mad with power."

Justice Miller looks towards Rachael and Officer Bailey.

"Who, may I ask, caught Mr. Flint?"

The two officers turn to face each other quickly before turning their attention back to him.

"Officer Clarke, Your Honor," Officer Bailey announces.

"Officer Clarke, would you take to the stand please?" he asks firmly.

"Yes, Your Honor."

Rachael makes her way towards the stand without a glance in my direction.

"Officer Clarke, would you please explain the events that took place on the date of the incident?" Justice Miller asks.

"We received an anonymous call at 11:40 pm, telling us that there was someone acting suspiciously around the jewelers. Myself and my colleagues followed the tip and made our way there immediately. As soon as we arrived, we found Mr. Flint checking the store for a way in. He had a satchel with him, but he dropped it and started to walk away. We detained Mr. Flint after that," Rachael explains.

"Did you retrieve the discarded satchel?" Justice Miller asks.

"Yes, Your Honor. It was empty. Mr. Flint didn't get inside the building. We spoke to the owner of the store, but he didn't report any lost property or damage."

Justice Miller looks at me again, but I look away, feeling ashamed of myself.

"Mr. Flint, anything else you wish to add?"

"No, sir," I respond.

"Thank you, ladies and gentlemen. I will take a brief recess while I review all of Mr. Flint's records. I will make my ruling in the next few hours."

He slams the gavel, then stands up and walks through the same door he had entered through earlier. Officer Bailey and Rachael are by my side again in moments and like before, they take an arm each.

"What now?" I hiss nervously towards Rachael.

"You will be taken to the 17th precinct and placed in a holding cell until Justice Miller is ready with his decision," she explains.

We leave the courtroom, walk back up the marble corridor and emerge onto the street. As we make our way back to the car, a thought hits me. *How did they know I was looking for a way in?* They didn't arrive until I started walking away. I need to know.

"How did you know that I was scoping the jewelers?" I look directly at Rachael.

She glances at me quickly, opens her mouth to respond, but Officer Bailey cuts in.

"We were watching you. We moved in when you started to walk away."

I tear my gaze away from Rachael and glance at Bailey, who seems thoroughly pleased with herself, radiating arrogance. My face falls, as does my mood as they load me back into the car and we head into Midtown Manhattan, towards the 17th precinct.

I pace the small detention cell of the precinct back and forth, ignoring a couple of comatose drunks, snoring loudly on the bench beside me. As the minutes tick by slowly, I'm becoming more fidgety and annoyed, and the foul stench emitting from the drunks irritates me further. I'm not feeling as positive for my freedom as I was this morning. Justice Miller was intense and no-nonsense towards me, but I hope that Rachael's testimony will be enough to set me free and that I won't have to wait long to find out. Whatever happens next, it sure as hell won't involve Tobias O'Malley. He took me in, I followed him and my so-called 'brothers' for years, and all they did was stab me in the back. I glance across the precinct and catch Rachael's eye. She is sitting at her desk, looking back and forth between her computer monitor and her paperwork. She glances in my direction, catches me staring as I smile at her, but she hastily looks back down without returning my smile and resumes her task. More and more, I think Rachael just wants to avoid me, and even though the thought depresses me, she is merely focused on her job. I sit on the bench beside the comatose drunkard, but his smell nauseates me. *Guess the floor will have to do.* I sit on the cold ground, rest my arms on my bent-up knees and place my head in between them. Maybe she's already seeing someone. Maybe she's married. My gut twists painfully, but I've never noticed a ring on her, which reassures me a little. I glance up when I hear footsteps. I stand and walk to the bars and see Officer Bailey approaching the cell, but there's no sign of Rachael. Maybe she's still at her desk. I peek over, but she's gone, further to my displeasure. Officer Bailey unclips the keys and unlocks the door.

"Time to head back to court," she says.

"Is Rach- erm- I mean, Officer Clarke coming with us?"

Officer Bailey scowls at me, obviously not as sympathetic towards me as her colleague.

"She is. She's bringing the car round."

She eyes me suspiciously, then looks back over her shoulder, before she swiftly turns to look back at me.

"You stay away from Rachael. She is a good woman and a valued friend. She doesn't need trouble in her life," she hisses violently.

I look at her, shocked by her outburst.

"I don't know what you're talking about," I quietly deny.

"Don't lie to me. You think I didn't notice you staring at her every five seconds? I'm not an idiot, Mr. Flint. Don't you become one either."

I'm being threatened by this woman. *How dare she?* I am suddenly overcome with rage, but I manage to suppress it.

"That's for me to decide, not you," I snap back quietly, my anger about to boil over at her audacity.

Officer Bailey purses her lips while her eyes bore into me, but she says nothing more. Instead, she grabs my arm firmly and quickly walks me outside towards the waiting police car where Rachael is sat in the driver's seat.

"What took so long?" Rachael directs towards Bailey, who places me into the back of the car.

"Sorry. Me and Mark were just having a little talk. Right, Mark?"

They both glance at me, waiting for my answer. I want to say that Bailey threatened me, but I know that Rachael won't believe me.

"Sure. She put me in my place," I respond coolly, my temper held back.

Rachael stares at me for a couple of seconds in contemplation, before glancing towards Bailey, who is now in the front passenger seat beside her.

"Okay. Well, we'd better go. We'll be late," Rachael informs.

We pull away into the busy Midtown traffic and back towards the court while I stew silently over Bailey's tenacious and unorderly tirade towards me.

The traffic is heavy, but we arrive back at New York State Supreme Court. Rachael and Bailey lead me back into the same room that I was in this morning. I sit in the same chair and glance up at the clock; it's now five past four in the afternoon. An audience starts to enter, just as eager as I am to know about my fate.

"All rise for Justice Miller," the bailiff announces again.

Justice Miller emerges and sits behind the bench. Like he did before, he glances at me, then looks away and clears his throat loudly.

"I have reviewed all the information that's been given to me by the NYPD, the testimonies provided by Officer Clarke and Mr. Flint, and I have just spoken with the Chief of Police on Mr. Flint's case. I have made my final decision."

My heart is in my throat. *This is it.* Hopefully, my bad decisions don't cost me years behind bars.

"I cannot condone your affiliation with Mr. O'Malley, Mr. Flint. However, there is no evidence of stolen property from the crime scene, and for that matter, no crime had been committed by you."

I'm not sure how to feel. The courtroom is in silence as we await the verdict. Justice Miller continues.

"Furthermore, I have found no criminal connections linking Mr. Flint to Mr. O'Malley, so I find no reason to charge Mr. Flint as an accessory to Mr. O'Malley's appalling crimes, nor for the felony he has been accused of. I hereby declare Mr. Flint cleared of all charges."

I'm shocked and relieved all at once. There are gasps and whispers of disbelief coming from behind me. Justice Miller turns his gaze at me.

"Mr. Flint, you are free to go. Case dismissed."

Justice Miller slams his gavel and leaves without another word as the audience behind me start to disperse.

I take a huge lungful of air and collapse into the back of my chair out of shock. I'm free. I can't believe my luck. Rachael appears by my side and helps me to my feet. She looks as gob smacked as me. I stand, but feel weak at the knees as I try to comprehend what's just happened. Barely recomposing myself, I look at Rachael, who smiles back at me.

"Congratulations, Mr. Flint."

I beam at her.

"Thank you... So, what happens now?"

"You just need to do one more thing. You need to come back with us to collect your personal effects, then you're free to go," she explains.

"Okay," I say simply.

Rachael and Bailey escort me out of the courthouse where I am greeted by the bitter but welcoming air. Rachael opens the back of the police car for me and I climb in.

I shift from foot to foot impatiently at the back of a long queue inside the Metropolitan Correctional Centre. Several other released inmates collect their belongings and leave the facility one-by-one. Rachael is in the corner by the entrance with her arms folded, waiting to escort me from the building. Finally, I'm at the desk, where a middle-aged woman looks up from her computer screen expectantly.

"Name and prison number, please," she asks in a hoarse voice.

"Flint, Mark. Prison number..."

Shit. I can't remember. Moments later, Rachael is by my side.

"Prison number, 5160," she answers for me.

Rachael peeks out the corner of her eye as I flash her a grateful smile. The middle-aged woman types furiously into the computer, then she rolls her chair back, stands up and disappears behind a side door.

"Thanks. Guess I'm not the only one with a good memory," I quip.

Rachael chuckles and looks at me.

"Guess not."

I chuckle with her and get a sudden urge to chance asking her out, but then the secretary returns carrying a brown paper envelope and reaches her hand into it.

"Okay. One cell phone, one wallet, one wristwatch and one photograph."

She places each item on the desk as she presents them to me. I hastily place the photo in my wallet and pocket it, followed by my cell and wristwatch.

"Thank you," I say.

Rachael takes my arm and escorts me outside into the, now, freezing dusk. She lets me go and I turn to face her.

"Good luck to you, Mark. Stay out of trouble."

"I intend to."

Rachael smiles, then she begins to walk back towards her police car with Bailey still at the wheel. I take a long breath. *This is your only shot, Mark.*

"Rachael," I call, and start to run after her.

She stops and turns around, arching her brow. I realize I didn't address her appropriately and I think she's going to chastise me, but she responds.

"Yes. What is it?"

I stop in front of her.

"I just wanted to ask... if... you would come out for a drink with me sometime?"

I feel a little silly and know what her answer is going to be. Her mouth falls open, about to speak before she peeks towards the police car. I find myself mirroring her and we both see Officer Bailey glaring at us, mainly me. I'm taken by surprise as Rachael grabs my hand and leads me around the corner of the building, out of sight.

"Mark, I'm sorry. I'm going to have to refuse," she says simply.

My mood slips.

"Why?" I feel crestfallen.

"Isn't it obvious? I'm a cop and you're-" She stops, unable to finish her sentence.

"-a criminal?" I complete it for her.

She looks at me, then lowers her head.

"I'm sorry. It just wouldn't work," she whispers.

She walks away from me, but I grab her hand gently and she turns to look at me.

"Are you seeing someone?" I ask, dreading her answer. *Detective Benson, maybe?*

"No, I'm not. Just let go, Mark," she says quietly, but authoritatively.

I do as I'm told and release her, feeling stupid and out of order, but slightly relieved, though it's short-lived.

"Is it because I once worked for O'Malley? Is *that* what puts you off?" I ask gently, but desperate to know.

"I have to go." Rachael is insistent, but I try one last time.

"Just… think about it. Please?"

She glances up at the sky and takes a deep breath before looking back at me. The light of the streetlamps illuminates her beautiful face. She smiles sweetly, her alluring hazel eyes sparkling.

"I'll think about it."

She turns and proceeds to walk back to her car. This time, I let her go. I watch her and the last thing I see is her shiny mahogany hair as she climbs delicately into the car. She is driven away into the hectic evening traffic and then she's gone. I commit her to memory, just in case I never see her again, wondering if that little talk was merely our final goodbye.

Chapter Three

I walk the streets of Manhattan with no real destination. A thought hits me, causing me to stop suddenly in my tracks. I ignore the angry pedestrians who push and shove their way past me. Rachael's right, we are two very different people. It's not what she said, but that's what she implied. I don't think she'll take my offer, that possibility was dashed when she found out about my history with Tobias. I'll just have to forget about her. Officer Bailey said that Rachael doesn't need trouble like me in her life. She's better off without me. I look down at the wilted red carnation still pinned to my breast pocket. Angered by what it represents, I rip it from my jacket and throw it to the ground, cutting my ties with Tobias.

This is your fault, O'Malley. No, it's mine. I never should have trusted him. I sigh heavily, my breath condensed by the cold air. With a heavy heart, I continue walking, pulling my jacket tighter around myself to brace against the bitter wind.

I roam Manhattan mindlessly, admiring the city's beauty. I observe the Empire State Building, immerse myself with the atmospheric and brightly lit posters and logos in Times Square and eventually find myself outside the Rockefeller Center. I sit on the wall, exhausted, and put my head in my hands, not knowing what to do. I am alone on the streets, again. I need to find a job and a place to stay. I contemplate my options, but I don't know where to begin. Suddenly, I feel strangely unsettled as if someone is watching me. *Tobias?* I look nervously over my shoulder and see a man, roughly my age who is tall and broad-shouldered with black spiky hair and blue eyes, wearing a denim jacket and black jeans, observing me. He looks strangely familiar, but I can't place him. I turn my full body to get a better look, then it hits me. Trent. We were school buddies together back in Chicago. I leap to my feet as we observe each other.

"Mark?" he asks, astonished.

"Hey, Trent."

He takes a step closer, then a large, all-tooth grin spreads across his face. He barrels towards me and swamps me in a bear hug.

"Good to see you again, man!" Trent exclaims excitedly.

I rasp, barely able to breathe due to his enthusiastic grasp around me. Thankfully, he lets go, and I take a grateful breath.

"What are you doing here?" he asks.

I grimace and his smile fades.

"Long story. How about you? I haven't seen you in over twelve years," I continue, now smiling.

Trent dropped out of school when he was sixteen and he moved here shortly afterwards with his mom. Grandma and I only visited them here once.

"I'm doing okay. I've had my ups and downs, but... life's good. How's your grandma? You know, Mom really misses her."

My face falls and I look down at my feet sadly. Trent seems to get the message as I hear him gasp.

"Oh… I see. I'm sorry, man."

He pats me on the shoulder sympathetically.

"It was a long time ago. She died suddenly from complications of the heart. Sorry I didn't tell you sooner."

He nods understandably, but I quickly change the subject.

"How's your mom? Grandma and I used to get on so well with her."

"She's doing okay. She occasionally gets emotional about Dad. I still miss him too."

He looks momentarily woeful, but he quickly regains his composure and smiles again.

"Where you staying?" he asks.

I shrug my shoulders.

"Nowhere. I'm probably going to sleep here on the street."

Trent's expression changes, this time looking befuddled. He shakes his head disapprovingly.

"No, you're not. I've got an apartment not far from here. You can stay with me," he offers.

I feel grateful for his generosity. Before I can respond, he puts his arm around my shoulders and we start making our way to his apartment.

"Thank you," I smile.

"No problem," he smiles back.

It's amazing that this morning, I felt cold, scared and alone. Now, I feel safe and cared for. In a brief moment, thoughts of Rachael, Tobias and my troubled childhood disappear, quiet for now.

Trent and I have been walking for a short while, not nearly for as long as I was walking earlier. He talks to me about his life since he moved here and continues to press me for answers on what I've been up to, but I refuse to tell him. Eventually, he gives up. We cross 8th Avenue and walk into a residential area on West 47th Street. Trent stops outside an old, white apartment block. He fishes his keys from his jacket pocket, unlocks the door and we both enter. We walk up a couple of flights of stairs before we reach Trent's front door which he also unlocks.

"Come in," he says, pushing the door open for me to enter first.

I walk inside and stand in the middle of his living room. His apartment is a lot nicer than I thought it would be. It's a sparsely decorated studio with wooden floors, a couple of beige couches, a shelving unit piled high with CDs and DVDs, a TV mounted onto the brick chimney breast and a table with a couple of blue chairs near the integrated kitchen. Trent enters, takes off his denim jacket and carelessly drops it onto the floor beside the front door.

"Nice place," I compliment, continuing to observe my surroundings.

Trent sits down on the couch and grins at me.

"It's not much, but it's comfy," he replies modestly. Trent's always been modest.

I sit down beside him and take off my worn shoes, relieving my sore feet.

"Want a drink or anything?" Trent asks.

"I'd love one. Whatever you're having."

He stands and strolls casually into the kitchen, opens the fridge and pulls out two bottles of Bud Light. *Budweiser? Good, I could do with some booze.* He walks back over to me and hands me a bottle. I take it gratefully and have a large sip. It's delicious and quenches my thirst instantly. Trent takes a sip of his own, then turns on the couch to face me.

"I'm so happy to see you again, Mark. We haven't spoken since you and your grandma visited twelve years ago. I've really missed you. Why didn't you call?"

There's hurt etched on his face, his lips forming a hard line. I finally surrender and tell him everything, about those wasted years with Tobias and about my recent jail time.

I have been rambling for nearly two hours, and when I'm finished, Trent is staring at me, wide-eyed and open-mouthed. The silence stretches between us and I begin to worry that it was a mistake to have told him everything, but he finally responds.

"So… You were in jail for something this… Tobias guy wanted you to do?" he asks, dumbfounded.

"Yeah. I can't make any more sense out of it than you can. Tobias and I had a falling out days before the job."

"Why? You told me you guys were close."

"We used to be. Tobias was like a father to me. He took me in like he did a lot of other young misfits, but he was molding us into terrible, misguided people. I realized I didn't want that future, so that's why I left."

Trent continues to stare. I take another long draft from my beer and continue.

"I explained to him that I wanted to start making an honest living, that I wasn't prepared to condone his actions anymore. I told him that I was leaving his crew first thing in the morning. He was furious, accused me of being 'ungrateful' for everything he did for me and further accused me of treachery. I apologized, then he softened a little and told me to do this 'one last thing'. Reluctantly, I agreed, but when I got there, the police were waiting."

"Shit. That's messed up," Trent curses under his breath.

"I know. A female officer named Rachael Clarke arrested me and took me to jail where I was kept over the weekend. I was only set free this afternoon."

Trent is quiet again and turns away from me for a few seconds. He seems lost in thought before he looks back at me.

"Thanks for telling me, Mark. I'm sorry that happened to you, but at least you're free. You can live your life. What do you intend to do with yourself?"

I think about his question for a moment.

"Honestly, I don't really know right now, Trent. For now, I have you, and I have a crush on Rachael. I intend to win her round."

The words tumble out of my mouth before I realize what I have said. Trent blinks at me, then crows with laughter.

"Wait, Rachael Clarke? The woman that arrested you? You certainly took time to commit *her* to memory."

I'm hurt by this.

"I'm glad you find me so amusing, Trent," I respond sarcastically.

Like a teenager, I stomp into the kitchen, away from Trent's laughter and pour the rest of my beer down the sink. He stops laughing and glares at me.

"Jeez, sorry. I don't mean to laugh. It just sounds ridiculous," he says.

I think about it briefly.

"Maybe a little. Look, it's late and I'm tired. I haven't slept well for some time. Where will I be sleeping?"

Trent stands, walks to the opposite couch and pulls it out into a bed. He strolls across the lounge and enters another room, presumably *his* room. He returns with some spare sheets, a duvet and pillows. He swiftly makes the bed, then glances at me as I continue to stand in the kitchen.

"Thank you for letting me stay," I smile.

"You're welcome."

I sit on the edge of the bed as Trent starts sniffing.

"What's that smell?" he says, his nose crinkling.

I sniff with him, lowering my head to my armpit, then realize. I absolutely reek.

"It's me. I haven't had a decent shower for a while," I confess.

He takes a step away from me and shakes his head disapprovingly.

"Towels are in the cupboard, just there."

He points to a door next to his bedroom. He walks past the kitchen and I follow after him. He opens another door down the hallway.

"Bathroom is here. You're welcome to use my body wash and shampoo. If you're going to win this girl over, you need a wash."

I smile at him and walk back to the cupboard he just pointed out. I open it and help myself to a white fluffy towel.

This is the softest I've ever had. I return to the bathroom, where Trent is still standing.

"Thank you," I say gratefully.

He grins widely and retreats back to his bedroom. I walk into the calming sky-blue bathroom and close the door, locking it behind me. The smell is fragrant and it's steamy in here; Trent must have had a shower recently. I strip out of my suit, the only clean clothes I own, and jump into the shower cubicle, sliding the door shut behind me. I twist the red-rimmed faucet and hot water cascades from the large shower head onto my face. I turn the temperature down a little and raise my face to the welcoming warm water. I shampoo my greasy, floppy hair three times, then I apply body wash to myself twice and scrub vigorously. I turn the shower off, step out, dry off and wrap the towel around my waist. I feel so much better and very refreshed. I collect my clothes that lie in a heap and head back to the living room towards my pull-out bed. I discard my clothes at the foot of the bed, just as Trent comes out of his room with pajamas and a navy dressing gown draped over his arm.

"Wow. You were in there a long time, but at least you don't smell like garbage now," Trent chuckles.

I hadn't kept track of how long I was in the shower for, it was *that* relaxing.

I laugh. "Thanks."

He hands me the pajamas and gown.

"You're welcome to these. I don't wear them anymore," he smiles.

I look down at the clean clothes and smile at him gratefully.

"I'll leave you to it. Good night, Mark," he says.

He enters his bedroom and shuts the door, leaving me alone.

I fold the towel neatly and get changed into my pajamas. I bend down to collect my suit jacket, remove what little I have out of the pockets including my cell phone and my empty wallet, and place them on the floor beside me. I climb into bed and lie down; it's comfortable and warm, a massive contrast to anything I have ever had. As I start drifting off to sleep, my cell buzzes, pulling me from my much-needed rest. I grumble angrily but roll over to pick up my cell. I have received a message from a number that I don't recognize, I open it and scan it quickly:

> *Forgive this intrusion. Don't ask me how I got your number, but if you are interested in knowing, meet me in Central Park tomorrow afternoon at three. I will be sitting near Bow Bridge.*

I reread the text a few times, trying to guess who it could be from, then a dark thought comes into my mind. What if it's Tobias? *Is he planning to ambush me?* I shake that thought from my mind, switch my cell off before picking my wallet up. I turn it over in my hand a few times, then pull out the photo. It's a picture of Grandma, still smiling at me after everything that I have done. I stare at her, illuminated by the streetlamp outside the window. I check to see if Trent's listening.

"Goodnight, Grandma," I whisper, kissing the photo.

Tears start trickling down my face, but I dash them away. I place the photo under my pillow and drift into a deep, but troubled sleep.

I wake early, still bothered by the mysterious text I received last night. I toss and turn, trying to get back to sleep, but it's hopeless, so I decide to get up and start my day. Trent is sitting at the dining room table, typing furiously on his laptop. He glances up at me briefly and returns to face the monitor.

"I hope I didn't disturb you. Sleep well?" he asks.

"Best sleep I've had for a long time. You?" I respond, truthfully.

He doesn't reply, he just gives me a slight grunt. I shake my head at him and walk into the kitchen. I open the fridge and help myself to a strawberry yogurt for breakfast.

"Want anything?" I ask.

No response. I eat my yogurt quickly and sit down next to him.

"What are you doing?"

I lean over to try and get a better look. He stops typing and looks at me.

"I recently lost my job at the Broadway Theatre for putting faulty bulbs in the stage lighting. Wasn't for me anyway," he answers, looking back at his laptop.

"So, what are you doing?" I ask again.

He sighs.

"I'm looking for a new job. What else?" he snaps.

"Okay, sorry."

I hold my hands up in a defensive gesture.

"I'll leave you to it," I acquiesce.

I walk back to my pull-out bed, grabbing the TV remote on the way. I sit down and switch the TV on. I browse through the channels, but nothing takes my fancy.

"I've got Netflix if you're interested," Trent calls over.

"Netflix?" I furrow my brow, having never heard of it.

"You haven't heard of it?" he asks astonished.

Trent abandons his laptop, sits down on the bed beside me and shows me how it works.

Trent and I have spent the last few hours watching episodes of Breaking Bad. I'm now addicted to it and insist we watch one more episode.

"Told ya. Awesome, isn't it?" Trent beams.

I shush him and return my attention back to the screen. He chuckles slightly.

"I have an interview this afternoon, so you'll be on your own later." He grins at me, obviously proud of himself.

I peek over at him quickly and answer with a grumble. He climbs off the bed and walks towards his bedroom. Last night's strange text pops unbidden into my mind. I pause the program, causing Trent to stop and glance over. He cocks his head to one side.

"What's up?" he asks.

I grab my cell from the floor and examine the text again.

"I need your advice on something."

He walks back over and turns the TV off. I now have his full attention.

"Oh?"

I hand my cell to him. He reads the message quickly before his eyes dart to mine.

"Did you reply to this?" He's nervous.

"No. I thought I would see what you thought first."

He looks at the text again and hands my cell back to me.

"Mark, this could be another setup, maybe from Tobias. You aren't planning on going, are you?"

Part of me says it's a bad idea. Trent could be right. It seems a little coincidental that I just got out of jail and then this text comes shortly after. I rack my brains as to who else it could be, then it hits me. *Rachael.* I asked her to think about meeting up with me; maybe she has.

"I'm going," I say, determined.

Trent blinks at me a few times, saying nothing. His mouth falls open, then he closes it and opens it again, obviously speechless as he rubs his eyes.

"You're mad," he chastises.

"Maybe I am, but I need to do this."

"Why? What is so important about this? Can't you just delete the text and forget about it?"

"I know it sounds crazy to you, Trent, but what if it's from Rachael? I need to know what she has to say."

He rolls his eyes, frustrated.

"Oh, come on, Mark. You can't seriously believe that this *Rachael* will just drop everything to come and see you."

I contemplate this for a second, then frown at him.

"I need to know," I reiterate, at a loss for what else to say.

Trent closes his eyes and pinches his nose, then he opens his eyes and looks at me.

"Do what you must. Just holler at me if anything happens," he answers.

He walks away into his bedroom and closes the door softly. I look at his closed door, then return my attention back to my cell and type a quick response:

I'll be there.

I've been browsing Netflix's library for a while, but nothing interests me. My mind is clouded by thoughts of the mystery meeting later. Trent emerges from his bedroom, wearing a fine, sharp suit and carrying a cardboard box, which he puts on the floor beside my bed.

"I doubt you have many clothes at the moment, so you're welcome to some of my old ones," he grumbles.

He still doesn't look impressed with me, his blue eyes lacking their usual friendly shine. I turn the TV off and look through the box.

"Thank you," I acknowledge.

I get to my feet and give him a light and reassuring tap on the back.

"I know you are concerned for me, and I appreciate that, but I need to go to this meet," I insist.

He gives me a tight smile.

"Yes, I *am* concerned for you, and with good reason."

He backs away from me slightly, out of my reach.

"I'm worried about you, Mark. If you feel like you must go, I can't stop you. Just be careful."

I look at him, surprised. Trent has never been the soft type.

"I'll be fine," I assure him.

He stoops down to collect his bag.

"Well, I'm off," he informs.

His eyes shine with concern and I give him a weak reassuring smile.

"Oh, before I go, my number and some cash, in case you need a cab."

He hands me a piece of paper and palms me twenty dollars, which I place in my pocket. After saving his number into my phone contacts, I give him an appreciative nod, then he walks past me, opens the door and leaves. I run my hands through my hair and return my attention back to the box that he just dropped. There's some really nice stuff in here. T-shirts, a couple of suits, some ties, jeans and converse sneakers. There are even fresh pairs of socks and underwear in here. I try to think what would be appropriate to wear later. If it's Tobias, I couldn't give a damn about how scruffy I look, but in the slight chance that it's Rachael, I want to look and smell nice. I decide on a blue and white checked shirt, black jeans, leather jacket and converse sneakers. I have a quick blast in the shower and afterwards, I get changed into my chosen attire. I run a comb through my hair, brush my teeth and look at myself in the steamed-up bathroom mirror. I use my palm to wipe the condensation away, so I can get a better look. *That will do.* As a final thought, I spray some of Trent's cologne on, before walking out of the apartment and onto the street to hail a cab.

It's 2:50 pm when the cab drops me off at Central Park West. I feel uneasy and start to regret my decision of coming here.

Christ… what am I doing? I contemplate returning home, but I shake my head, take a deep breath and enter Central Park. I walk past Strawberry Fields as joggers run in the opposite direction and tourists snap photos happily while riding in horse-drawn carriages. I've missed a simple stroll in the park; it used to be a favourite pastime for me and Grandma, the only good memory I have as a kid. I feel tears pricking the backs of my eyes, but shake my head to subside them. *Hold it together, Mark.*

I arrive at Bow Bridge and check my watch which tells me it's 3:05. I'm a bit late, but I still have no idea who I'm looking for *or* who to watch out for. I look around suspiciously. No familiar faces yet, until I spot a young woman with mahogany hair, blowing gently in the slight fall breeze, sitting on a bench with her back to me. I breathe deeply and take a cautious step towards her. I realize who she is… Rachael. I beam inwardly. She looks stunning, not her usual police self at all, but straight, glossy hair that hangs down her shoulders. She is wearing denim jeans, a black winter coat and beige boots. I stand behind the bench she's sitting on and lean down close so that I can admire her perfect features from the side.

"Evening," I croon softly.

She turns and looks up at me, her hazel eyes catching me off-guard. She looks away again without a smile.

"Evening, Mark."

I sit down beside her. She peeks over with a ghost of a smile playing on her lips. I reciprocate. She takes a nervous breath.

"How've you been?" she begins casually.

"Not bad. I'm staying with a friend. We ran into each other yesterday."

She continues to smile warmly, then giggles softly.

"That was lucky!" she quips.

Her expression swiftly changes from care-free to serious.

"He's not affiliated with-" she begins, but I raise my hand, knowing exactly who she was about to refer to.

"No, not at all."

She sighs with relief, then changes the subject quickly.

"I've been thinking about what I said to you yesterday."

I look away from her, anxious where she may be going with this.

"Rach-," I try to start, but she holds her hand up, immediately silencing me.

"I don't think you are a bad man, Mark. I think you got in with the wrong crowd due to desperation. I've looked at your file thoroughly today."

I listen intently as she continues.

"I don't know how I feel about you. I'm confused about my emotions for you, but I think I have a good idea of how you feel about me."

I definitely know how I feel about Rachael. She gives me butterflies every time we're together. Her beauty and smarts are compelling. I feel like she can see right through me and for a brief moment, I feel exposed. She looks away, inhales deeply, then resumes.

"I wanted to ask... if you'll join me for dinner tomorrow, so we can talk about our feelings for each other a little more."

I'm shocked by what I'm hearing. *Yesterday, she said 'no' to drinks. Now, she's inviting me to dinner.* I'm thrilled by her offer, but before I accept it, there are some things I need to get off my chest.

"I know you didn't say it yesterday, but I know what you meant, Rachael. We *are* from two different backgrounds, but you're right, I'm not a bad guy. I was young, stupid, homeless and desperate, and Tobias preyed on that. It was the biggest mistake I have ever made, but that's behind me now. I promise you."

She looks intent with thought, resting her chin against her nimble, slender fingers.

"I'm glad to hear that. I'm sorry that happened to you, it couldn't have been easy."

I shake my head slowly.

"It's in the past. With that said, I would love to come out to dinner with you."

She smiles.

"Good, I assume you have my number?"

"Um…"

I take my cell from my pocket and check the contact list, only Trent is listed. I look at her and furrow my brow slightly. She smiles sweetly and takes a notebook and pen out of her bag.

"I'll write it down for you, just in case."

She scribbles quickly, tears off a shred of paper and hands it to me.

"Here's my number, just so you know that it's me this time," she chuckles.

"I'll text you a time and place, but please, keep this to yourself until we're sure of what we want."

She seems concerned all of a sudden. *Why?*

"Don't worry, not a word," I reassure.

She nods, satisfied with my answer.

"I'll see you tomorrow then."

I beam at her.

"Looking forward to it."

She places her hand on my arm slightly, stands, then walks away without a backward glance. Her brief, delicate touch has elevated my mood and I melt inwardly. *Wow. She's willing to give me a shot. I'm a lucky son-of-a-bitch.* I stand, leave the park with renewed purpose and make my way to the nearest subway station.

I arrive back at Trent's apartment, but he's not home. I enter the kitchen and open the fridge, but nothing seems to take my fancy. Instead, I opt for a glass of water and sit on my couch bed, thinking more about the brief but sobering meeting I just had with Rachael. She mentioned that she's confused about feelings she has for me. *What does that mean?* I'll ask her tomorrow at dinner. All I can do for now is wait for her text. Sitting here alone without Trent is boring and the silence is beginning to grate on me. I take my cell out of my pocket and send him a quick message:

Where are you? M.

I place the cell on the foot of my bed and wait to see if he replies. I surf through the TV channels and settle on the news, but don't take much notice. I get up and walk to the window, still holding my glass of water. I stare out at the other apartment blocks across the street and listen to the hustle and bustle of Manhattan's late afternoon traffic. I sigh and down my water, place the glass in the sink and return to the couch. My phone buzzes; I've received a reply from Trent:

> *Back later. How did the meeting go? Who was it?*
> *Tell me everything. T.*

I ignore the text, but mentally prepare myself for the barrage of questions he's going to throw at me when he gets back. I get changed into a white shirt and loose grey pants while I continue to ponder to myself. I hope Rachael doesn't change her mind about tomorrow, the thought is agonizing. I watch one episode of Breaking Bad, still waiting to hear from Rachael, but as the credits roll, I've still heard nothing. She *did* give me her cell number. *Should I call her? No.* I might frighten her away, it's best to leave her be and let her mull it over. Frustrated by my nagging thoughts, I switch Netflix off, get up from the couch, and head into Trent's bedroom. When I enter, I'm overwhelmed by the state of it. *It's a mess!* Unwashed plates and glasses scattered on his desk, clothes strewn all over the floor and the bed is unmade. *Jesus.* I tut at the mess and decide to clean it up before he gets back. At least it provides a distraction from anxious thoughts of Rachael.

I have made the bed, put Trent's dirty clothes into the laundry and placed the dirty plates and glasses into the dishwasher, all of which took me well over half an hour to do. Trent still hasn't returned home, and I still haven't heard from Rachael. I huff, aggravated and sit cross-legged on

Trent's now tidy bed and play Call of Duty on his PlayStation console.

I've spent hours trying to get to grips with this silly war game, but after being killed for the hundredth time, I switch off the console in a mood and check my cell. It's ten o'clock. Still no Trent and still no word from Rachael. Feeling frustrated and weary, I head to bed, pulling the duvet up to my chin and drifting into a peaceful slumber.

Chapter Four

I open my eyes and blink rapidly as the light streams in through the curtains. I rub the sleepiness out of my eyes and glance at my wristwatch; 9:45. *Crap.* I've been asleep for nearly twelve hours. I leap out of bed and hurriedly slip on my grey pants and white shirt, which lies in a crumpled mess on the floor beside me. Trent looks over from the kitchen. He's at the stove, frying something that smells enticing. He blinks at me with a surprised expression.

"You've been asleep a while. You okay?" he asks.

I walk slowly into the kitchen and lean against the counter.

"I'm fine. How did your interview go?"

He returns his attention back to frying eggs and sausages.

"Not bad, I think. They said they'll let me know soon."

He dishes up the food and walks to the dining table where he places the two plates down. I eye the breakfast; the smell is mouth-watering, but my stomach is still in knots from last night.

"Thank you for making breakfast, Trent, but I'm not hungry."

I am in fact, famished but I ignore my stomach's protest as I eye the breakfast. Trent picks up his knife and fork, then frowns.

"You've got to eat, Mark. You're getting thin. You'll get sick. Please eat."

I sigh, resigned, sit at the table and start wolfing down my breakfast. It delivers what it promises, it's delicious and kills my hunger instantly. Trent grins, seemingly satisfied and continues with his food.

"Oh, by the way. How did this mystery meeting go? Who was it?" he asks with his mouth full, spitting fragments of food while he speaks.

I roll my eyes. *Here we go with the no-holds-barred questioning.* I swallow a mouthful and answer.

"Woah, slow down. The meeting went fine."

He leans across, more interested.

"Well? Who was it? I assume it wasn't Tobias, considering you're still in one piece."

I look away from his quizzical gaze, get up from the table and clear my plate, my appetite vanishing.

"Mark?" he calls.

I hear the shuffle of his chair against the hardwood floor as he follows me into the kitchen. I scrape the remnants of my breakfast into the trash and place the dirty dish into the sink.

I turn back to face him, knowing I won't hear the end of this.

"It was Rachael," I answer as I walk past him.

I catch a surprised glance from Trent on my way to the couch. Trent abandons his half-eaten breakfast and comes to sit beside me. I slowly turn my face to his and raise my eyebrows with a 'what now' expression.

"What did she say?" he asks, blunt as ever.

I sigh.

"She wants to meet up for dinner, that's if she texts me first," I explain patiently, as if talking to a child.

Trent still has a confused look on his face.

"Why? Has she got feelings for you?"

"I'm not sure."

He frowns, looking even more perplexed.

"But she arrested you, Mark."

I shrug at him.

"*And*? If we have feelings for each other, you can't deny us that."

My voice is now starting to rise. I don't like to be questioned. He holds his hands up in a defeated gesture and gets up.

"I'm not denying you anything, I'm just trying to protect my friend," he says, wounded.

"Protect me? From what?"

"Yourself," Trent responds quietly.

Before I have time to answer, he walks into his room, leaving the door ajar. I don't understand why Trent is so concerned for me. He has never trusted the police. Every time I have tried to ask, he refuses to tell me why. I'll try and get it out of him someday, but the sound of a text alert gets my attention, prompting me to grab my cell excitedly and look at the message:

> *Mark, meet me at Storico at 7 pm tonight. It's an Italian restaurant near Central Park. Rachael.*

With trembling fingers, I respond:

> *I'll be there. Looking forward to seeing you.*

I need to make sure I look good for my rendezvous with Rachael. I run my hands through my floppy, unkempt hair and decide that I need a haircut, but I don't know this city well enough to know where to get it done. Maybe Trent will know. I stand slowly and knock softly on his bedroom door, but there's no answer. I push it open slightly and poke my head around. Trent is sitting at his now clean desk near the window with headphones on and browsing the web, his back to me. I stroll in and tap him on the shoulder. He spins in his chair and removes the headphones from his ears.

"What?" he says, sounding like I've disturbed him.

"Do you know a good barber?"

He raises a brow.

"*Why*?"

I stare at him with a 'why do you think' expression.

"Because I need a haircut," I scoff.

Trent smirks at me.

"Oh really? I never would have guessed," he chuckles, before continuing in a less sarcastic manner.

"My friend, Rex, can come by and do it for you. I think you'll like him; he's very gay."

I cock my head to one side.

"What are you implying?"

He grins widely and shrugs his shoulders.

"Just sayin'. Don't worry, he has a boyfriend."

I chuckle.

"Can he come today?"

Trent scratches his chin before shrugging again.

"Dunno'. I'll have to call him. Does it *have* to be today?"

I nod once and Trent seems to understand.

"Are you seeing that police chick again?"

Jesus. Am I that transparent that everyone can see right through me? First, Rachael. Now, Trent. I sigh.

"Yes, I'm seeing *Rachael* tonight."

His brow knits together and it looks like he's going to protest more, but thankfully, he holds his tongue.

"I'll give Rex a call," he replies nonchalantly.

He places his headphones back on and turns to face the laptop again. I contemplate complaining about how he talks about Rachael, but I relent. Instead, I pat him gently on the shoulder. He turns to look at me once more and I hold my thumb up, by way of thanks before I proceed to walk out of his room.

"Mark?" Trent speaks up, surprising me.

I turn around to face him.

"Thanks for cleaning my room."

I smile, then leave his room, closing the door softly on my way out.

A few hours later, there's a knock at the front door.

"That'll be Rex," Trent announces.

He places his Stephen King novel down on the side table next to the couch and arises. I also jump to my feet.

"I'll get it," I offer, and hurry to answer the door.

Rex is tall, quite muscular and tanned. He has long sun-kissed blonde hair which is tied into a ponytail, and sparkling brown eyes. He is wearing a tight grey Ralph Lauren polo shirt which shows off his toned chest, and black jeans. I smile at him and offer my proffered hand.

"You must be Rex. Mark Flint."

He displays perfect white teeth and takes my hand enthusiastically.

"Mark! I am *so* pleased to meet you. Trent has told me all about you," he gushes.

I pale and swallow.

"*Everything*?"

Rex continues to grin.

"Don't worry, sweetie. I don't judge."

I breathe a sigh of relief. *I like him already.* I stand aside, smiling, and wave him in. He picks up his duffel bag from the floor and strolls inside. Trent is slumped back on the couch, but as soon as he sees Rex, he stands up and makes his way over.

"Rex. Thanks for coming on such short notice."

Trent and Rex high-five each other. They're obviously close.

"My pleasure. Now then, where will I be doing this?" Rex asks as he stares admiringly around the apartment.

"In the bathroom," Trent says simply.

"Marvelous. I'll go and set up."

Rex smiles and claps his hands together, then heads in the direction of the bathroom. I turn to Trent.

"Nice guy," I say.

I catch Trent smirking in amusement as I follow Rex into the bathroom.

I've had my hair washed, blow-dried and cut to a more reasonable length. It's still long and floppy, but it doesn't cover my eyes nearly as much. Rex stands back and admires his handiwork.

"Much better!" he declares proudly. "Do you like it?"

He hands me a compact mirror and I look at myself.

"I love it. Thanks."

"Great."

He smiles as he begins to sweep up the hair clippings. I head out of the bathroom and return to the living room. Trent looks up at me and nods in appreciation.

"Not bad."

I smile and sit down beside him. Rex appears from the bathroom moments later, his duffel bag hanging over his shoulder. Trent walks over and shakes his hand appreciatively.

"Thanks again. What do I owe you?"

Rex's mouth twists with disdain.

"Oh, nonsense. We're old friends, Trent. It was a pleasure."

"Well, maybe we could meet up for drinks soon?" Trent suggests.

Rex claps his hands and hops on the spot excitedly.

"Oooh! I'll look forward to that," he enthuses with exuberance.

Rex turns his attention to me.

"I hope you can join us for that too, Mark."

I smile at them both.

"I'll consider it. Thanks."

"It was a pleasure meeting you," he says to me warmly.

"Likewise," I return.

Rex heads for the front door.

"See you soon," he shouts to us both before opening the door and exiting.

Trent sits back down and looks at me.

"You look loads better; less like a bum now."

I shake my head at him, then laugh.

"Gee, thanks," I joke.

Soon, we are both in fits of laughter.

It's almost time for me to meet up with Rachael. I'm a nervous wreck, and my gut twists painfully in anticipation. I've never been on a date before, so this will be a first. Trent insisted I have a shave. I smile to myself as I recall his words that he spoke earlier while we were waiting for Rex's arrival.

"Women don't dig hairy men, buddy."

I pick up his razor and start shaving.

Afterwards, I have left myself a smattering of facial hair, which I prefer. *Less itchy.* I've opted to wear a white shirt, navy pinstripe jacket, and pants to match, courtesy of Trent's goodwill pile. It's a little loose, but it'll do. I'm also fashioned with a navy-blue tie and shiny black shoes. Finally, I strap on my wristwatch and spray myself with Trent's Hugo Boss cologne. I'm now ready for my date. I exit Trent's room and stand in the middle of the lounge. Trent examines me closely.

"You look knockout, buddy. She'll love it."

I beam inwardly. It feels nice to receive a compliment from him. I look down at my watch which reads 6:30 pm.

"I should go," I say.

Trent follows me to the front door and produces his wallet. He pulls out sixty dollars and hands it to me.

"Here, you should take this."

I look at the money and step back.

"Trent. Thank you, but I can't take this," I answer, feeling guilty, but he frowns at me.

"You can and will. You don't want a lady paying for dinner on your first date."

I take the cash reluctantly and surprise him with a quick hug.

"Thank you... for everything," I whisper, overcome with emotion.

He taps my back awkwardly.

"It was nothing. I wasn't gonna let my pal freeze on the streets."

I let go and smile at him, and he nods towards the front door.

"Go on, get outta here. You'll be late."

He smiles back as I open the door and rush down the stairs. Stepping out onto the street, I yell "Taxi!" and raise my hand.

One pulls up in front of me and I jump in. The driver turns in his seat to look at me.

"Where to?" he asks as he chews gum loudly.

"Storico, please," I respond.

He turns back to face the road and pulls out into the loud evening traffic.

The traffic is heavy and we are currently in gridlock. None of the vehicles in front of us have budged for some time and I'm growing increasingly impatient. I look at my watch that now reads 6:50 pm. *Shit! I'm meant to meet Rachael in ten minutes.* I sit back in my seat and try to relax, but my stomach is in knots and I can't stop fidgeting. I'm starting to feel nauseous. This is my first proper meeting with Rachael, and I can't even be punctual. *Have I blown it already?*

"Come on. Please move," I pray silently.

My prayers are seemingly answered as the traffic begins to flow again until finally, we make it out of the traffic jam caused by road works.

I jump out of the cab at 7:10 pm. A little late, but hopefully, she'll be forgiving.

"Thanks," I say to the driver and palm him fifteen dollars.

I push my way through the bustling crowds, getting closer to my destination. I instantly spot her; she's standing outside a building which looks significant, almost like a courthouse. I freeze and observe the building. I notice a sign, close to where she's standing, that reads '*New York Historical Society Museum*'. I exhale; it's not a courthouse. I approach her slowly and like when I saw her in the park, she takes my breath away. She has her hair tied into a messy ponytail and she's wearing a long slim-fitted red dinner dress, black cardigan and glossy scarlet heels to match. She looks utterly radiant. I lick my bottom lip appreciatively as she turns her face and our eyes lock, igniting every nerve in my body. She smiles as I reach her.

"Hi, Rachael. Sorry I'm late," I apologize.

"Hi, Mark. Don't worry, I only just arrived too."

She giggles, sounding irresistible with a hint of nervousness like me. I look her up and down, admiring her slim physique.

"You look… stunning."

She grins warmly and bites her lip briefly.

"Thanks. You've scrubbed up well."

I look down at my attire before looking back into her enchanting hazel eyes. I straighten my tie and clear my throat.

"Shall we go in?" Rachael offers.

I look at the entrance of the museum building. *The restaurant's in here?*

"In here? I mean… sure," I respond.

She surprises me by linking her arm through mine as we walk into the building together. We make our way through the lobby, our arms still linked as we head towards Storico, located on the right side of the hall. Inwardly, I wonder what made her choose this venue.

"My dad used to bring me and my sister here a lot," she explains, answering my unspoken question.

I glance at her, but she stares straight ahead, smiling to herself. Curiosity hits me.

"Tell me about your family," I prompt.

Her smile fades and she remains silent. We walk through the glass doors and into the restaurant.

"Good evening. Table for two?" the waiter asks, looking first at Rachael, then at me.

"Please," she responds, smiling sweetly.

He collects a couple of menus and gestures with his hand.

"Right this way, please."

He smiles and ushers us to a small table in the corner. Rachael shrugs out of her cardigan and places it on the back of her chair, revealing perfectly toned arms. I unbutton my jacket and sit opposite her. She catches me staring and I quickly divert my gaze to admire the restaurant's warm, opulent surroundings. It has yellow and white furniture with a romantic eighteenth-century Venetian vibe. I glance across the table at Rachael, eager to know more about her and wondering why she didn't answer my question earlier. I'm about to ask again, but she's busy scanning the menu. I pick up mine and do the same.

"I know what I'm having. How about you?" Rachael says.

She places her menu back on the table as I continue to scan mine quickly. The turkey Bolognese sounds interesting. *Odd. I thought it was only made with beef.* I tilt my head up to find her watching me expectantly.

"I've decided," I say.

She smiles and summons the waiter, who scurries over and stares at Rachael a bit too eagerly, much to my chagrin.

"I'll have the vegetable spaghettI and a glass of red wine, please."

The waiter scribbles on his notepad, then diverts his attention to me.

"I'll have the turkey Bolognese and a glass of red wine too, please."

He scribbles again.

"Thank you," he says politely, then he collects the menus and heads towards the kitchen.

Rachael blows out a deep breath, visibly nervous, before she fixes me with her intrigued gaze.

"Tell me more about yourself, Mark. How did you find yourself here, in New York?"

I stare back at her and sigh.

"My parents abandoned me when I was six, so my grandma took me in. She died shortly after I turned seventeen."

Rachael parts her lips slightly and shuts her eyes painfully, but when she reopens them, they're filled with sympathy.

"I'm so sorry," she says solemnly.

I shrug.

"Well, it's in the past. Tobias picked me up off the streets. I spent a lot of wasted years with him and eventually, he brought me here, to New York. You know the rest."

I'm desperate to steer the conversation away from that forbidden chapter of my life.

"Tell me about your family," I attempt.

She smiles fondly and opens her mouth to answer, but the waiter returns, and she remains silent, waiting for him to leave. He places our red wine in front of us before beating a hasty retreat, providing Rachael with a chance to speak.

"My father is loving, but God, he's stern. He has been part of the force, coming on thirty years now, but he's been Chief for the last decade. It's how I got my job."

I pale. *Her father is the Chief of Police? The same man Justice Miller spoke to? Shit.* I try to look unfazed by this revelation she has divulged.

"And your mother?" I ask gently, having recomposed myself.

"My mother is a lawyer in the courts. She met my father during a case where he was the arresting officer. I also have a younger sister, Louise. I helped Mom and Dad raise her when she was a baby when they were busy with work."

She smiles fondly again when she mentions her sister.

"She's studying to be an ob-gyn," she continues.

"Wow, that's quite a family you have. All of them have important roles in the community."

She nods happily.

Internally, I'm a mess, now that I know who her father is, but I'll try to forget about that for now and enjoy our evening.

"May I ask where you live?" I ask.

She blinks a few times. I hope I haven't offended her.

"Not far from here," she states as our meals arrive.

"Enjoy," the waiter says, then leaves us to it.

We both look down at our plates; it smells delicious. I take a sip of my wine as we both tuck in.

"What about you?" she asks, pointing her fork at me.

I look up from my meal and raise my eyebrows.

"Who's this friend that you're living with?" she continues.

After swallowing a mouthful, I reply.

"His name is Trent Wilkinson. We live in the Broadway area. We went to school together back in Chicago."

She stares at me, nonplussed. "Chicago?"

I chuckle at her expression, her full lips twisted in confusion.

"I'm surprised you don't know that about me. I was born in Chicago."

She giggles slightly and responds.

"Must have missed that part."

She then returns to her meal.

"I've heard Broadway's a nice area to live in," she continues after a mouthful.

"It's lovely," I agree.

She puts her knife and fork down, and places her hands flat on the table in front of her. She has my full attention immediately.

"Shall we get down to the nitty-gritty? As I expressed yesterday, I'm confused about feelings I have for you," she starts.

My appetite vanishes.

"In what way?" I ask.

"That's the problem, I just don't know."

She continues to look straight at me. I swallow.

"Rachael, I want us to be together, but only if you're comfortable."

The words tumble out of my mouth quickly. Tears brim in her beautiful eyes.

"I want us to be together too, but I'm not sure if we can be."

My mood free falls.

"Why?" I ask.

The waiter collects our plates, agonizingly halting our conversation. *Yet again.* When he's gone, she looks back at me.

"I just don't want my career to be at risk. I don't think anyone will agree with our relationship."

I understand completely. She's probably worried about Officer Bailey, and more than anyone else… her father. I take a deep breath and attempt to comfort her.

"I know it will be complicated… us being together, because of my past, but try not to worry about what others think of us. We're both adults, and you're free to make your own decisions. If you decide it's too much of a risk, don't take it and I will leave you be."

My heart drops as I say this, but I remain determined. She seems to be considering what I have said, but she shakes her head slowly at me.

"Check, please," she calls to the waiter, who nods and makes his way over.

"I'll pay," I offer, producing the cash from my pocket.

She arches her finely manicured brow at me, looking at the money suspiciously.

"My friend lent it to me," I explain quickly.

"Ah."

The waiter arrives and places the check onto the table. I pick it up and read it; fifty-eight dollars and seventy cents. *Damn, I'm a bit short.* I place the cash on the table and glance over at Rachael guiltily, but she smiles.

"I've got this," she says.

Before I can protest, she swipes her card, paying the check in full.

"Thank you. Have a nice evening," the waiter smiles.

Rachael stands up and collects her cardigan from her chair while I retrieve the cash from the table. I stand, button my jacket back up and we leave the restaurant together. We walk arm in arm through the museum lobby then we step out into the chilly evening air as I check my watch. *Wow, nine o'clock already.* I turn to face Rachael.

"Thank you for dinner, Rachael. I really hope to see you again soon."

She looks back at me.

"Would you like to come back to my place? We could continue our conversation there," she offers.

The butterflies are back in my stomach. "Sure."

She grins slowly.

"It's a bit of a walk. Shall we get a cab?" she asks, but I shake my head.

"I could do with the walk," I respond, smiling.

Her grin widens, then she turns right, and we walk together towards her apartment.

We make small talk while continuing to walk with our arms linked, but neither of us is brave enough to engage in a full conversation.

After a twenty-minute trek, we arrive at her apartment block on West 60th Street. It is a very tall red brick building, at least thirty floors high. It stands on the street corner and is surrounded by trees that have long ago lost their leaves. She takes my hand and leads me towards the green front door. A doorman steps forward as we approach. He opens the door and we both breeze in.

"Evening, Tom. How's the family?" Rachael greets the doorman warmly.

He smiles and tips his hat to her.

"Good evening, Rachael. The wife and kids are great. Keep me on my toes though," he puffs jokingly.

Rachael giggles and Tom the doorman directs his kind gaze at me.

"Sir," he greets, tipping his hat at me also.

I smile at him, but don't respond. Rachael takes my hand again and leads me through the immaculate marble lobby and towards the elevators. She presses the call button, then we stand and wait. A loud ping announces the elevator's arrival, we step in and Rachael presses another button. The doors slide shut and we ride up in silence. I glance over at her, but she stares at the closed doors in front of us. I look across at the elevator buttons, curious to know which floor she lives on, floor fifteen is lit. *Jeez, that's high up.* The elevator pings again and the doors open. We step out and we walk down a short corridor. She unlocks her front door and steps inside. She slips out of her cardigan and hangs it on the hook by the door. I walk past her; there is a spacious kitchen directly on my left, then I emerge into the living room. It is simply decorated with cream walls and a matching rug with an oak coffee table standing in the center. There is a large burgundy couch and two matching armchairs sit either side of the rug. A large TV rests on a glass cabinet with a PlayStation console underneath and a potted plant rests on the window sill. *Much larger than Trent's place.* I walk further into the living room. She closes the door and approaches me slowly, coming to a stop right in front of me. She is so close I can smell her sweet fragrance. *Roses.* We stare into each other's eyes, neither of us saying anything.

I break the silence. "Thank you again for tonight."

"You're welcome," she whispers.

Suddenly, she leans in and kisses me very gently on the cheek, then she breaks away and slumps into one of the armchairs. I'm frozen to the spot and raise my hand to my cheek.

She kissed me. The first time I have been kissed by anyone. It was over quickly, but I crave more. I glance down at Rachael, who has her head in her hands. I take off my jacket and sit on the couch beside her armchair. She's very quiet and very still.

"That was nice," I say.

She looks up from her hands and gives me a weak smile.

"I apologize," she croaks.

I look at her, dazzled, and smile.

"Rachael, you don't need to be sorry. I enjoyed it."

She gets out of the armchair and joins me on the couch. She looks into my eyes and appears to be searching for something in them.

"Hold me," she whispers.

I pause, briefly unsure of what to do, but then outstretch my arms and hold her like I have never held anyone before. I feel a warmth inside me like I've never felt. In this moment, I have never been so happy or so at home.

Chapter Five

⌒

Minutes go by and neither of us says anything. I continue to cradle Rachael silently, her head resting gently on my chest. I can feel her soft, warm breathing through my shirt. I lower my face to the top of her head, taking the opportunity to softly inhale more of her sweet scent. *Wow, someone should bottle this.* She looks up and pulls away, forcing me to release her. She pulls the hair tie from her hair, allowing it to fall in a mahogany wave over her slender shoulders as she delicately combs it through with her fingers.

"You're beautiful," I compliment.

She smiles shyly, then looks down at her hands.

"Thank you. No one's ever said that about me."

She's picking at her fingernails nervously. I take both her hands in mine.

"Never? But you are. Have you ever had a relationship before?" I ask, suddenly very curious.

Her eyes brim with tears and she looks away from me, pulling her hands from mine.

"I was in a relationship about two years ago. My fiancé was travelling. I didn't go with him, due to my work commitments. He cheated on me while he was abroad, so I called off our engagement," she explains.

"Fiancé?"

She responds with a small nod. I'm overcome with rage. *How the hell could someone do that to her?*

"He's a fool," I growl, more to myself.

She shrugs slightly, then wipes her eyes.

"Have you been in a relationship before?" she asks.

I chuckle.

"Me? Never. All the girls at school would stay well away from me. Who'd want to date me?" I scoff.

She puts her hand tenderly on my forearm.

"I would."

I grin at her as she smiles sweetly, but her expression shifts back to serious.

"We need to keep our relationship a secret for now, Mark, just until I can figure out how to tell everyone."

I blink at her and raise my eyebrows in disbelief.

"Please?" she whispers.

I sigh heavily.

"Okay. If that's what you want, then I won't speak a word."

She smiles, obviously satisfied with my answer.

"But I want to tell Trent," I add quickly.

She stares at me in alarm.

"Don't worry. Trent is very secretive. You can trust him."

She opens her mouth but closes it again before she exhales.

"Sure, but no one else. *Okay?*"

She's insistent, pointing her finger at me sincerely.

"Cross my heart," I swear, placing my hand on my chest.

She smiles, now at ease. I look down at my watch, it's now 10:10 pm. I get up and put my jacket back on.

"You're leaving?" she asks with a lilt of disappointment in her voice.

She wants me to stay. I pull her up, pressing her against me.

"We both have a lot to think about," I explain.

She looks down solemnly. I lift her face gently back up with my index finger and smooth her hair out of her face.

"I'll call you tomorrow," I reassure her.

She nods and stands back from me.

"I'll show you out."

I let her lead the way as I follow her to the door; it gives me an opportunity to watch the gentle sway of her hips as she walks. I suck in my bottom lip and resist an urge that begins to bubble inside me. *Mark, control yourself.* She opens the door and walks with me to the elevators where we both ride down to the lobby together. We step out and stride past Tom the doorman who bids me goodnight, I walk towards the green main entrance, then stop and turn to Rachael.

"Until tomorrow," I say.

She smiles warmly, then I open the door and walk to the edge of the sidewalk. I raise my hand to hail a cab home. One screeches to a halt and I turn to face Rachael again who is standing in the doorway.

"Until tomorrow." She recites my words and waves at me.

I smile back at her as I climb into the cab. I give the driver Trent's address, then he pulls away. I turn in my seat and wave at Rachael with a huge grin plastered on my face. The taxI rounds a bend and I can no longer see her. I sit back in the leather seat, feeling triumphant. I went out to win her tonight and it looks like I have, but we still have a long way to go.

The streets are quieter and far less busy than earlier. It takes less time to get back to Trent's than it did to meet Rachael. *Why wasn't it like this earlier?*

I jump out of the cab and hand the driver a large tip due to my good mood. I head inside Trent's apartment and climb the stairs. Upon entering, I slip my shoes off and toss my jacket to the couch. Trent doesn't appear to be home, but as soon as I shut the front door, he comes barreling out of his room, stopping me as I try and retreat to the bathroom.

"How was it?" he asks eagerly.

I groan, exasperated.

"My date was great, but I ain't telling you anymore. Goodnight."

I hurriedly walk over to the pull-out couch, removing my tie along the way, and lie down. It goes surprisingly quiet. I was expecting Trent to throw all sorts of questions at me. I glance up slowly, but Trent appears to have given up as he is no longer standing where I left him. I get back up off my bed and proceed to get undressed. Trent walks back in, catching me off guard as I stand in his lounge half-naked, wearing only my boxer briefs and socks. I grab the duvet from the bed and cover myself.

"Jesus!" I exclaim angrily.

Trent ignores my protest and continues to grin stupidly, before walking further into the room and sitting on a blue chair beside the dining table.

"So... what happened?" he asks, slapping his knees with his hands as he sits.

I rake my hand through my hair in annoyance and think of what I can say to shut him up.

"We went out for dinner, then she invited me back to her place."

His mouth drops open in surprise.

"You went back to *her* place?" He leans in.

I rub my eyes in irritation.

"Just to talk."

Trent continues to stare at me.

"Anything else?" I ask impatiently.

"Did you...?"

I look at him, appalled.

"No. I did not."

My good mood is forgotten. I feel bombarded by Trent's persistence.

"One more question?" he presses further.

"*What?*" I grumble.

"What happens between the two of you now?"

I think about what I can say to him, but Rachael did tell me she doesn't mind if I tell him.

"We're dating. What do you *think* happens next?"

He looks at me in shock.

"But you mustn't tell anyone," I warn.

"You know I won't," he says as he gets to his feet.

"Not even Rex," I call after him.

He turns to give me a blank expression, then closes his bedroom door, finally leaving me in peace. I lay back down on my bed but feel restless. I punch my pillow in an attempt to get comfortable, still to no avail. I can't help thinking about Rachael. She's risking her career for me. *Can I ask her to do that?* One way or another, we will find a way to be together happily without risking anything. With that pleasant thought, I finally drift to sleep.

My eyes flutter open to welcome the early dawn. I'm feeling happy, sated and very relaxed after a restful sleep, the best I've had in years. I get out of bed and have a stretch. Trent is sitting at the dining table with his headphones on and drinking his morning brew. He looks up and removes his headphones.

"Morning," he says simply.

"Good morning, Trent," I return, as I make my way to the kitchen and pour myself a cup of coffee, then sit opposite him.

"Are you seeing Rachael today?" he asks.

"Not sure. I told her I would call. Why?"

He shrugs.

"Just wondering."

I purse my lips at him and am about to question him further, but his phone buzzes against the table. He picks it up and frowns at the number.

"Hello?" he answers clearly, then listens intently. "Yes. Speaking."

I look at him suspiciously, but he holds his index finger up to his lips and disappears into his room to continue his conversation in private. I finish my coffee before depositing my empty cup into the dishwasher.

Trent hasn't come out of his room for the last five minutes and it sounds like he's still on the phone. I decide to fire up his laptop and look for a job of my own. If I want Rachael to take me seriously, getting honest work is a good start. Trent finally re-emerges but is silent. I look up expectantly.

"Well?" I prompt.

Trent looks at me.

"That was the guy I had the interview with."

"And? What did he say?"

He smiles gleefully.

"I got the job. I start in a few days," he beams.

"That's great! Congratulations!" I enthuse, pleased for my friend.

"Where are you working?" I continue.

"With Rex, as a receptionist at the Neapolitan Hotel."

I give him a thumbs-up gesture and return my attention to the laptop.

"What are *you* doing?" he asks, sitting beside me and peeking across.

"Looking for work," I answer, my eyes still locked on the monitor.

I can feel Trent's eyes on me, but I don't look back; I'm fully immersed in my task.

"Well. Good luck. I'm going out."

Trent stands and grabs his jacket before leaving.

I've been job hunting for a few hours now, but everything I have seen either doesn't appeal to me or I don't have the right qualifications. Frustrated, I shut the laptop down and rub my face. *Who would hire me anyway?* I don't have much work experience, my grades from school were poor and I just got out of jail. None of that should matter; I need to keep trying. Trent is still out, probably celebrating with Rex somewhere. I contemplate calling him to see if I can join him. *Yeah, I think I will.* I pick up my cell, but it starts ringing. Without checking the number, I answer it.

"Hi, Mark. I just wanted to hear your voice."

It's Rachael. She sounds desperate, which worries me instantly.

"Hey, what's wrong?"

"Could you meet me... now?"

"Sure. Where?"

She's silent for a moment.

"Maybe... at the Unisphere, in Flushing Meadows? It's over in Queens," she finally answers.

"I'm coming now."

She hangs up.

I get dressed in double quick time, before rushing outside and running to the 50th Street Subway Station. I quickly purchase a Metro Card, which I should have done sooner, and jump onto a crammed train just before the doors close.

I spend the journey worrying about Rachael, about us. She sounded troubled and it makes me think she's having second thoughts. I dismiss the thought and wait anxiously to arrive at Flushing Meadows.

I alight from the train at Mets-Willets Point Station and rush towards Flushing Meadows-Corona Park. I can see the Unisphere straight ahead. I make my way hurriedly through the metal gates, into the park and rush towards the fountain in search of Rachael. I stop in front of the Unisphere and look up at it. I feel the icy water of the fountain slightly splashing me. I look around at my surroundings, and all I can see are children playing frisbee and couples walking hand in hand. I wonder idly if that could be me and Rachael someday. I look in the opposite direction and see her walking towards me. She looks crestfallen.

"Oh, Mark. Thanks for coming."

She throws her arms around my neck. I wrap my arms around her and rock her gently.

"You know I would come. What's wrong, Rachael?"

She lets go and grabs my hand then leads me towards the surrounding wall of the Unisphere to sit down. She wipes her eyes with the back of her hand before turning to face me.

"I can't help worrying about us, Mark. I thought about what you said. I know I shouldn't care about what people think of us, but I'm so scared about it all."

She wipes her nose. *Good thing I have tissues.* I pull one out from my pocket and hand it to her, she takes it gratefully. I stroke her face and wipe away a stray tear with my thumb.

"I know things aren't easy... for either of us at the moment, but if you are having second thoughts..." I can't even finish the sentence, the thought of losing her is too painful.

She looks at me and shakes her head.

"No. Of course not. It's just that... I had a call from Dad today and he could tell something was up. The problem is he can read me like a book, Mark. He is going to prompt further until he finds out. I know he will."

I take her hand reassuringly.

"I'm inexperienced with this sort of thing. I'm not really the best person to ask. I've never had to deal with these feelings before, but if it makes it easier, why not introduce me to your parents? We can just tell them the truth and get it out in the open."

She looks at me in alarm.

"Meet my parents? I think it's too soon."

"Just think about it. You can't live with this uncertainty and neither can I. It's not fair on either of us."

She nods and seems to be agreeing with me. Finally, her mood seems to lift a little.

"Maybe I could meet your friend, Trent first?" she suggests.

I think about this and wonder what his reaction would be. *Not good, I bet.*

"I'll try, but Trent doesn't trust the law. I've never understood why, but I will convince him and get back to you, but for now, try not to worry."

She turns and looks towards the Unisphere and admires it, I mirror her. She looks back at me and smiles, then playfully jabs me in the ribs, tickling me.

"Hey," I protest, and tickle her back in defense, invoking a childish, but delectable laugh from her.

We are both in fits of laugher and are soon in a full-blown tickle fight. She loses her balance and falls back into the pool of water surrounding the Unisphere, pulling me in with her. We are both drenched but are in fits of laughter. I step out and take Rachael's hand, pulling her out with me. I shake myself off as best as I can as Rachael takes off her flats and pours the water out of them while we're still in hysterics. People walk past us, staring with disapproval, but we just don't care.

"Okay. That's my shower for the day," she laughs, as she places her shoes back on and wrings the water from her long hair.

We are still laughing at each other.

"Let's go for a walk, dry off." I chuckle, holding out my hand.

She takes it without hesitation, and we walk hand in hand in the park. *Like a regular couple.*

We talk; she tells me that she's been a member of the police force for seven years. We poke gentle fun at Officer Bailey's moodiness. It turns out Stephanie and Rachael have been best friends since they were children; it's a revelation for me. Rachael stops and looks at her watch.

"I'd better go. I have to be at work in an hour."

She lets go of my hand and gives me a brief peck on the cheek.

"Rachael," I call as she walks away.

She turns to look at me.

"Don't worry about anything. I'll sort it," I reassure.

She produces a dazzling smile.

"I know you will."

I return her smile as she turns to walk away again.

"Rachael," I call once more.

She looks over her shoulder and giggles.

"Yes, Mark?"

"Be safe at work. I love you."

I can't believe I said that out loud.

Her mouth drops open in astonishment. She runs back over and looks up at me. Our eyes lock, hazel into blue.

"I love you too," she whispers.

Her lips are suddenly on mine, taking me by surprise. We hold each other close, our wet clothes sticking to each other as we continue to embrace. I savor everything she has to offer. *I love this woman and I can't believe she loves me.* Sooner than I would have liked, she breaks away and briefly presses her forehead to mine.

"Talk later," she breathes, then she begins to walk away.

I watch the gentle sway of her hips like I did before as she slowly strolls away, until she turns a corner and is out of sight. I'm breathless, I confessed my love for her, and to my surprise, she loves me. *Rachael Clarke loves me!* I clap my damp hands together happily and leave the park, feeling victorious once again.

Chapter Six

I stroll back to Mets-Willis Point Station, elated, but freezing due to my soaked clothes. I casually weave my way through the crowds, who stare and grimace at my wet clothes. I enter the subway station, swipe my Metro Card, push through the turnstyle and emerge onto the platform to catch a train back into Midtown Manhattan. The train rumbles and grinds to a halt at the platform and I step on-board. All of the seats are taken, but I happily stand. The doors slide shut and the train pulls away loudly. I hold on tightly to the handrail above me. When I was making my way to Flushing Meadows this morning, I was wary and anxious about what Rachael wanted, but now I come away with a new sense of purpose, wet, but thrilled all the same. However, my pride is replaced with uncertainty. I need to think of a way to convince Trent to meet Rachael, but I know he'll hate the suggestion. I need to ask him and get it out of the way. The train rolls into the 50th Street Station and I step off quickly.

On the short walk back home, I try to come up with a plan to put Trent at ease, but I have no idea how to initiate the conversation.

I climb the stairs of Trent's apartment, unlock the door and head inside. Trent stands in the middle of the living room with his arms folded when I enter. He stares at me and raises his eyebrows at my damp clothes.

"Where were *you*?" he asks.

Christ, he's scolding me as if I wasn't old enough to go out alone.

"Out. With Rachael," I respond curtly and shove past him.

"It looks like you did more than go out with Rachael. What did you do? Swim across the East River?"

I chuckle at the pleasant memory, but then head into the kitchen. He follows me in and watches carefully as I pour myself a glass of water.

"Mark, what's going on? Are you and her serious?"

I look at him with a quizzical expression.

"We love each other, Trent. That's all that matters."

He seems satisfied as he nods and heads back into the living room.

"Good. What happened to your clothes?" he asks as he sits down on one of the couches.

"Like you said. I swam across the East River," I joke.

Trent hoots with laughter.

"Fine. Don't tell me."

I put my half-drunk glass of water in the sink and sit on one of the dining chairs.

"Can I talk to you seriously for a moment?" I ask, changing the vibe.

He frowns.

"Sure. What's on your mind?"

I take a calming breath.

"You know I said that me and Rachael love each other? Well, there's something that's preventing us from moving forward."

Trent leans in closer.

"Which is?"

I pick at my knee and continue.

"She is concerned about what people may think of us, considering our contrasting backgrounds. She wants some reassurance."

Trent rubs his chin thoughtfully.

"*Right...?*"

He gestures with his hand for me to continue.

"I need you to do me a *huge* favor."

He twists his mouth in contemplation and raises his eyebrows expectantly before he realizes what I'm asking of him. His expression changes from intrigued to horrified as he jumps out of his seat and walks around the room frantically.

"No. I can't," he groans.

I leap up and follow him.

"Trent, please. I need this from you," I implore.

He stops and glares at me, his blue eyes are wide with fear as he shakes his head.

"I'm sorry, I just can't."

We stand in the middle of the living room, staring at each other.

"I don't know why you have such a problem with the law, Trent, but I promise you, Rachael is different."

He shuts his eyes and rubs his forehead, he seems agitated. When he reopens them, they're blazing.

"I haven't told anyone this before, not even Rex."

He turns his back to me. I approach him, keen to know what he is about to tell me.

"When I was a kid, my father was wrongfully arrested for a murder he didn't commit. It was simply a case of mistaken identity. I remember my mother trying to back up my father's innocence, but the police just wouldn't listen."

He stops and puts his head in his hands. I place my hand on his back reassuringly.

"Go on," I prompt softly.

He looks up at the ceiling.

"My father committed suicide in jail. He was convinced that he would never be free, and it got too much for him. The cop that arrested him was a crooked cop who was let go from the force shortly after my father's death, but because of that error, my mother had to raise me alone. She continues, to this day, to blame herself."

His voice cracks on the last word and it sounds like he is sobbing, his back and shoulders shake with tension. I have never seen him so distraught before, but now I see him in a totally different light.

"Thank you for telling me."

He wipes his eyes and looks at me.

"Hopefully, you understand now."

I nod at him.

"I understand completely. I'm so sorry about what happened to your dad."

He wipes his eyes again.

"It's in the past, nothing can be done now."

He walks to the window and stares blankly out to the street below.

"Rachael... isn't like the cop who arrested your father," I reassure him.

Trent looks slowly over his shoulder, his mouth twisting in disbelief.

"I need your help. Do it for me?" I implore him again.

He looks away and continues to stare out the window, then he rests his forehead against the glass, obviously in anguish.

"Set it up," he finally acquiesces.

I pat him on the shoulder.

"Thank you," I answer.

I turn on my heel and sit on the couch to text Rachael.

It's been four hours since I texted Rachael, and there's still no word from her. I'm really starting to worry. I know deep down she's fine and capable, but I just can't help myself. I try to do things to occupy my mind. I have tried watching TV, surfing the net and accompanying Trent to the grocery store, but nothing has worked. I can't wait anymore. I grab my cell, sit on the couch and call the 17th precinct. After a few minutes on hold, a woman answers the phone.

"Hello. You've reached the 17th precinct of the New York Police Department. Officer Bailey speaking, who may I ask is calling?"

I groan inwardly. *Damn it. Of all the police that work there, it had to be her.*

"Hello. Is Officer Clarke around please?" I speak softly, hoping she doesn't recognize my voice.

"I will go and check. Who's calling, please?"

I pinch my nose and reluctantly answer. "Mark Flint."

I hear a very slight gasp.

"Mark Flint? Can I help you with anything?" she asks, more sternly.

"I would like to speak with Rachael, if you don't mind, officer," I answer a bit more forcefully than I intended.

"She's out on a call at the moment, but I will let her know you called."

She didn't even check! I feel like she's making up excuses, but I give up.

"Okay. Thanks for your help."

I rapidly hang up and throw my cell onto the couch beside me. I don't know what her problem is with me, but at the moment, I just don't care. I want to know that Rachael is safe, so I decide to call her cell instead. Unsurprisingly, it goes through to answerphone.

Rachael's clear, soft voice simply states "Hi, this is Rachael. Leave a message."

The beep sounds, and I speak into the phone.

"Hey, it's me. I was just checking to see if you're okay. Call me when you get this."

I hang up and decide to go out for a run as the tension is killing me, but what can I wear? I head over to Trent's goodwill box and rummage through it. I find an old pair of grey sweatpants and a white shirt. *Trent thought of everything.* I slip them on quickly, and head out the door, wanting to rid my nagging thoughts of Officer Bailey's denial and Rachael's whereabouts.

I've been running through Central Park for the last half hour. I've run under Trefoil Arch, past the Bethesda Fountain, and I now stand on Bow Bridge as I catch my breath. I glance towards the bench where I met up with Rachael after I was freed from prison. This is where our affair started; this is where my redemption started. I smile at the warming memory and continue with my run until I stop at Ramble Rustic Bridges, completely out of breath. I place my hands on my knees, my breath evaporating in the cold afternoon chill. I look up and admire my beautiful surroundings, trees and a stunning, old wooden gazebo. I'm hot and sweaty, but I feel invigorated. The sound of my cell ringing distracts me, I pull it out of my sweatpants and answer.

"*Hello?*" I wheeze, still out of breath.

"Caught you at a bad time?" Rachael's soft voice relaxes me instantly.

"No. Not at all."

I sit inside the gazebo.

"I got your message, and Stephanie told me you called. Everything alright?"

"Everything's fine. I was just worried about you and I wanted to ask you if you would be free for a drink sometime. Trent has agreed to meet you."

She's quiet, but I feel her smile radiating down the phone.

"I'm good. Exhausted mainly. We are very busy down here today, but I'm off-duty tomorrow, so I'll be free then."

I try to remember if me or Trent have anything planned for tomorrow, but nothing jumps out at me.

"Tomorrow? Great. I'll text you our address."

"Great. I'd better go. See you tomorrow."

She hangs up. I smile to myself, get up and sprint back home.

Trent and I can't be bothered to cook dinner, so we order pizza. We sit on the couch and watch crap midweek TV. I still haven't told him about tomorrow, but decide I have to.

"Rachael is coming over for drinks tomorrow," I blurt out.

He slightly coughs while taking a slug of his beer and wipes his mouth with the back of his hand.

"*Great,*" he says sarcastically.

I purse my lips at him.

"You could be a little more optimistic about it."

He shrugs and takes another long draft of his beer.

"I can't say I am looking forward to it."

Suddenly, I don't feel much like eating. I get up, discard my half-eaten slice of pepperonI pizza and stomp past him angrily while he looks at me in surprise. I turn and fold my arms.

"Then I will just have to prove you wrong about her," I say.

I turn on my heel and march into the bathroom, slamming the door shut on the way in. I sit on the edge of the bath and think that maybe I overreacted a little. I need to try harder to control my temper. Trent told me why he has such a problem with the police, and he took me into his home when I had nowhere to go. I'm suddenly hit by a wave of guilt. I open the door gingerly and peek out. Trent is still sitting on the couch. I walk over slowly, but he refuses to look at me.

"I'm sorry. I didn't mean to be rude."

He still doesn't look at me, but I see his shoulders slump.

"You took me in when you could have easily let me freeze on the streets. I owe you everything, and if you're not ready, I will let Rachael know," I continue.

He huffs and finally turns to face me.

"It's not a problem, I will meet her."

He stands and nudges me with his shoulder jokingly.

"Just control your temper. You're acting like a stubborn teenager," he laughs.

I grin and laugh with him.

"Sure, and thank you."

He nods, still grinning at me. I turn and head for the pull-out bed. Trent yawns loudly.

"Are you watching this?" he asks, pointing at the TV.

"No."

He picks up the remote, switches off the TV and makes his way to his room.

"Sleep well," I call.

"You too."

I think that went well and I feel loads better. I get undressed hastily and climb into bed.

I wake suddenly. I'm not sure what woke me. I look around the room, but no one's there. I groan and roll over in bed to peek at my phone; 6:15 am. I try to get back to sleep, but I am now fully awake. I'm excited, but nervous about later. Hopefully, Trent will see Rachael in a positive light. I rub my eyes and get out of bed. I need to go for a run, so I get changed into my sweats and head out.

I take my usual jogging route through Central Park. I'm hot, sweaty and out of breath after an hour. I return home to find Trent curled up in the corner of the couch reading a book. I stop and stare at him; he looks in my direction before giving me a brief smirk and returning back to his Stephen King novel.

"You got up early," he says, shutting his book and placing it on the arm of his chair.

"I couldn't sleep."

He sniffs slightly.

"Me too." He looks me up and down. "Went for a run?"

I look down at myself and make my way to the bathroom.

"I'm going to have a shower," I call, not answering his question, and close the door behind me.

Rachael is due to arrive in a few hours and we've got nothing to offer her that she might like, so I head out to the store around the corner to grab some drinks and snacks. As I walk through the convenience store, I can't believe just how boring this task is. I have bought some white wine, beers for Trent and some nuts and chips. I pay for the items and start heading back. When I arrive home, I'm shocked to find Trent vacuuming. I grin and head to the kitchen to place the drinks in the fridge and the snacks on the counter, then I sit at the dining room table. Trent turns the vacuum cleaner off and stows it away in the storage cupboard. I can't help but laugh at him, he frowns at me.

"What's funny?" he says gruffly.

I stop laughing but struggle to keep a straight face.

"You look like you need an apron and a head bandana," I tease gently.

His frown deepens.

"I like my place to be tidy. You could help out a bit," he teases back.

I laugh loudly.

"You like your place tidy? What about the mess I found in your room?"

He narrows his eyes playfully.

"Well, if you like cleaning bedrooms so much, you can help me with the rest of the place."

My grin widens as I get to my feet and help Trent with his chores. I'm excited about today.

For most of the afternoon, Trent and I continue to clean the apartment in peace. We barely say anything to each other, except for Trent barking orders at me occasionally. We are both startled by the sound of the intercom buzzing. Trent turns on the spot suddenly and shoots me a panicked look.

"It's her."

The fear is evident in his voice, but I give him a reassuring smile and answer the intercom.

"It's me," Rachael breathes softly.

"Come in," I say simply, and buzz her in.

I look over at Trent, who now seems to be trembling. I walk over and give his shoulder a reassuring squeeze.

"I can't do this. I'm going out for a while," he says suddenly.

Before trying to make his escape, I grab his forearm and sit him down on the couch. There's a loud knock at the door, so I give him a final look and a thumbs-up gesture.

"You'll be fine," I whisper.

He looks at me, wide-eyed, as I turn and make my way to answer the door.

Rachael looks as stunning as ever, simply dressed in skinny jeans, a loose-fitting blue blouse and white chucks. She smiles at me before I take her in my arms and kiss her quickly.

"Welcome. Come in."

She takes my hand and I lead her into the living room. Trent doesn't turn around to greet us, he's frozen to the couch. We walk over to him, and he finally peeks up at us.

"Trent, this is Rachael," I introduce her calmly.

Rachael offers her hand.

"Pleased to meet you, Trent. Mark's told me about you," she greets.

Trent continues to stare at her blankly. Finally, his manners register. He stands and shakes her hand weakly without saying a word.

"Please, take a seat, Rachael. Would you like a drink?" I offer.

She settles onto the couch opposite Trent and grins up at me.

"Just some water for now, please, Mark."

I smile, then face Trent.

"Something stronger, whiskey," he breathes.

I look at him, frustrated, but choose not to argue. I look over at Rachael awkwardly. She gives me a slightly unsettled look, purses her lips and gives me a brief, if not awkward smile. I head to the kitchen to prepare the drinks. I watch the two of them closely. Trent seems to be observing her and Rachael looks down and twiddles with her hair nervously.

"Mark tells me you were friends at school." Rachael tries to engage Trent in conversation, raising her head up to face him.

I listen and look over at Trent.

"Mm, hmm," Trent responds.

"You were in Chicago together, right?" she tries again.

"Yep."

I palm my face and clear my throat. He glances over and I attempt to signal him to talk to her properly. *Come on, Trent.* I collect the glasses hurriedly and hand Trent his whiskey, which he downs immediately, then I hand Rachael her water, which she takes gratefully. I perch on the arm of the couch where she's sitting and rest my arm around the back of her shoulders. Trent continues to say nothing, he just stares, lost for words. I gesture at him subtly again to talk. Finally, he gathers his bearings.

"So, Rachael… Mark tells me you're a cop?" he starts.

I rub my forehead with my fingers. *Could this be any more awkward?* Rachael looks up at me nervously and returns her stare at Trent.

"I am. What do you do?"

Trent is silent for a few seconds but then responds.

"I work as a receptionist at a hotel."

Rachael's eyes widen slightly.

"Really? That's interesting. You must meet so many people."

I look at her and then at Trent. He seems to be visibly relaxing a little.

"Yeah, I suppose I do. I haven't actually started yet. I start tomorrow."

"Oh, congratulations."

Trent finally cracks his first smile of the evening.

"My sister always wanted to be a chef at a hotel, but Dad wouldn't let her," Rachael continues.

"Why?" Trent asks.

She is quiet for a moment, but then answers.

"He wanted her to do something *'more useful'*."

She rolls her eyes at the memory. Clearly, her father seems to be overbearing and I now understand why she is concerned to introduce me to him. Trent seems intrigued by this information as well.

"I think being a chef *is* useful. After all, it involves serving the public, no different from what you do," he says.

I've never heard Trent be so philosophical.

Rachael giggles and looks back up at me. I look down at her; she seems to be giving me an expression that she needs rescuing from Trent. I slap my knees and stand up.

"I think we have discussed work enough. Who's up for a game of poker?" I declare.

"How about strip? Me and Mark play it all the time. Don't we, bud?" Trent jokes.

I whip my face round to him and scowl.

"*What?*" Rachael has turned beet red.

I look at her, embarrassed.

"He's joking, we don't really... *Right, Trent?*" I say, through gritted teeth.

"Nope. Just plain, boring poker."

He grins playfully and starts to laugh, enjoying his little joke. Trent grabs the deck of cards from the coffee table, shuffles them and starts to set up on the floor.

"Straight flush. I win again," Rachael announces triumphantly.

Rachael and Trent seem to be getting on famously now; she grins at him.

"Jeez, Rachael. I didn't think you would be this good." He smiles at her and she grins right back.

"Another game?" he asks excitedly.

Rachael looks at her watch and scrambles up from the floor.

"Is that the time already? Sorry, I need to go. I have work early in the morning," she informs.

"Me too, but you already know that," Trent chuckles.

Me and Trent both stand with her. She is now putting her shoes on hurriedly as we both watch her like she's some sort of exotic animal. She turns and smirks at us both.

"Thank you both for a lovely evening," she acknowledges.

I follow her to the door.

"You owe me another game," Trent calls after her.

"Try and stop me," she calls back.

I open the door for her as she leans in to kiss me.

"Thank you," she whispers.

I melt inwardly.

"Anytime," I respond.

She hurries down the stairs without a backward glance. I close the door and rush to the window where I see her climbing into a taxi. I knock on the window, prompting her to look up as I give her a wave. She grins, blows me a kiss, then she's gone. I turn to see Trent sitting on the couch with his hands behind his head, looking visibly relaxed.

"Nice girl. You've landed on your feet with her, buddy."

I can't help but smile at him.

"See? What did I tell you?"

He looks at me and ruffles his spikey hair into place.

"I'm going to bed."

Trent stands from the couch and retires to his bedroom. I make my way to the bed and lie back. That went a lot better than expected. Hopefully, she is feeling more confident about us being together. There's hope for us yet.

Trent left for his new job early this morning after spending most of breakfast raving about Rachael. I'm going to have a lot of quieter days now that Trent is gone. I have spent most of the morning researching to find a job myself, but I've still found nothing. I'm becoming more frustrated as the day drags on. I have heard nothing from Rachael and I feel lonely without Trent. I have always hated my own company since my parents walked out on me, I shake my head to clear my thoughts, refusing to think about them. I've been trying to occupy myself by watching TV and playing on Trent's PlayStation, but nothing works. I pace the apartment, not really sure what to do, so I decide to go out for some fresh air.

It's a mild but bright day. The streets are heaving and full of life as ever. People bump and push past me as they rush around on their lunch break. I walk through the busy streets and stop outside the Empire State Building, staring up at it, mesmerized. I let my mind drift back to Rachael meeting Trent, grinning at the memory. Trent hasn't stopped buzzing about her and I am pleased that they got on better than I could have hoped for. An uneasy feeling pulls me away from my pleasant memory, and my skin crawls as if I am being watched. I look around in all directions, but nothing jumps out at me straight away. I scold myself for having such stupid thoughts. *No one's watching me.* I start to make my way back home, but the feeling that I'm being watched or followed gets worse. I look over my shoulder several times, a lot more often than I would like. I walk faster, trying to escape my uneasy feeling until eventually, I'm running. I turn a corner sharply and run straight into a man in a suit who is talking loudly on his cell.

"I'm so sorry," I apologize.

He pauses his conversation and looks at me angrily.

"Watch where you're going!" He stomps away and continues his call.

I said I was sorry. I swiftly turn on the spot and continue to walk home as quickly as I can.

I arrive home, slam the door shut and rush to the window, looking outside. I don't see anyone or anything suspicious. Trent is still at work and I know I won't be able to call him for reassurance. I sit down and place my head in my hands, then I'm startled by my cell ringing. I pull it out of my pocket and answer.

"Yes?"

"Afternoon," Rachael says softly.

I am so pleased to hear from her.

"Hey. You okay?" I ask.

"Yes, I'm fine. Are you okay?"

She sounds concerned.

"Yeah, of course. Just came back from a run," I lie.

I don't want to worry her. She says nothing and we both hang on the line. The silence is agonizing and I can't stand it anymore.

"How's work?" I break the silence.

She draws out a long breath before answering.

"I just thought you would like to know that we may have a lead on Tobias."

I run my free hand through my hair, pulling at it a little before I start to pace around the room.

"Really? Where is he?"

She exhales again.

"Sorry, Mark. I'm not allowed to tell you for your own safety, but I am leaving with my back-up in a few minutes to chase the lead."

My mouth drops open and my stomach free falls.

"Rachael. Tobias is a very dangerous man."

"I know that, but it's my job."

I groan inwardly.

"I know, but…" I pause.

"But what? This man needs to be taken off the streets."

"I know. Just… please be careful. That's all I was going to say."

I can now feel her warm smile through the phone.

"Of course. I'll call when I get home… I need to go."

I'm scared. I don't want this call to end, but I don't have much of a choice.

"Bye, Rachael. Please be careful. I love you."

"I will. Goodbye, Mark. I love you too." She hangs up.

I drop my phone to the floor in shock and twist at my shirt in apprehension. I knew me and Rachael's relationship would be difficult due to her dangerous job, but now she is going after Tobias. I know what he is capable of, and the thought of the two of them confronting each other makes me nauseous, but there is nothing I can do. I won't interfere with her career. I can't do anything but wait and hope that she'll be okay.

Chapter Seven

Hours have passed since Rachael called and I've been getting more and more agitated throughout the day. I hear the front door close and Trent strides in, smiling, but his smile fades when he sees me.

"Jesus. You're a mess. What's the problem?" he asks, glancing at me.

I stare back, pleased that he has finally returned.

"Nothing. Tell me about your first day. How was it?"

I try and change the subject, not feeling keen to discuss what Rachael told me, but Trent narrows his eyes and walks towards me.

"Stop trying to distract me. What's the problem?"

He stops in front of me, places his hands on my shoulders and gives me a little shake. I know I'm not going to get out of this, so I tell him.

"Rachael went after Tobias today. I haven't heard anything from her for hours."

Trent lets go of me.

"Tobias? You mean the guy that you used to hang around with?"

"The very same. He's dangerous, Trent."

He continues to look at me, then shakes his head slowly.

"I'm sure he is, but Rachael will be fine."

Trent tries to comfort me, but it sounds like he doesn't believe his own words.

"How do you know?" I test him, but he doesn't answer.

He turns away and throws his bag into the corner of the room.

"Let's get dinner started," he suggests, not answering my concerns.

I push my food around my plate. I'm hungry, but my stomach is in knots with fear. I try another mouthful, but I struggle to swallow it. Trent eyes me from across the table.

"You going to finish that?" he asks quietly.

I look at my barely touched steak.

"No," I answer sadly.

I look down at my feet, nagged by my dreadful thoughts of what may have happened to Rachael. I hear Trent clear away the dishes, then he comes back over to me.

"Come on, let's get your mind off of this."

He pulls me up from my chair and leads me into his room. He sits me on the edge of his bed and places a PlayStation controller on my lap. I look up at him.

"I'll race ya," he smirks.

I crack a half-hearted smile and let Trent challenge me.

Trent switches off the console after a few sessions of Gran Turismo.

"Heard anything yet?" he asks.

I check my phone; it's ten to midnight and there are no missed calls or texts. I shake my head at him regrettably.

The sound of the intercom startles us. We look at each other, perplexed. Trent gets up from the edge of his bed.

"Who could that be? It's so late," I ask.

He shrugs and exits the bedroom. The doorbell rings, I listen intently, but I can't make anything out, just Trent mumbling. A few seconds later, he re-enters the room.

"Mark, you might want to come in here."

He's nervous. *Who was it?* I follow him into the living room to find both Rachael and Bailey, still in their uniforms, standing in the middle of the room. *Thank goodness. She's okay.* However, my relief is quickly replaced by concern. Rachael looks at me sternly before turning and smiling at Trent.

"Thank you." Rachael addresses Trent.

He nods and retreats into his bedroom behind me. I stare at his closed door, confused as to what's going on. *Thank you? For what?* I turn slowly to return my steady gaze at Rachael and Bailey. I lick my lips slowly, trying to say something, but nothing comes out. They continue to glare at me, and I finally have the courage to speak.

"Did you get him?" I start.

Rachael looks over at Officer Bailey who continues to regard me angrily.

"We got him," Rachael answers professionally, but I feel like there is more she isn't telling me.

I step forward, keen to touch her, relieved that she's okay, but she holds both her hands up to stop me and gives me a slight shake. I stop and turn my attention to Officer Bailey who steps towards me.

"During our interrogation, Tobias claimed *you* were the leader of his crew, and that he was merely the front man," Bailey elaborates bitterly, eyes blazing.

My mouth falls open in shock.

"What!? That's crazy. Compare my file to his, he is wanted for all sorts of crimes. The judge said I was clear," I exclaim, almost shouting.

I look over at Rachael in disbelief. Her eyes soften, but she tears her gaze from mine and looks down at the floor. Bailey continues to blaze.

"Mr. Flint, you will need to come with us." Bailey produces the handcuffs.

I step away from her, but she moves closer. I look at Rachael desperately.

"Please," I beg, but Officer Bailey gets hold of me. I struggle in vain.

"I haven't done anything!" I shout, trying to shake Bailey off, but she grips me tighter, snaps the cuffs around my wrists and wrestles me to the floor.

"Stop!" Rachael demands.

Bailey and I both turn to look at her while she presses me firmly against the cold, ceramic floor.

"Rachael, you know what this man is capable of. We must take him in."

Rachael closes her eyes and when she opens them again, she looks at me with determination.

"I believe Mark. He's not the leader. Tobias is a lying son-of-a-bitch. We shouldn't be taking him seriously," she states aggressively.

Officer Bailey tries to argue. "But it's our job to-."

Rachael cuts Bailey off mid-sentence.

"-to arrest the bad guy, which Mark is not. The judge said he has no criminal convictions. We have nothing to hold him on."

I smile at Rachael. *My savior. My shining light.* Bailey continues to look sour-faced at Rachael as if she can't believe what she is hearing, but eventually, she removes my cuffs and marches to the front door. I get back to my feet, rubbing my wrists. She stops and turns to face me.

"I will be watching you *very* closely, Mr. Flint."

Bailey points her long finger firmly at me, shaking it after each word that she angrily spews. She turns her attention suddenly to Rachael, now directing her finger at her.

"You need to get your priorities in order, Rachael. He is no good for you."

"It's not my priorities that are the problem, Stephanie. It's yours."

The two women glower at each other, full of scorn. Without another word, Bailey leaves. Rachael darts me a quick look and makes her way to the door herself.

"I'm sorry if I destroyed your friendship," I apologize whole-heartedly.

"It'll be okay. I'll talk to Stephanie," she reassures.

We smile at each other.

"You can tell me anything, Mark. *Was* Tobias right? Were you *really* the leader of his crew?"

She's asking this time, though far less provocatively than her colleague. I stare at her and slowly approach her. She watches me as I take both her hands and look her in the eye with sincerity.

"I promise you. I was not the leader. That bastard betrayed me. Now, he will do anything to ruin me," I answer calmly.

"That's all I needed to hear," she says.

After a minute of staring, we hear angry beeping coming from outside. Rachael looks towards the window.

"I'd better go."

She turns to head out, but I pull her back to me.

"I'm just glad you're alright," I say softly.

She smiles and kisses me quickly on the cheek. Without another word, she gently pulls away and exits the apartment. I follow her out and watch as she rushes down the stairs.

I walk back inside just as Trent re-emerges from his bedroom and looks from me to the front door with a puzzled expression.

"What the hell just happened!? You know I don't want police in my house." He's fuming.

"I didn't invite them, Trent. Rachael's colleague tried to arrest me."

He steps back in disbelief. "Arrest you!? On what charge?"

I shrug my shoulders and sigh heavily.

"Tobias was caught, then he says *'I was the leader',*" I state patiently with a hint of rage.

"Bullshit. You don't look like the sort that could lead a criminal organization," Trent spits angrily.

"Oh, *thanks…*" I respond, reassured, but slightly offended.

He didn't mean it like that.

"No. I mean that in the nicest way possible. You're not *him*. You're a good man, Mark."

It's good to know that I have two people on my side when the world is against me, but after an eventful evening, exhaustion kicks in.

"Look. I'm tired, I'm going to bed."

I turn away and sit on my bed. Trent nods and heads back into his room. I punch my pillow and hang my head, trying to calm down.

How could he do this to me? Tobias and I were always close. I was always loyal to him until I had no reason to be anymore. He betrayed me, but he sees *me* as the traitor. He wants revenge, any way he can get it.

It's cold and dark. The rain is cooling my heated face. I'm standing in an alleyway near the Hudson River. Tobias looms over his latest victim, his spy, Adam. A pool of blood surrounds his corpse while Tobias' revolver is still smoking. He blows the barrel successfully and grins at me.

"See that, Mark? Easy," he sneers.

I look down at Adam's dead body and cringe. I want to protest, but I don't have the nerve. I know he will kill me next if I do. I simply return his grin with a weak smile.

"You know why I had to do it. Right, Mark? He was going to sell us out. I killed him to protect us," he explains in an eerily fatherly tone that he always uses.

I glance down at the body and feel utter guilt.

"Someday, Mark, you will take my place," he continues.

He reaches into the breast pocket of his jacket and pulls out a red carnation. He sniffs it slightly, and deftly drops it onto Adam's corpse. Tobias' calling card. He turns on his heel and casually strides away. I look down at the floor and feel weak. I know now, that I cannot continue this lifestyle.

"You're an idiot, Tobias. Adam was loyal to you. He was loyal to all of us." I call after him, angered by what he has done.

He looks over his shoulder at me slowly, before charging at me and grabbing my shirt, pushing me hard against the brick wall.

"What did you call me?" he seethes, bearing his yellow, decaying teeth.

All I can smell is his bitter breath of cigars and brandy. I am quivering with fear.

"*Nothing. Sorry,*" I rasp.

He smiles, then drops me to the floor.

"Good," he responds kindly, as if nothing happened.

He grasps my arms and helps me to my feet, pats me clean and straightens my shirt. He begins to walk away, and like an inept sheep mindlessly following his shepherd, I walk in his shadow and trail after him back to our dilapidated hideout.

I can't shake the image of what Tobias did to Adam. One of his most loyal followers got a bullet to the heart. I sit in the corner and watch Tobias as he throws some wood into the burning barrel for warmth.

"I can't do this anymore," I relent.

Tobias turns on the spot and pulls his revolver from his pocket and strokes it gently.

"*What?*" he breathes.

I swallow nervously, staring at his gun.

"I can't do this. It's too much," I elaborate.

He approaches me slowly and crouches down in front of me, leaning against my chair. He admires his weapon, turning it menacingly in his hand, before drawing his green eyes back up at mine.

"You're like a son to me, Mark. I did everything for you, and this is how you repay me?"

My heart is in my throat; I know I need to choose my words carefully.

"I know you did. I'm sorry, but everyone in this gang has either been murdered or arrested. I just want a normal life."

He laughs. "A normal life is no good, Mark. I know, I used to live one myself. Didn't work out. Don't fool yourself; you are cut out to be like me."

He gets back to his feet. I shake my head and can't face him anymore.

"I'm sorry, my mind is made up. I leave in the morning." I'm nervous but determined.

"After everything I have done, you just want to walk away? That's ungrateful, Mark. I looked after you when you were cold and alone. You're going to sell me out to the cops, aren't you? You traitor."

He's quivering with rage and looks to be turning purple. My heart is in my throat and I fear for my life as I continue to eye his gun.

"I'm sorry, Tobias," I squeak.

Strangely, his anger subsides.

"I'm a generous man. I'll let you go free. All I want in return is for you to do one last thing."

I'm relieved, but suspicious as well.

"What do you want?" I ask nervously.

"Meet me in Barretto Point Park tomorrow. You will receive the job there. Do it, then you're free."

I sit bolt upright in bed and gasp in a lungful of air. I'm trembling and drenched in sweat. I take a calming breath and rub my face. I'm a mess of conflicting emotions.

Did I betray him? I was only trying to do the right thing. Maybe I should have ridden it out with him. I shake off the ridiculous thoughts. *If I stayed, I would probably be dead now.*

I mentally slap myself. *Get a grip.* I just need to focus on my new life with Rachael and forget about Tobias. After all, he's locked up now, so he can't hurt anyone any more.

I haven't slept since my nightmare. I've been too unsettled. I groan and curse quietly before I roll out of bed. I grab my navy dressing gown and slip it on quickly. The sun starts to rise on the horizon, promising another bright day, unlike my mood. I make my way to the kitchen and switch on the kettle to make myself coffee. Still dazed by my nightmare, I reach into the cupboard to get a mug, but drop it to the floor where it shatters.

"Shit!" I hiss.

I am rummaging through the cupboards, looking for a dustpan and brush when I hear Trent's bedroom door open. Within seconds, he enters the kitchen and stands over me.

"Mark. What are you doing?" Trent admonishes.

I raise my head to look at him, but I hit my head on the rim of the cupboard.

"Ow… Sorry, Trent. I was going to clean up the mess I made."

He glances down at the shattered mug.

"I can see that. Don't worry, I'll deal with it."

He steps over the mug fragments and heads to the cupboard under the sink. He collects the dustpan and brush and quickly sweeps it up.

"I'm sorry I woke you," I apologize.

He stands up and places the broken china into the trash, folding his arms as he looks at me.

"What's going on? Couldn't sleep again?"

"Nope. I keep getting nightmares, but the one from last night was so real."

He frowns at me and scratches his chin slowly.

"Maybe you should see a doctor or something," Trent suggests.

I think about it momentarily but can't face it.

"I can't. I don't want to explain to some shrink what I have done in the past."

Trent pats me on the shoulder and looks at me sincerely.

"Then speak to Rachael."

My mouth twists at this idea as well.

"She knows enough."

He sighs and walks into the living room and I follow after him.

"I'm just trying to help."

"I know. Thank you, but I will deal with it on my own."

Trent contorts his face and stares for a couple of seconds.

"Okay," he responds quietly.

"Let's get breakfast started." He changes the subject.

Trent volunteers to make breakfast. He jokes that he doesn't want me breaking anything else, which cheers me up a little. The smell of Trent frying eggs makes me feel queasy. He occasionally turns to check on me as I sulk on the couch, but neither of us speak any more about my nightmare. After a while, he approaches me with caution, as if I'm dangerous, and hands me a plate. I look at the egg on toast placed before me.

"I don't want it," I say miserably, and place it on the floor beside me.

He narrows his eyes with concern.

"We've been over this. You need to eat. You'll waste away."

He retrieves my plate and places it back on my lap. "Bon appetite."

He turns and walks to the dining room table to start his own breakfast. I eat it slowly just to make Trent happy. Maybe I will talk to someone about my woes. I need to get the burden off my back.

Trent has gone to work, and I have the apartment to myself. I have felt out of sorts since my nightmare. I rake my fingers through my floppy hair and look out the window. It's a sunny day, strange for mid-November, but it doesn't reflect my mood. The traffic and pedestrians are in full swing, with everyone rushing to work. I wonder to myself what problems *they* might be facing today, probably less severe than mine. I shake my head. I can't sulk here all day, so I get changed and go out to explore.

I feel better already; the slight breeze gradually blows my troubles away. I'm becoming more familiar with this amazing city, and it feels more like home to me than Chicago ever was. I continue walking, lost in my own thoughts on this chilly, but bright Sunday morning. I find myself at the Rockefeller Plaza. This is where Trent and I were reunited after so long. I grin at the memory as I rub my hands together in an attempt to keep warm, my breath evaporating in the increasingly bitter air. I notice a large crowd down the street who are chatting loudly and excitedly about something while snapping photos on their phones. I make my way over to blend in with the crowd and look in their direction. A huge truck is slowly making its way towards us, and on the back of it rests a massive spruce. There are news vans and camera crews everywhere. This must be the famous Rockefeller Christmas tree. I have seen many photos of it but have never been lucky enough to see it this close. I watch in awe; it's stunning. The truck grinds to a halt in front of the enthusiastic crowd as they snap more photos. Two large men step out of the truck and jump onto the back of the trailer. They begin to undo all the straps around the tree as a large crane makes its way over. The crowd gradually disperses, giving me a chance to get a closer look. I watch as the crane is put into place, then it winches the tree off the trailer and places it onto a wooden stand in the center of the plaza. It's quite a sight; maybe I should ask Rachael if she wants to come here with me when the tree's lit up. *Has she ever been to the light-up ceremony?* Maybe I could make it a date. *Yeah, maybe I will, but when is it?* I look around to see if there are any signs that could give me an idea of when the ceremony will take place, but there aren't any. I see a cop trying to control the excited crowd. I make my way slowly towards him, exhaling nervously.

"Excuse me?" I ask.

He turns and smiles politely.

"Do you know when the light-up ceremony is?"

He looks puzzled momentarily but smiles again.

"It is normally held at the end of November. I think it is the 30th this year, but you will need to double-check."

"Thank you so much," I respond, and start to walk away.

As I make my way through the bustling crowd, I spot someone in the distance. *She looks familiar.* I walk cautiously towards her and am amazed to notice it's Rachael. I rush over enthusiastically, desperate to see her.

"Rachael," I shout through the crowd, but she doesn't hear me.

I am close to her now.

"Rachael!" I call, louder this time.

She turns, and I freeze. It's not Rachael, but she looks strikingly similar.

"Oh, I'm sorry. You look a lot like my girlfriend," I explain, embarrassed.

The young woman stares at me, then chuckles slightly.

"Rachael?" she asks.

"Um… yeah."

"You're not talking about Rachael Clarke, are you?"

"Yes. That's right," I respond, not thinking.

She laughs. "The amount of times that people have mistaken me for Rachael. We might as well be twins. I didn't realize she has a boyfriend. Finally."

I'm so confused, but then it hits me. I know who this is.

"Forgive me. I'm Louise, her sister."

Crap. I just told a member of Rachael's family that I'm dating her! What will she say?

Chapter Eight

"Nice to meet you," I say hastily.

I attempt to make my escape, but she follows after me.

"Wait. Who are you?" Louise asks.

I refuse to look at her.

"Mark Flint," I grumble.

I hear no response, so I turn to face her. *Maybe she ran off? Nope. Still there.* She stands in front of me, gaping.

"*The* Mark Flint? The one my sister was investigating?"

I have to try and rectify this. Rachael is going to kill me.

"Look, I was falsely accused. I was cleared of all charges. Rachael didn't want me to tell anyone about us. Will you keep this quiet… Please?"

My words tumble out quickly, but Louise listens.

"I won't breathe a word," she smiles.

I let out a relieved sigh.

"Thank you."

I'm freezing now. *Time to head back home.*

"It was nice meeting you," I say quickly.

I turn and make my way home as fast as I can.

Trent is on the phone when I come in. He looks up and puts his finger to his lips.

"Yes, sir. Thank you."

I sit on the couch and listen curiously. He smiles and chuckles a little.

"I understand."

He continues with his call. *Who is he talking to? His boss, maybe?* He nods slightly and walks away from me so I can no longer eavesdrop on his discussion. He says something else and laughs. At last, he ends the call and pockets his cell away, grinning enthusiastically.

"I've done it," he declares triumphantly.

I blink a couple of times at him and rub the back of my neck.

"Done what?" I ask, perplexed.

"You owe me a 'thank you', my friend."

"Why?" I ask, scratching my chin.

"I have noticed how you've been struggling to get work due to your... um, past. So, I've arranged for you to meet my boss at the hotel where I work. He's going to discuss opportunities with you."

I blink at him again, lost for words momentarily. Finally, I speak.

"Thanks for your help, Trent, but working at a hotel isn't really my thing."

Trent's smile fades.

"It's a start, right? You never know, it might grow on you."

I think about this for a moment, then sigh.

"Sure, I'll give it a go. When's the interview?"

Trent grins at me.

"Interview? It's not an interview, Mark. My boss just wants to meet you. Tomorrow morning, 11 am," he says.

I slump back into the couch.

"Sure."

He gives me a long look and heads towards his bedroom.

"Hey, Trent."

He looks over his shoulder at me.

"Thanks again," I smile.

He smiles back.

"Anytime, bud."

He enters his room and closes the door behind him.

I pace back and forth, feeling anxious about meeting Trent's boss in the morning. I've never had a real job before, so I don't know what to expect, but Trent is right, of course. I have been struggling for so long, and now he has handed me a lifeline. I need to grab this opportunity with both hands and go for it. I sit on the edge of my bed and think about what I will be offered tomorrow. My cell starts to vibrate beside me; I pick it up and look at the number. I smile and answer.

"Evening, Rachael. Good da-."

"What the hell are you playing at!?" she hisses, interrupting me.

Man, she's pissed. What have I done now?

"I'm not sure what you mean."

I rack my brains trying to think what I may have done. She groans angrily down the phone.

"I just had my sister on the phone. 'I met Mark at the Rockefeller Center this morning!'. You told her that we're dating! You promised me, Mark. How could you?" She shouts bloody murder down the phone.

My blood drains from my face. *She said she wouldn't tell anyone!*

"I'm *really* sorry. I didn't know." I stop, lost for what else to say.

"You didn't *know?*" she bellows.

I rub my face, annoyed.

"I didn't know she was your sister. I spotted her and thought it was you. We started talking and it slipped out. I'm sorry. But please, stop haunting me with my past. I'm trying to right the wrong in my life."

I'm feeling a little angry myself now; she gasps at my outburst and sobs a little.

"Please don't get upset. I really am sorry, Rachael."

I try to soothe her, feeling guilty. She sniffs and continues.

"No, I'm sorry, Mark. Why should I care what people think of us? I'm a grown woman."

I nod.

"I told you not to care about what people think when we met up at the Unisphere, remember? If we are going to be together, you need to introduce me to your family sooner or later," I explain, calming down gradually.

"You're right,"

I breathe a sigh of relief now that she now seems to understand.

"I'm meeting Trent's boss tomorrow. He might be giving me some work. Think about what I said and let me know what you decide."

"Sure. Good luck tomorrow," she whispers.

We are both quiet, but continue to hang on the line. I can't bear the silence.

"Listen, I need to go… Speak soon," I breathe.

"Sure."

I quickly press the end button on my cell and throw it onto the bed beside me. I flop down and cover my eyes with my arm, feeling irritated, but unsure whether it's at myself or Rachael. I was probably a little harsh on her, but I was only telling her the truth. I know I didn't start out great in life, but I did explain to her that I'm trying to right the wrongs. Hopefully, she considers this and agrees to let me meet her parents. I will make sure that if that day comes, which I hope it does, I will be able to prove everyone wrong and become a better person who can date Rachael without anyone questioning us. This is my mission. This is what I'm going to achieve. I won't rest until I have it.

I open my eyes and remove my arm from my face. It's dark outside and the room is pitch black. I must have dozed off. I sit up and switch on the free-standing lamp beside me. Tobias is standing at the foot of my bed, holding a knife. I can't help but stare at him in disbelief. He bears a slow evil grin.

"Hello again, Mark," he says coolly.

I rub my eyes.

"Tobias? But you're in prison."

"Yes, I am. Who put me in there?"

He glares at me and strokes his blade with the tip of his index finger.

I blink at him and try to answer, but I can't believe what I'm seeing. I hastily grab my cell where I dropped it earlier and dial Rachael's number. It doesn't ring.

"The number you have dialed has not been recognized. Please try again later."

I drop the phone in shock. She's blocked my number.

"You're driving her away, Mark. No one is here to help you."

He walks around the bed, still grinning wickedly.

"What's wrong? Not going to speak to your old friend?" he crows.

"We were never friends," I whisper, but his sinister grin becomes broader.

"You are a little traitor, Flint. After everything I did for you," he hisses.

His eyes now blaze with anger, as he slowly paces towards me. I jump off the bed and run to Trent's bedroom door. I slam my fists desperately on the door.

"TRENT!" I scream.

There is no answer from him and I turn to see the knife-wielding Tobias slowly approaching me again. I try to stay away from him.

"You're alone, Mark. I'm the only friend you had, and you threw it away."

I feel faint, my heart in my throat. I have nowhere to run. Suddenly, he lunges at me with the knife and slashes me across the chest, ripping my shirt. I feel the warmth of blood trickling down my body. The pain is sharp and unbearable. I collapse onto my hands and knees, weak from blood loss.

"Please... Stop..." I rasp.

He laughs menacingly and lunges again.

I wake up, screaming. I look around, but no one is there. I look down and lift my shirt hurriedly. *Nothing, just a lot of sweat.*

Moments later, Trent bursts into the room and looks directly at me, then he scans the room quickly before visibly relaxing. He sits down beside me, I'm shaking violently. His eyes shine with concern, he puts his hand on my shoulder and gives me a brief, friendly shake.

"You alright, bud?" he asks.

I jolt away from him.

"Get off!"

I scramble to the opposite side of the bed. Trent's eyes widen in surprise at my hasty retreat and his lips form a thin line.

"What's wrong?"

I shake my head frantically. He frowns and stands up, his hands raised as he grabs a dining chair and pulls it up close to me. He sits down on it, crosses his legs and continues to observe me.

"You can't have been screaming for nothing."

He tries to keep his voice neutral, but it's betrayed by obvious concern.

I shake my head again and place my head in my hands. I feel like I need to have a good cry but know I can't do it in front of him, I don't want him to think I'm weak.

"Just a stupid dream."

He combs his fingers through his messy hair.

"It was Tobias again, wasn't it?" he murmurs.

I look up at him.

"How did you know?"

Trent responds with a simple shrug.

"Just a hunch."

I give him a weak smile. He stands and places a hand gently on my shoulder. I flinch slightly but don't leap away this time.

"You are safe here, but please, I implore you to get some help."

"I can't," I whisper.

Trent blinks at me.

"Mark, please."

"I can't," I repeat, more forcefully.

He frowns again and walks back into his bedroom. I lie flat on my back and stare up at the ceiling. I check my hands which are still trembling. I scold myself for denying Trent's help. *Get a hold of yourself, Flint.* Tobias is locked away, but these nightmares are coming on so suddenly, they're getting worse and I don't know why. I rub my forehead, desperate to be rid of my nightmare. My cell rings, startling me. I pick it up; it's Rachael. I'm not in the mood at the moment, so I let it go through to voice mail. Seconds later, she tries again. I sigh and answer it, knowing that she won't give up.

"Hello," I manage.

"Hey. Trent just called, he said you needed me. What's going on?"

I groan inwardly and silently curse Trent's persistence.

"Rachael, I don't want to talk about it."

"Mark, you can tell me anything. If you want us to be together, you need to be open with me. Just tell me what's wrong." She's getting desperate.

I take in a large breath and exhale. *Here goes.*

"I keep having nightmares about Tobias. They are getting worse," I answer quickly.

I hear her gasp in surprise.

"What happens in them? Tell me more."

"Just flashbacks of the old days with him, and then these... messed up dreams, where he haunts my new life. I feel alone."

"You're not alone, Mark. You have people around you that care about you."

I scoff in disbelief.

"It's true, Mark. I love you, Trent loves you, and by the sound of it, Louise already loves you. Tobias is locked away. He's not going anywhere for a long time, except for the super-max," she reassures.

"Super-max?"

"Yes. He was convicted yesterday. He's been sentenced to life behind bars and we'll be transferring him soon."

"That's great, but I don't know how that's going to make me feel any better."

"Speak to me or Trent. We care about you, so don't shut us out."

"Okay, I'll try. Thank you, Rachael."

"Don't thank me, thank Trent."

"Sure. I'll speak to you later. I love you."

I feel her warmth through the phone.

"I love you too."

I press end on my cell. I feel elevated, much better. Trent slinks out of his room and shoots me a quick glance.

"Thank you, Trent."

He sits at the dining room table.

"Anytime. I was worried about you. Feel better?" he asks.

"Much. I'm sorry I haven't expressed how grateful I am to have you and Rachael on my side."

He smiles.

"Just don't shut us out. We want to help you."

"I won't," I smile.

He sniffs, then gets to his feet.

"Enough of this mushy talk. You have an important meeting to attend. You still good for it?"

"As I'll ever be," I answer, getting off the bed.

"We'd better get ready to go," he smiles.

I'm showered, shaved and dressed in a charcoal pinstripe suit and navy tie. Trent sits back on the couch and examines me when I enter the lounge.

"What do you think?" I ask.

He gets up and looks at me closely while he rubs his chin thoughtfully.

"Perfect," he exclaims.

I smile at him and collect my bag.

"Let's go," Trent continues.

We walk together down 7th Avenue, through the brightly lit Times Square before turning left onto West 42nd Street. Trent has given me little information about his boss, which is irritating. All I know is his name is Kevan Levitt, and he originally came from Ireland. We stand outside the hotel. It looks like an old building, nineteenth-century perhaps, though it is relatively modern at the entrance.

"This is the Neapolitan Hotel. Don't be nervous, everyone's cool here."

He nudges me playfully in the ribs.

"Get it? Everyone's *cool* here. You know?"

I chuckle slightly, but furrow my brow too.

"Can we go in now, please?"

Trent recomposes himself, then leads the way inside, past two smartly dressed porters who open the doors for us. I trail after him quickly as we walk through the marble lobby, its floors striped with light and dark shades of brown. We head towards the elevators. He presses the call button where we stand and wait. The elevator pings loudly and the doors slide open. We both calmly step inside.

"You aren't coming with me, are you?" I ask.

I only just realize that Trent still hasn't left me. He looks across at me.

"I need to take you to Mr. Levitt's office. His orders," he explains.

I'm getting butterflies in my stomach as we ride up to meet Mr. Levitt. I've never had a real job before so this is all completely new to me. Another loud ping pulls me from my uncertain thoughts as the elevator arrives on the fifth floor. We both step out and walk down a long corridor with beige walls and a dark red carpet. We pass various bedroom doors before Trent swipes his access card and leads me through a staff door at the end of the hall. We stand outside a mahogany door and I am reminded of Rachael's silky hair. I envision her, my Rachael, my shining light, dressed in white, her hazel eyes and her soft wanting lips draw me close.

"Ready?"

Rachael vanishes from my vision as I am snapped out of my reverie by Trent's voice. I shake my head and blink a few times.

I clear my throat. "Yeah."

He knocks loudly and confidently on the door. A second later, a deep voice summons.

"Come in."

I look at Trent and he gestures with his hand for me to enter first. With a shaking hand, I twist the doorknob and enter the room which is decorated with cream walls, blue carpet and various hotel awards plastered on the wall. A middle-aged man with white hair and specs, wearing a sharp suit is sitting behind his mahogany desk looking at a computer screen. When I enter, he looks up and smiles.

"Ah. Mr. Flint, I presume," he greets warmly.

He has a convincing American accent, though with a slight hint of Irish too.

I swallow. "Yes, sir."

His smile grows wider as he stands from his seat before turning his attention to Trent.

"Thank you, Trent."

Trent nods and backs out, shutting the door softly behind him. I look back at Mr. Levitt who continues to smile at me.

"Take a seat, son." He directs his hand towards the chair opposite him.

I walk over and sit down, as does he. Mr. Levitt quickly reads something on his computer before he turns back to me.

"It seems you don't have a lot of work experience, Mr. Flint," he starts.

I swallow the lump in my throat and desperately try to find an answer.

"No. I'm afraid I don't," I manage.

He regards me with his brown eyes.

"Your friend speaks very highly of you, though. Could you tell me what you have been doing with yourself recently?" he asks.

I die inside. I hoped that I wouldn't be asked this question. I'm tempted to lie to him, but I know that would be a bad idea.

"It's a little complicated."

He relaxes in his chair and removes his specs.

"What's complicated, Mr. Flint?"

I decide to get it over with quickly.

"I have just been released from prison, sir. I was wrongfully accused of something."

I look down at my shiny shoes, ashamed, but when I peek up, he is leaning over his desk and seems to be examining me.

"I can tell," he says simply.

I'm astounded by his response, but what surprises me the most is that he is still smiling at me.

"What Trent has told me about you, Mr. Flint, speaks more to me than a wrongful prison sentence. You would make a fine addition to my team here."

I look at him, wide-eyed.

"I don't know why, but I like you. I think you are trustworthy. You have only confirmed how I feel by telling me the truth when it would have been easier to lie. I find it very noble. It's a valuable trait to have, Mr. Flint."

He looks at one of the hotel awards in his office before turning back to me.

"Would you like to work for me?" he asks.

"Yes please, sir," I enthuse.

"Well then, welcome aboard."

He stands and offers me his hand. I arise quickly and shake his proffered hand enthusiastically.

"You start tomorrow at lunchtime. You'll be met in the lobby by a young lady named Melissa. She will be showing you how things are done here."

"Thank you for the opportunity. I won't let you down, Mr. Levitt."

I grab my bag and make my way to the door before turning to face him again.

"Oh, before I go…"

Mr. Levitt looks up expectantly.

"What's my role here?"

Mr. Levitt smiles and chuckles slightly.

"Apologies. You will be a cleaner."

Cleaner? Well… It's a start.

"Thank you."

"The pleasure's mine, Mr. Flint. Good luck tomorrow," he smiles, then waves me out.

I exit his office and head straight to the elevators, buzzing with excitement. I step inside the waiting elevator and ride it back down to the lobby. I look around and spot Trent and Rex sitting behind a desk, chatting animatedly to each other. Trent peeks over in my direction and I give him a quick wave. He mutters something quickly to Rex, then rushes over to me.

"Well?" he asks excitedly.

I look down at my feet and his smile fades.

"Mark?"

"I'm in."

He beams at me and slaps me hard on the back.

"Good job!" he applauds.

"I have you to thank."

He surprises me by blushing a little. I look towards Rex and give him a wave and a thumbs up. He smiles and waves back.

"I'd better get back to work. See you at home," Trent says.

He strides back to his desk where he continues his conversation with Rex. *Finally, my luck is beginning to turn.*

Chapter Nine

I walk through Broadway, too excited to head home. It is my last day before I start work, so I'm taking this opportunity to walk the streets of Manhattan for a while. I feel like I have been walking for hours; my legs are aching, but I just don't care right now. I make my way through Times Square, which is as noisy and vibrant as ever, though a bit too much for my liking. Excited tourists chat loudly and take photos of the bright surroundings. I walk past the small NYPD station and stop, wondering if I might spot Rachael. She isn't standing outside the front, so I walk around the side of it, but I still can't see her. A police cruiser pulls up and then I see her. Rachael emerges from the car, followed closely by a female cop I don't recognize. They are locked in a conversation as they watch passers-by closely. I watch them, hoping she will be on her own eventually so I can go and speak to her. Finally, the female cop nods at something Rachael says before she jumps back into the cruiser and speeds away. I rush over the street towards Rachael.

"Rachael," I call.

A taxI screeches to a halt as I stupidly rush into the busy street. He beeps angrily and leans out of his window.

"What do you think you're doin'?" he berates me.

I hold my hands up and step back onto the sidewalk. Nearby pedestrians stare at me as if I'm stupid and the irate taxI driver speeds away. I glance back in Rachael's direction, hoping she hasn't left, but luckily, she's still there. She's staring in my direction along with a couple of her colleagues. One of the male police officers is about to approach me, but Rachael holds him back and crosses the street towards me.

"Mark, hey. What are you doing here?"

We have a quick hug and she pecks me on the cheek.

"I was just out for a walk."

She looks me up and down and finally notices that I am wearing a suit.

"Damn, of course. Your meeting with Trent's boss. How'd it go?" she asks.

"I got it. I'm a cleaner at the Neapolitan Hotel."

"Congratulations. I'm so proud of you."

I grin and look at my watch. *Lunchtime.*

"When's your lunch break?" I ask, not wanting to part from her yet.

"I'm always on call, Mark, but we can have a quick bite now if you like."

I smile and take her hand. We push our way through the tourists in Times Square and wander the surrounding streets looking for a suitable place for a quick lunch. She stops outside Joe's Pizza and leads me inside.

"They do fantastic pizza by the slice here," she says.

We make our way to the counter and we each order a slice of Margherita pizza. We sit at a table in the corner and tuck in. *Wow, she's right.* This is the best pizza I've ever eaten.

"I thought a lot about what you said yesterday," she begins.

I stop and stare at her mid-chew.

"You're right. It's not fair for either of us to have this relationship in secret."

I swallow my mouthful, but say nothing, letting her finish.

"I called my mom this morning and mentioned I'm dating someone."

She chuckles a little to herself.

"Of course, she was overjoyed, and they want to meet you tomorrow night."

I look at her. *Jesus. Meet her father, the Chief of Police?*

"I'm sorry, Rachael. I start work tomorrow."

"When do you finish?"

"I'm not sure, but I start at lunch, so I should be finished by five-thirty. I'll let you know."

She thinks about this, then nods.

"I will pick you up then."

After settling that matter, we chat happily to each other, but a troubling thought crosses my mind, spoiling my good mood.

"Rachael, I need to ask you something."

She looks up, also mid-chew, but swallows quickly.

"Oh?" she says, as she sucks her fingers.

I'm distracted momentarily by what she's doing, but I regain my focus.

"Can I ask where you caught Tobias?"

She grins.

"He was found on the docks near the Hudson River. You should have seen the dirty warehouse he was living in. I think his prison cell is an upgrade. At least he has a toilet and a bed in there," she laughs.

I chuckle, but my mind flashes back to one of my nightmares; Tobias and I were there. *Has he been there all this time?* I consider telling Rachael about my nightmares in greater detail, but I'm interrupted by Rachael's police radio crackling to life.

"We have an emergency in Queens. Please respond," the distorted voice calls.

Rachael presses a button.

"This is Officer Clarke. I'm on my way."

She looks at me and frowns, as do I.

"Sorry. I need to go. See you tomorrow."

She jumps up from the table and rushes outside. A couple of police cars speed past, sirens blaring, before one pulls up in front of her. She climbs in, then the car speeds away. It was a young male officer driving this time and I suddenly feel very jealous, I shake it off. *That's ridiculous. They're only work colleagues.* I look down the street, but she's long gone. I turn sharply on my heel and head back to the apartment, now nervous about work and meeting her father, the Chief of Police, tomorrow night.

The apartment is silent when I arrive back. No Trent. I get undressed out of my suit and change into a loose pair of sweat pants and a grey shirt. I sit on the couch and switch on the afternoon news, but I am not paying attention to it. I wonder briefly what the emergency in Queens was about, but I'm more concerned about Rachael. I hope she's okay. *Come on, man. She's a police officer, she's trained for this sort of stuff.* My mind drifts to the male officer that was driving the police car that Rachael got into. If I ask, would she tell me who he is? There's no harm in asking. I rest my feet up on the couch and continue watching the afternoon news, but soon I start to feel weary. I jump awake and shake my head, not wanting to fall asleep, but it soon takes hold of me and I drift off.

I am awoken by the front door slamming shut. Trent breezes into the living room, glances over at me briefly and grins before depositing his bag on the floor by the kitchen island.

"Good day?" he asks, sounding exhausted.

I grin at him broadly. He shakes his head playfully.

"I take it from that smile that you saw Rachael today."

I nod and reply. "I took her out for lunch."

Trent switches off the TV and sits cross-legged on the couch beside me.

"That's nice," he replies simply, then switches on his laptop.

I get up off the couch and head to the box of clothes to see what would be appropriate to wear to work tomorrow. I don't want to wear anything smart if I'm a cleaner. I choose some old, over washed blue jeans and a simple white shirt. Trent glances over.

"They do provide uniform, you know."

"Just want to be prepared."

He nods his head in acknowledgement and returns to his laptop. My next task is to choose clothes for the meeting with Rachael's parents tomorrow night. I'm pleased she has finally agreed to let me meet them, but I can't help having a sense of unease about it all. Rachael has already admitted that her father is stern, though she did add that he is also loving; maybe that will win out. I sure hope so. Desperate to clear my troubled thoughts, I grab my cell quickly and punch in Rachael's number; she answers almost instantly. That's surprising. I was expecting to leave her a voice mail.

"Evening, Mark," she says.

"Evening, Rachael. How was the emergency?"

She sighs heavily.

"Complicated, but dealt with."

I'm curious and attempt to probe her further.

"May I ask-."

"It's classified." She stops me quickly.

"I'm sorry. Am I still seeing you tomorrow?"

"Of course, if you still want to go."

I think about backing out, but decide I must do this.

"Of course."

"Great. I will pick you up at five-thirty from work. What's the address?"

"I'll text it to you."

I don't know it in full, but I'll look it up.

"Wonderful. See you tomorrow."

"Good night. Looking forward to it," I say, trying to sound genuine.

"Good night."

I know that Rachael is probably more afraid than me about tomorrow, but I will be sure to put her at ease and prove everyone wrong once we get there. I look up the address of the Neapolitan Hotel and send her a quick text. I wait, but there is no reply. I shrug and am suddenly overcome with exhaustion once again.

I wake bright and early, excited about my first *real* day at work. I leap out of bed and have a quick shower. I heard Trent leave early this morning, but I will meet up with him when I get to work. I get changed into the clothes I chose last night and make my way to the kitchen. I decide on a quick breakfast, opting for a cinnamon and raisin bagel. I sit at the dining room table, finish my bagel and drink my coffee. Once I'm done, I brush my teeth and check myself in the mirror. I scowl at myself; my hair's starting to get long again. *Damn. Why does it grow so fast?* I hastily try and bring it under control with my fingers, but fail. I groan at myself, annoyed. I must schedule another haircut with Rex, but for now, it'll have to do. I grab my coat and bag, and head out the door, ready for my first day at the hotel.

I arrive outside the hotel after a ten-minute walk. It was a nice stroll, aside from nearly being trampled by other commuters. I've been pushed and shoved more times than I care to remember, but it didn't bother me really. I hold my head up and stride through the double doors. I look over at Trent's desk, but he isn't there. I step further in and find Mr. Levitt standing beside the marble reception desk.

"Welcome," he greets me with an outstretched hand.

I shake it enthusiastically and take a quick glance at the young woman standing beside him. She can't be any older than twenty-five, she is fairly short with long strawberry blonde hair, smells strongly of perfume and is coated in makeup.

"I like to see you so punctual, Mr. Flint. This is Melissa, she will be working alongside you," he explains.

She steps towards me slightly, offers me a warm smile and extends her hand at me like Mr. Levitt just did. I shake it slightly.

"Pleased to meet you," Melissa murmurs.

I look back at Mr. Levitt as he grins at us both.

"Glad to see you both getting on already. Well, I'll leave you to it."

He strides casually through the marble lobby and back towards the elevators. I turn my attention back to Melissa who continues to stare at me, which makes me very uncomfortable. I lick my bottom lip, wondering what I should say now.

"Um… so, what now?" I decide to ask, breaking the silence between us.

Her smile fades before she turns and walks away.

"Follow me," she says quietly.

I rush after her as she heads for the elevators. We ride up in silence, but she has started to chew gum a bit too noisily. I clear my throat feeling uncomfortable, but thankfully, the elevator arrives at our floor. She steps out first, we walk down a corridor past several bedrooms until we reach the staff access door. She swipes her access card and enters. We walk down another long corridor, past Mr. Levitt's office, then she opens a white door at the end.

"This is the staff room. Leave your bag in here." She points towards the lockers.

I place my bag and jacket into the first available locker that I find. I face her again but she says nothing, just turns and exits. I follow her down the corridor. She looks at me out the corner of her eye, but when I return her glance, she hastily looks away and picks at her fingernails. *A nervous habit, I presume.* She opens another door on the opposite end of the corridor and gestures me with her hand to enter first. I walk past her and we seem to be in the utility room. The walls and floor are concrete and there are a couple of wooden shelves with cleaning products lined on them. Melissa steps in behind me, evident from the sound of increasingly loud gum-chewing, and she turns on the light. It buzzes noisily into life above us. She gives me a long, sharp stare and I feel more uncomfortable than I did before. Finally, she speaks.

"This is where all the cleaning equipment is kept. When a guest checks out, you collect things from here, then go and clean that room before the next guest arrives," she explains.

I nod, listening carefully. She looks at the clock above us.

"Guests will be checking out soon. We had better get ready."

She scoots around me and grabs the janitor trolley filled with new bed linen and cleaning materials, then she picks up the vacuum and thrusts it at me. I take it from her and watch as she also collects the mop and bucket. We head out of the utility room, then she locks the door behind her. I follow her towards the elevators and I press the call button. We stand and wait in awkward silence. I clear my throat again, feeling gradually more uncomfortable, but the elevator arrives. We wait for the hotel guests to clear out first.

"Morning," I greet an old couple warmly.

"Morning," the old lady smiles.

Melissa steps in without a word and I begrudgingly follow after her, bringing the equipment with me. The doors slide shut as we make our way back down to reception. She glances over at me again.

"So, do you have a girlfriend?" she asks, which takes me completely by surprise.

What an inappropriate question!

"Yes," I state, continuing to glance at the closed doors in front of me.

"*Good,*" she answers, but it sounded very sarcastic.

We arrive on the ground floor and as soon as the doors open, Melissa storms out, leaving me to carry everything she left behind. I struggle with it all, but Rex spots me and rushes over, grabbing the bucket from me, preventing me from spilling water everywhere.

"Thanks," I smile.

He smiles back at me, then shoots Melissa a nasty stare, but she ignores us both.

"Sorry about *her,*" Rex apologizes.

I shake my head and shrug my shoulders.

"Don't worry about it, Rex. Not the worst I've experienced. Trust me on that."

He walks over to the lobby with me and drops everything at my feet.

"Thanks again, Rex. My hero." I chuckle.

Rex laughs with me.

"Oh, it was nothing. I gotta go, darling. Don't let her give you grief. Okay?"

"Sure thing. See you later. Say 'hi' to Trent from me."

"I will. So long. I'll be at the desk if you need rescuing again!"

I laugh.

"Okay, Rex."

Rex walks back to the desk, where a customer is waiting. I look over at Melissa. She gives me a venomous stare that feels like it could slice right through me.

"So, are we going to get started or what!?" she yells angrily, which makes guests turn around in utter shock and disgust.

I'm so embarrassed. *How did this woman get a job here? She's unbearable.*

"*Yes,*" I reply coolly.

Me and Melissa work in silence as we start to dust and polish the lobby. After a while of awkward glances from her, she collects the cleaning equipment and heads back to the elevators.

"Are you coming?" she asks grumpily.

I turn away from my task of cleaning the reception desk and scowl at her.

"When I'm finished with what I'm doing, yes."

We glower at each other briefly, but she luckily regains her professional demeanor.

"Come to the first floor when you're done. The bedrooms are next."

Before I have the chance to answer, she heads into an elevator and makes her way to the first floor. I blow out a breath in frustration. I don't know how I'm going to cope working alongside someone who seems to hate my guts for some reason. I glance quickly at a young female receptionist who grins at me sympathetically and rolls her eyes, this makes me chuckle slightly.

"Have you had trouble from her too?" I joke softly.

She sniggers. "We all have."

I quickly finish what I am doing and make my way to the first floor, stopping only briefly to shoot a look back at the sympathetic receptionist.

"Wish me luck," I joke.

She laughs loudly.

"Luck," she responds, as I step into the waiting elevator.

I find Melissa in one of the guest bedrooms, cleaning the bathroom. I step inside and she glances up.

"Christ, what kept you?" she snaps.

"Sorry," I respond sullenly.

"Well. You can start by vacuuming the bedroom."

She turns her back to me and continues scrubbing the bathtub. I go out into the corridor to retrieve the vacuum, while mimicking her snarky voice. I'm tempted to shout something sarcastic at her, but a few guests walk past, so I wisely hold my tongue. I need this job desperately and I'm not going to waste my time arguing. I start vacuuming, but feel miserable. *This is going to be a long day.*

Contrary to my earlier beliefs, my day goes faster than I had expected. I am feeling rather pleased with myself. I've managed to clean eight bedrooms in five hours. Melissa has been giving me the cold shoulder all day, only speaking to me to give sharp and authoritative instructions. I have managed to hold in my frustrations all day as I have been busy thinking about Rachael, about us. *Speaking of which.*

I check my watch; thirty minutes until Rachael arrives. I rush to the staff room to retrieve my bag and jacket, then head to the restroom. I remove my work clothes and change into a smart blue checked shirt, denim jeans, leather jacket and smart shoes that I packed last night. I look at myself in the mirror, again battling with my scruffy hair, but it's still a mess, though it's better than it was. I stuff my work clothes into my rucksack and rush out, stumbling hard into Trent.

"Whoa. What's your hurry?"

He looks at me puzzled, noticing that I've changed my clothes, then he smirks.

"Date night?" he asks.

I shake my head.

"I'm meeting Rachael's parents tonight."

Trent's eyes widen a fraction, then he grabs my arm and pulls me back into the restrooms.

"I don't know if you should go through with this, Mark. It's too soon," he hisses.

I cock my head to one side, confused.

"Why?" I ask.

He begins to pace around uncomfortably.

"I just have a bad feeling about this. I'm just looking out for you."

I approach him and place a hand on his shoulder. He finally stops and looks at me.

"I know you are, but I'll be fine. I'm only meeting her folks. What could go wrong?"

I won't admit it to Trent, but I know exactly what could go wrong.

Trent responds with a weak smile. I check my watch again; I'm running late.

"Listen, I need to go," I say.

I shrug off my bag and hand it to Trent.

"Could you take this home for me?"

Trent continues to stare at me, nonplussed.

"Please?" I beg.

He reaches out and takes it from me. I give him a grateful smile before I rush out without a backward glance. I dash through the lobby and give Rex a quick wave on my way out. He looks surprised as I hurry past him, but I don't have time to hang around. I push through the double doors and out into the freezing fall air. Rachael is standing on the sidewalk, leaning against the hotel wall. She looks more stunning than ever. She is outfitted in a long black dress and stilettos. Her hair is swept over her right shoulder, revealing her slender neckline. My mouth dries and I'm lost for words. *Christ. I'm acting like a twelve-year-old who just picked up a dirty magazine.* She looks towards the hotel doors and sees me standing and staring. A slow sexy grin spreads across her face when she sees me. My heart skips a beat. *Holy hell.* She begins to approach me.

"Hello, Mark. How was work?" she asks smoothly.

I finally find my voice.

"Interesting," I state.

She smiles and offers me her hand. I take it happily and we walk to the parking lot, a block away from the hotel. She collects her keys out of her purse and presses a button on the fob. A white Mercedes flashes to life, I look at the car with awe.

"Nice car."

She beams at me.

"Thanks," she chuckles.

I walk around to the driver's side door and open it. She looks puzzled.

"Just thought I would be a gentleman," I explain modestly.

Her face lights up and she glides smoothly into the driver's seat. I close her door and stroll over to the passenger side where I step in and settle into the plush leather seat. She glances over and gives me a small smirk.

"Are you sure about this?" she asks.

I give her a reassuring glance and take her hand.

"We'll be fine," I reassure.

She nods and blows out a long breath before putting the key into the ignition and the car purrs into life. She gives me a final glance, then pulls out of the parking lot and into the busy evening traffic.

Chapter Ten

———— ∼∼ ————

We're stuck in rush hour traffic in the middle of the Hugh L. Carey Tunnel. Rachael reaches over to the car stereo and switches on the evening traffic report, but I'm not really paying attention to it. I'm bristling with nerves and I feel Rachael is too. I peek over at her, but she continues to glance straight ahead. As the traffic inches forward a fraction, I rub my hands nervously against my jeans which seems to get her attention. She turns off the radio.

"Are you okay?" she asks.

"Sure. You?" I return.

She responds only with a soft sigh. She is very quiet, and the silence is driving me crazy.

"Who was that man?" I ask.

She looks at me, confused.

"The man that picked you up yesterday, after we had lunch," I clarify.

She turns her attention back to the road, but I can't see her expression.

"His name is Scott Davis. He's a rookie on the force, only joined us four weeks ago. I'm showing him the ropes."

I look out the passenger window.

"Why do you ask?"

I shrug. "Curious."

She chuckles softly.

"You seem curious about a lot of things."

I laugh.

"I've always been that way."

She reaches over and gives my leg a gentle squeeze but says nothing more.

We've made it out of the tunnel and emerge into Brooklyn. After a while, she takes a sharp left off Ocean Parkway and into a suburban neighborhood. I glance quickly at the street sign, *Marlborough Road*. It's a quiet street, surrounded by trees and smart, delicate houses. She pulls into a driveway on the left and switches off the engine.

"Here we go," Rachael says, her eyes rounded with worry.

I give her hand a gentle squeeze to reassure her. She steps out of the car and I follow after her. We walk over a perfectly manicured lawn and up a few stone steps of a large white house. We step onto the wooden porch and approach a pair of large dark wood double doors. She takes a nervous breath, then knocks loudly and we wait. A moment later, the double doors open and a slim, tall, middle-aged lady stands before us. She has mahogany hair like Rachael, albeit slightly paler, and kind brown eyes. She bears a warm, welcoming smile.

"Rae. It's been too long," she says sweetly.

Rachael steps in and hugs her. *Rae? I like it.*

"Hi, Mom."

They release each other before Rachael turns to me.

"This is Mark," she introduces me to her mother.

"Mark, this is my mom, Sara."

I step forward and offer Mrs. Clarke my hand, but she takes us both by surprise by folding me into her arms and hugging me hard. I hug her back weakly.

"Welcome to my home. Come in, you must be freezing."

She waves her hand in the direction of the hallway. I step in anxiously. Rachael takes my hand and smiles.

"Come and meet the rest of the family," Mrs. Clarke says, ushering us further in. We follow closely behind.

"Colin, Louise. Rachael's home," she calls.

The first thing I hear is loud footsteps barreling down the stairs. I look at Rachael, who rolls her eyes.

"*That* would be Louise, but you've already met *her*."

She points her thumb in the direction of the noise. Louise makes it to the bottom of the stairs and rushes towards Rachael, hugging her hard. She then turns to me.

"Good to see you again," Louise says happily.

Rachael grabs her arm.

"Don't breathe a word to Dad," she hisses.

Louise holds her hand to her mouth.

"Sorry," she whispers and smiles apologetically, before heading away into another room.

Rachael rolls her eyes again and leads me into a plush living area. There is a large fireplace with a warm fire already lit, two cream couches stand opposite each other and at the back of the room, there is a stain glass window. I look around in amazement.

"It's not much," Rachael says modestly.

"It's fantastic," I compliment.

She leads me to one of the immaculate couches where we sit. A moment later, Mrs. Clarke re-enters the room followed closely by who I can only assume is Mr. Clarke. Like his wife, he is tall, except he has black hair and blue eyes, and has a stern look on his face. He smiles warmly at Rachael, but gives me the briefest of looks. I smile at him but he furrows his brow and grunts. Rachael stands, as do I.

"Colin, this is Mark." Mrs. Clarke points in my direction.

I step forward and extend my hand as a greeting to Mr. Clarke.

"Pleased to meet you, sir."

He doesn't return my handshake but glares at me and his frown deepens. His mouth twists with uncertainty, then he walks past me towards Rachael, greeting her fondly.

"Colin, manners," Mrs. Clarke hisses at him angrily.

He lets go of Rachael and comes to stand in front of me again, begrudgingly shaking my hand.

"Pleased to meet you," he says gruffly, before turning and leaving the room without another word.

I look at Mrs. Clarke who watches her husband with disapproval as he leaves, then she races after him. I look at Rachael who has paled a little. I sit back down, and she sinks beside me.

"I don't think he likes me," I whisper, half-joking.

She looks at me.

"Mom will talk to him."

We sit and listen to the crackling fire, but otherwise, the room is deathly quiet until Louise enters.

"Mom says dinner is ready."

We stand and follow her into the dining room. Mr. and Mrs. Clarke sit opposite each other at an impressive oak table. Mr. Clarke is still frowning, and Mrs. Clarke looks at him with a look of fury, but when she spots us, she stands politely.

"Louise. Take a seat beside your father, please," she instructs.

"Rachael, Mark, you sit here on the right, next to me."

We take our seats while Mrs. Clarke rushes off to collect our meals. I look towards Mr. Clarke, but he looks straight through me. Rachael finally pipes up, killing the silence.

"Work's been busy recently. How's college, Lou?"

Louise beams.

"It's great. Difficult though."

Mrs. Clarke returns and places the plates on the table in front of us. We are having chicken dressed in a white sauce with baby potatoes and green vegetables. However, unlike the rest of us, Rachael has a roasted vegetable tartlet.

"I'm vegetarian," she explains.

Of course. She had vegetable spaghettI on our first date.

"Ah," I acknowledge and start my meal.

"So, Mr. Flint. What have you been doing with yourself?"

Mr. Clarke is finally talking to me. I look up and face him nervously.

"I work as a cleaner at a hotel with my friend."

Mr. Clarke chuckles to himself.

"A cleaner? Perfect job for an ex-convict," he responds sarcastically.

"Colin!" Mrs. Clarke warns.

He looks over the table at her and I try to respond positively.

"Just trying to change my life around for the better, sir."

He grunts and we all continue to eat.

"That's nice, Mark," Mrs. Clarke answers.

I smile at her gratefully.

"What about you, Louise? How is your ob-gyn course going?" Mrs. Clarke asks.

Louise glances up.

"I love it. I was just telling Rae that it's getting harder."

"It will get harder, dear, but it will pay off in the end," Mrs. Clarke responds.

"Dad. Did you hear that we caught Tobias O'Malley a few days ago?" Rachael asks.

The table falls silent as Mr. Clarke takes a sip of his brandy.

"Did your boyfriend assist? I'm aware that he used to be *very* familiar with him," he asks, stressing the word 'boyfriend'.

I bristle a little.

"No. We found him on our own. He was on the docks by the Hudson."

"Glad to hear it," he responds.

Rachael scowls slightly at her father, then gets back to her meal. Louise starts to chatter loudly to her parents, but at the moment, I'm not taking much notice. I feel discouraged by Mr. Clarke's scrutiny and I'm not sure whether I want to be here anymore. Rachael and I finish our dinner in silence, only having an occasional glance at each other. When we are done, Mrs. Clarke stands again and clears the dishes. Rachael takes my hand under the table and offers me an apologetic smile.

"Sorry," she mouths.

I respond with a shrug. She stands and we head back into the living area where we sit by the fire again before Mrs. Clarke enters.

"Coffee, anyone?" she offers.

"No, thanks," Rachael and I both respond in unison.

Mrs. Clarke turns slowly and heads towards the kitchen. Mr. Clarke hasn't joined us in the living room. *He probably doesn't want to be around me.* I try and take reassurance that at least Rachael's mother and sister seem to like me, but I'm unsure what can be done about her father. I'm distracted from my thoughts by the sound of raised voices coming from the kitchen. Me and Rachael turn towards the source of the noise.

"I'd better check that out." She stands and I grab her wrist.

"Please don't."

She looks down at me and blinks, surprised.

"Louise," she calls.

A second later, Louise appears in the doorway.

"Keep Mark company."

Rachael shakes me off and heads towards the kitchen. I can do nothing but watch helplessly. Louise sits beside me. I look at her and try to distract myself.

"So, you're studying to be an Ob-Gyn?" I ask.

"Yeah, but my true ambition is to be a chef, but, well... you've met Dad."

"He doesn't want you to be a chef?"

I remember Rachael and Trent's conversation about Mr. Clarke dictating Louise's career path and I suddenly feel a pang of sympathy for her.

"Nah, he wants me to do something 'useful', like the rest of the family."

"Never give up on your dream. You'll get there one day."

She smiles sweetly and places her hand gratefully on my shoulder.

"Thanks, Mark."

The raised voices get louder and I'm sure I can hear Rachael. I get to my feet.

"What are you doing?" Louise asks, shocked.

"I need to help her," I state, before striding towards the kitchen.

Louise runs over and puts her hands on my chest to stop me.

"You can't," she says, panicked.

"I need to."

I try to get past her, but she grabs my arm. Her eyes shine with concern, I take pity and sit back down. Moments later, Rachael storms out of the kitchen followed closely by her parents. Mr. Clarke is red in the face, as is Rachael. I've never seen her so full of scorn before.

"You can't decide for me. I'm not a child, Dad!" She turns to her father, screaming.

"You're my daughter. I'm just trying to protect you," he shouts back.

"Protect me? From what!?" She clenches her fists angrily.

"Him," he shouts, pointing in my direction.

Everyone stares at me. *I just want to curl up and die right now.*

"That's enough, Colin. Stop it," Mrs. Clarke demands.

Mr. Clarke scowls at his wife and grunts. Rachael marches over to me and grabs my arm.

"Come on, Mark. We're leaving."

She pulls me up and storms to the front door as I follow her. She opens it wide, then freezes. She turns slowly to face the rest of her family who are staring at her in bewilderment.

"If you can't accept the life I have chosen, the good man that Mark truly is, then I want no part in this judgmental family," she says quietly, but scornfully.

She pulls me outside, slamming the door loudly behind us. She presses her key fob, unlocking the car and I jump in, as does Rachael. She places her face in her hands and takes a calming breath. I look out the window and see Mrs. Clarke rushing down the drive.

"Wait," she shouts.

Rachael sighs and winds down her window.

"I'm sorry. I'm not mad at you, Mom. I'm mad at Dad."

Mrs. Clarke leans in the window and starts to sob a little.

"I'm so sorry, to both of you, especially you, Mark. I will speak to your father."

Rachael softens a little and hugs her mom.

"Thanks for dinner," she whispers, then closes her window, pulls out of the driveway and speeds away.

We drive in silence through Brooklyn and back towards the Hugh L. Carey Tunnel. I try to think about something to say to lighten the mood, but my mind is blank. I glance anxiously at Rachael who keeps her focus firmly on the road ahead. I clear my throat, she looks over briefly and I give her a quick smile, but she quickly looks away again. I run my hands through my hair and breathe out the held breath I hadn't even realized I was holding. Rachael sniffs and wipes her eyes.

"I'm sorry. This was my idea. It's my fault," I try.

She peeks over at me again.

"You don't need to be. This isn't your fault. My father just doesn't know when he's off-duty. He thinks he needs to police everyone and everything, 24/7."

I reach over, desperate to comfort her, but decide that would be a bad idea while she's driving, so I place my hand back on my lap.

"I'll take you home," she offers, taking me by surprise.

"I was hoping I could stay with you tonight. That's if you don't mind. I don't want to push my luck any further."

I think I see a ghost of a smile on her beautiful, but woeful face.

"Sure."

I light up inside. I've never stayed over at a girl's house, not even when I was a teenager. In fact, she is the only girlfriend I've had. As Trent once put it, I've really landed on my feet with her. We continue the journey in peace. Rachael has switched the traffic report back on to kill the silence, but like before, I'm not really paying attention. I spend the majority of the journey trying to think how the dinner with her parents got so out of hand. I smile to myself with a redeeming thought; Rachael cares about me enough to stick up for me. Mrs. Clarke and Louise were lovely and so welcoming the second I arrived, but Mr. Clarke seemed to hate me straight away, most likely because I've been in jail. *Does he think it's wrong for someone like me to be with a girl like his daughter? I'm just not sure.*

"What are you thinking about?" Rachael interrupts my train of thought.

"Nothing really," I lie.

She looks at me as if she wants to pick my brains further, but thankfully, she says nothing and pushes down on the gas, accelerating us through the night. I should send Trent a quick text. I know what he's like, if I'm not back soon, he'll worry. I fish out my cell and tap out a quick and simple text:

Staying at Rachael's tonight.

I hit send and relax back into my seat. Faster than I had expected, he replies:

Cool, have a good night.

I switch off my cell, not wanting to be interrupted, and place it back in my pocket.

We approach her apartment complex. She takes a sharp left and pulls into the underground garage. It's relatively deserted as I can only see a few other cars parked in here. She parks smoothly into her designated space and switches off the engine. I risk a quick peek in her direction. She looks so forlorn, and it pulls at my heartstrings.

"What if you leave it for a few days, then call your mom?" I suggest.

She doesn't look at me, nor does she respond. She reaches into the back seat of the car and grabs her purse.

"Let's get inside," she says as she slowly steps out.

I scramble out after her, she presses the key fob to lock the car and heads towards the elevator. I rush over to her and take her hand in mine, grasping her soft fingers delicately, but she doesn't return the gesture. I start to worry that after what happened tonight, Rachael will change her mind about us and call it off. I dash that unbearable thought away. We ascend in the elevator and arrive on floor fifteen. We walk to her front door as she quickly fetches her keys out of her purse and unlocks it.

"After you," she says.

Not wanting to argue, I comply and head inside. She follows behind and slams the door shut, which startles me. She strolls past me and throws her purse on the couch before heading into the kitchen.

"I need some wine. Want some?" she asks gruffly.

I respond with a nod and watch her closely. She grabs two wine glasses out of the cupboard, pulls a bottle of red from the wine rack and pours it into the glasses. She looks over at me, catching me staring at her. She grins as her mood begins to lift.

"Sit down, Mark. Make yourself at home."

I remove my shoes and sit on the couch. She walks over, hands me my glass of wine and sits down beside me. She turns to face me, regards me carefully, then takes a large swig from her glass.

"That feels so much better," she murmurs, more to herself.

She places her wine on the table in front of us, then bends down and peels off her stilettos, one after the other, then folds her legs beneath her on the couch before throwing her shoes over to the corner of the room.

"I don't know why I bother with him," she says under her breath as she massages the soles of her feet.

Who? Me? She notices my shocked expression. Suddenly, she bursts out with laughter.

"Don't look so shocked, Mark. I was talking about my father."

I let out a sigh of relief. I hadn't realized that I was making that expression. I laugh with her, but then she stops laughing and looks at me more seriously.

"Mark," she starts, but we are interrupted by Rachael's cell phone buzzing.

She rips her gaze from me and darts a disapproving look at her purse. She stands quickly and rummages for her cell. She pulls it out and checks the number, then furrows her brow angrily and denies the call. I frown.

"Who?" I ask.

She raises an eyebrow with an 'isn't it obvious' expression. I can guess, so I ask no more. Her cell rings again.

"Christ sake," she grumbles loudly and answers it.

"Hello, Mom," she answers angrily.

She pinches the bridge of her nose and sits down opposite me.

"I don't care that Dad is trying to call me, Mom. I don't want to talk to him after what he just did."

She sounds pissed. She stands back up and walks towards the window.

"I don't care that he wants to talk to me. The answer is *no*."

I look at her, concerned. She groans heavily and grabs a cushion, holding it to her chest for comfort.

"Look, Mom. I'm tired and I don't want to talk about this anymore tonight. You tell Dad that no matter what his fucking opinion is on Mark, I... Don't... Care." She stresses every word.

"Goodnight."

She punches the end button before hastily switching her cell off and dropping it on the couch. She picks up her wine and downs the glass.

"What did she want?" I ask.

She puts her glass down and stares at me.

"It doesn't matter, I don't want to discuss it."

I hold my hands up in apology.

"Anyway, what I was going to say before we were *rudely* interrupted was, I'm sorry about my father. He behaved in a despicable manner."

She leans against the armchair and stares at me lovingly. I return her gaze with a warm, reassuring look of my own and smirk at her.

"I don't blame you. Please don't be sorry. Thanks for sticking up for me over there."

She sits down and continues to hold the cushion to her chest.

"He has always been so stubborn," she says, looking down.

I take a sip my wine and place my glass next to hers. I walk over and lift her face gently with my index finger.

"You don't need to feel bad about what happened. I'm serious, I've had worse."

I search her face for a clue that she will stop being so hard on herself. She still has a bitter look of sadness, but she rewards my comfort with a warm smile that melts everything inside me. She lifts her face to mine and kisses me sweetly and passionately. It's over too soon though, as she breaks away. I sit on the armrest beside her and finish my wine. Rachael stands and puts both our glasses in the kitchen sink, throwing the cushion back onto the couch in the process. She wanders back towards me.

"It's late. We both have work in the morning," she says softly.

"I don't start till midday," I scold her playfully.

She giggles.

"Okay. *I* have work in the morning then."

I laugh.

"In all seriousness, I'm going to get ready for bed. I'll fetch you a spare duvet and pillow shortly," she says.

"Thanks, Rae."

She smiles, then turns and walks into her bedroom, closing the door softly.

I stare at the closed door for a moment and wonder what I should do with myself. I slap my hands on my knees, stand up and look around the room. I sigh, then pick up her purse and cell where she discarded them on the couch and place them neatly on the coffee table beside me. I'm exhausted, so I start to get ready for bed. I remove my socks and pants so that I am left wearing only my boxers and shirt. I place all the cushions into a tidy pile on one end of the couch and lie on my back staring up at the ceiling. I try to come up with a plan as to what I could do to impress her father and make it a little easier for Rachael to deal with. I don't want her to fall out with her family because of me. She is lucky to have one. I had to grow up with no parents or siblings, only my grandma loved me, but she's gone too. I roll onto my side and try to clear my negative thoughts. I want to stay motivated to put things right for her. The sound of Rachael's bedroom door opening pulls me from my thoughts and takes me by surprise, considering that I am half-naked on her couch. I jump up and grab my pants, hastily trying to pull them on. She breezes out and sees me standing in my boxers. She freezes and her mouth drops open in surprise. I stand before her, feeling my face go beet red. Here I am, hairy bare legs, and she stands before me in a cream silk robe which shows off her perfectly shaped legs. *Rachael, in white, just like my dream.* I lick my lips instinctively and desperately try to cover myself up with my hands.

"Ready for bed, I see," she giggles as a slow smirk spreads across her face.

"You caught me," I chuckle.

Her smirk gets bigger.

"Not the first time I've caught you, Mr. Flint."

I shrug innocently.

"It'll be the last," I gloat.

She arches her brow.

"Oh *really*? Are you challenging me?"

Again, I shrug innocently.

"I was caught off guard last time. I made it too easy for you."

"Better have your wits about you next time."

She leans against the door frame of her bedroom, legs crossed and biting her bottom lip. Her seduction and wittiness set me alight with passion and lust, another new feeling that I've never experienced. She stands up straight and continues to beam at me. She gestures with her head for me to enter her room.

"Are you coming or what?" she smirks.

My mouth drops open. *Sleep in bed with Rachael. Should I?* Without much thought, I drop my pants to the floor and slowly step towards her. She watches me closely as I enter her room before closing the door behind us. I look back at her; she now has her back to the door and I feel her eyes look me up and down. I look around at her room; it has a feature wall at the back with cream and purple flowers on the wallpaper, but the rest of the walls are cream. The room is dominated by a stunning bed with a high fabric headboard and cream sheets. She has lit some candles which are flickering softly on the window sill beside me. I turn to face her as she walks towards me slowly and pushes her robe from her shoulders. Underneath, she is wearing a revealing black silky gown, now exposing her delicate arms and perfect curves. I stutter, trying to think of something to say, but she puts her index finger to my lips, silencing me completely. She regards me with a warm sexy gaze.

"Do you mind?" she whispers.

I have no words, so I shake my head. She grins, moves her hands to the hem of my shirt, pulls it over my head and drops it to the floor beside me. I'm now standing only in my boxers. She places her hands on my chest and gently pushes me back until I feel the bed at the backs of my knees. I sink onto it slowly, not daring to take my eyes off her. She sits beside me and places her hand in mine. We look into each other's eyes, blue to hazel. Suddenly, she lunges forward and her lips are on mine. We kiss firmly and passionately, both of us sinking back onto the bed so we are laying side by side, consumed in each other. I close my eyes and give in to her, knowing how much I want this, how much I want her. She draws away suddenly, prompting me to open my eyes and look at her. I gasp out of amazement. *Oh my god.* Without me noticing, she's removed her gown and is kneeling in front of me, fully exposed and revealing the true extent of her perfect curves. My mouth dries and I feel my body responding. She looks anxious all of a sudden, but I smirk at her and place my hands slowly and delicately on her hips. She lies on her back as I continue to caress her. After a while, she pushes me off gently and looks down at my underpants, which I also do, feeling nervous.

"It's okay," Rachael reassures.

I swallow and slowly slide them off. Her eyes widen when she sees me, but I remember something *quite* important.

"I don't have any protection," I say, feeling disappointed all of a sudden.

She cocks her head to one side, but continues to smile. She sits up, opens her bedside drawer and fishes something out before throwing it at me. I look at her with surprise and she shrugs. I'm pleased that she is more prepared than I am. I put it on haphazardly with shaking fingers, but she takes my hands to steady me and places it on properly. Without thinking, my ardor takes over as I climb on top of her. *This is it. I am about to lose my virginity to this woman, the woman I love. Rachael Clarke.* With one final look at her wanting face, my nerves melt into the abyss as our lust fully takes over and we make love slowly and passionately.

Chapter Eleven

———⟡———

We lie in post-coital bliss as our breathing slows. I lie on my back with my arms behind my head, my chest glistening with sweat. I look across at Rachael, who is curled around me like silk. She strokes her nimble fingers through my smattering of chest hair while she glides her smooth foot up and down my leg delicately. She looks up at me, notices me staring and smiles slowly.

"I love you," I whisper.

"I love you too," she whispers back.

I grin, then lean down and kiss her gently on the forehead. She rolls onto her back and stares up at her sparkly lampshade on the ceiling, looking lost in thought. I turn on my side and hug my pillow to my chest.

"You were prepared fast," I chuckle.

She looks back at me and looks momentarily confused, but her expression changes quickly from flabbergasted to cheeky. She shrugs slightly and grins a gleaming white smile.

"Someone had to be."

I laugh and smooth her hair out of her face.

"Did you plan this?" I ask.

She shakes her head and looks strangely sad about something. I'm about to ask what is troubling her, but she answers quickly.

"The protection was left over from-." She trails off and sits up in bed, exposing her naked back.

I think about what she's trying to say, but quickly figure it out. *Her ex-fiancé.* I choose not to probe her anymore, but another question nags at me. I sit up with her and pull her to me. She rests her head against my chest.

"Why did you keep them after all this time?" I ask, gently. She peeks up.

"I was waiting for you."

My heart melts at her loving words and I grip onto her tighter, totally in love and never wanting to let her go.

"Do you have another one spare?" I whisper playfully.

She looks up at me again, then pulls away and sits back on her heels, observing me. I stare at her as her eyes shine with menace. Soon, she jumps on me and we kiss each other amorously.

I stir from my blissful sleep and rub my eyes, feeling a little disorientated. I look down to my side to find Rachael sprawled across my bare chest, sleeping peacefully. I stroke her face softly with the backs of my knuckles as I watch the gentle rise and fall of her chest as she breathes softly. She mumbles something incoherent in her sleep. I freeze, not wanting to disturb her, but she stills and is quiet again. I look out of the window; it's still dark, but there's a tint of orange on the horizon, promising sunrise. I try to settle myself back to sleep, but struggle. I gently peel myself away from Rachael and sneak into the living room. I switch on the free-standing lamp in the corner and fetch my pants from the floor where I discarded them last night. I smile to myself, remembering my first sexual experience. I feel so elevated and at peace with myself for the first time in years. I pull on my pants and head to the kitchen to make breakfast in bed for Rachael. I open the fridge to see what I can use; I find eggs, spinach and a tomato. *Perhaps, an egg white omelet?* I've never made one before, but I remember Grandma making them for me all the time. I'll give it a go. I try to get the recipe up on my phone. *Crap, no web browser. I need to replace this old thing.* I walk over to where I placed Rachael's phone and pick it up. *Damn, it needs a password to unlock it.* I head back to the kitchen and hunt in the cupboards. Luckily, I find a cookbook. Rachael must be into cooking; her sister is too, maybe they got into it together. I open the book and find a simple omelet recipe. I start to busy myself in the kitchen, finding a frying pan and greasing it. I crack the eggs, separate the white from the yolk and start whisking vigorously. As I beat the eggs, I get the sense that I'm being watched. I turn instinctively to find Rachael in her silk robe, watching me.

"Good morning," I say, returning to my task.

She wraps her arms around my shoulders and kisses me on the cheek.

"Good morning," she whispers.

She nips my earlobe which makes me jump in surprise. I look at her.

"Behave," I admonish jokingly.

She pouts playfully.

"*Must I?*" she says, batting her eyelashes at me before waltzing out of the kitchen, giggling to herself.

I shake my head in mock disapproval and pour the mixture into the now hot frying pan. She sits at the breakfast bar and watches me innocently. I make my way over and comb her hair away from her face.

"Much better," I croon, kissing her on the lips.

She smiles, then peeks over my shoulder and giggles again.

"What's funny?" I chuckle.

She points towards the stove with her chin.

"The omelet is burning."

I swing round and see quite a bit of gray smoke emitting from what *was* Rachael's breakfast.

"Damn it."

I rush over and turn off the heat quickly. The omelet is now a *little* black, I dish it onto a plate and look at it with disgust.

"I'll make another one," I offer.

She shakes her head.

"It's okay. I'll eat it. How bad can it be?" she says.

Nervously, I place it in front of her. She looks at it and stifles a laugh. I shrug apologetically.

"I tried."

She tucks in. After a mouthful, she contorts her face and coughs slightly. *That can't be good.*

"Mm. Delicious." She coughs again.

I smirk at her and take the plate.

"I'll have that. Let me make you a fresh one."

I start to eat it myself, but as expected, it's revolting.

"Jeez, that's foul."

Rachael laughs.

"You tried."

I scrape the remains into the trash as she continues to laugh at me before joining me in the kitchen.

"I got this," she says, taking the spatula from me and making us both breakfast where I just failed.

I place my knife and fork down on my empty plate.

"That was *infinitely* more delicious than mine," I compliment.

She grins and takes a sip of her black coffee, then peeks at her watch. She jumps off her stool making me jump.

"Shit. I'm late for work."

She rushes into her bedroom. I follow her and lean against the door frame, tutting playfully. She throws a pillow at me which I catch, laughing at her as I watch her get dressed quickly.

"You're a bad influence," she giggles.

I shrug and smirk.

"That's me."

She rushes past me and ties her hair in a tight, neat bun before grabbing her jacket. I collect my things and we both head out the door. I follow her into the underground parking lot and help her into the car. She rolls down her window hastily.

"I would give you a ride home, but-."

I hold my hand up.

"It's okay. I could do with a walk," I answer.

She leans out the car and kisses me.

"Thank you for a memorable evening," I acknowledge.

She beams. "I'll see you soon, Mark."

She then rolls up her window and speeds up the ramp and out of sight. I stroll out of the parking lot and start to make my way home. I roam happily in the cool morning breeze and take a huge breath. I feel sated and free, knowing that me and Rachael are going to be okay, more than okay, but at the same time, I feel uneasy. I don't like the fact that she's a cop. It's a dangerous profession, but I promised her and myself that I wouldn't interfere. I just hate the thought that she is on the front line every day where she could get injured, or worse. *Stop it, Mark.* I'll have to let it go. Not wanting to ruin my good mood, I continue my long walk home to get ready for work.

I finally make it home. I fetch my keys out of my pocket and unlock the door. I'm surprised to find Trent asleep on the couch, but as soon as I close the door, he jumps awake. He turns over on the couch and looks up. He smirks when he sees my radiating smile.

"I take it from that look that you had a very good evening." He winks and chuckles.

I scowl at him.

"None of your business."

He raises his eyebrow suspiciously.

"Oh, come on. Just a little bit of detail," he begs.

"No," I state seriously.

He crows with laughter and looks like he is about to press me further. I attempt to change the subject.

"How come you're not at work?" I ask.

He sits up.

"Something called a day off," he quips.

I stroll past him, making my way to the pull-out bed where I sit down and ignore Trent's probing stare. I fish my cell from my pocket and find a missed call from Trent early this morning, and a message from Rachael. I smile inwardly and open it:

> *Thank you for last night, I had a fantastic time. Call you when I get home. I love you. XX*

My smile widens. I text her back:

> *Me too. Hope to do it again soon. Looking forward to speaking to you later. Off to work myself now. Love you too. XX*

I put my phone down on the bed and look up at Trent.

"Did you call me earlier?" I ask.

He looks up from his book.

"Yeah, just to see if you were coming home or spending another night with Rachael."

I nod, collect my work clothes and head to the bathroom to get changed.

I finally make it to work, albeit ten minutes late. I hope Mr. Levitt doesn't notice, but he's the least of my worries as I push through the double doors. Melissa is standing in the lobby with her arms folded, giving me a sinister look. I glare back at her as she checks her watch.

"You're late," she grumbles.

"Not by much," I try, but it obviously falls on deaf ears.

"What do you think Mr. Levitt would say?"

I continue to glower at her. "Sorry. It won't happen again."

She smiles a crooked grin.

"Glad to hear it. Well, let's get started."

She turns on her heel and marches away. I want to shout after her that she isn't the boss and that she should stop acting like one, but decide to hold my tongue. I really can't be bothered, and I feel like she has soured my good mood. I hang my head and trail after her towards the janitor closet. Like yesterday, she thrusts the vacuum and mop at me. I snatch them from her. She is really trying my patience today.

"I can't carry everything," I seethe.

She turns and looks at me before heading back into the closet without a word. When she re-emerges, she is only carrying a few detergent bottles and cloths. She walks towards one of the guest bedrooms. I struggle along with the bucket, mop and vacuum. My hands are so full and I feel like the handle of the bucket is slicing into my hand. I lose my grip and spill soapy water all over the red carpet. She turns and tuts at me.

"*Mark*. Now look what you have done. Mr. Levitt will be furious."

I feel myself getting angrier and I can't take it anymore.

"Well, I did ask *nicely* if you could help me, but for some reason, you've harbored some sort of vendetta against me since I told you I have a girlfriend. I don't know how that's any of your business, but we are here to work *together*."

I finish my tirade as she blinks at me and her mouth falls open in shock. I have never been so pissed off with anyone in my life.

"Now, if you'll excuse me, I will get this mess cleaned up. After all, it is *my* mess. If you can be bothered, keep guests away from the wet floor. *Okay?*"

Absentmindedly, I throw the mop at her and storm back to the janitor's closet. I open the door and grab a sponge, cloths and a couple of wet floor signs, but then feel a little daft. I should have just used the mop I was holding, but because of my rage, I didn't think of that. I rub my face, attempting to find my happy place and make my way back to the water spillage. I place wet floor signs around the spillage to avoid any more accidents and start drying the carpet as best as I can. Once I'm done, I make my way to the second floor to start my duties up there. Melissa is already cleaning when I arrive, but she keeps her distance from me. *Good.* I don't want her gawking at me anyway. I pull my thoughts away from her and start to clear the discarded breakfast trays that are littered outside the bedroom doors. I try to let my mind drift back to Rachael while I clean. Last night, I had a lot of firsts: Meeting her parents, taking a drive together, staying the night at a girl's apartment, but most notably, my first sexual experience. *Boy, would I do that again in a hurry!* My mood lightens immediately. I hope Rachael is having a better day than I am. I look forward to our phone call tonight and I hope that we can meet up again soon.

My day is finally drawing to an end, which I'm grateful for. Melissa hasn't breathed a word to me since my outburst, but I just don't care. *Who does she think she is, talking to me like that?* I won't let her sour and jealous mood spoil my fun. I clock out of my shift and make my way outside. It's raining hard, so I put my hands over my head in a vain attempt to shield myself from the rain and rush home.

When I arrive home, I notice Rachael's police car parked outside. I beam, eager to see her. I rush up the stairs and burst through the front door. Trent and Rachael are standing together in the living room. I smile at both of them.

"Nice to know you two are getting on so well," I joke.

They don't smile or respond. They both have a grim expression plastered on their faces. I glance at Rachael who remains stone-faced, and my smile fades. She takes off her police cap and steps forward slowly.

"Mark," she breathes.

I walk towards her.

"What?" I ask, feeling anxious.

Her frown deepens and she looks towards Trent. I mirror her and also turn to Trent, but he stares at me, not giving anything away.

"What's going on?" My anxiety is building.

She looks back at me and grimaces.

"Mark. Tobias has escaped."

I pale and feel like I could faint. *Tobias has escaped? Oh, shit.*

Chapter Twelve

I stare at Rachael, unsure how to respond, then turn my attention to Trent, who stares at the floor. I'm unable to speak a full sentence.

"But, how?" I whisper.

Rachael rotates her police cap in both hands, fidgeting with it uncomfortably. I know it's going to be bad.

"We were transporting Tobias to a super-max upstate. The police van was intercepted by two trucks, which blocked both the rear and front of our van, but that's not the worst bit," she explains.

I stare at her as she takes a photo out of her breast pocket and hands it to me. I take it from her and examine the photo. He looks strangely similar to Tobias, but slightly different too. I look closer, trying to figure out who he is, but I can't place him. I hand back the photo.

"Who is he?" I ask.

She cocks her head to one side and raises an eyebrow.

"You don't know?" She's surprised.

I respond with a shake. She rubs her forehead a little and resumes.

"His name is Curtis O'Malley... Tobias's younger brother."

I can't believe what I'm hearing. I didn't know Tobias had a brother; he never mentioned him. I'm distracted by Rachael as she continues to speak to me.

"I was suspicious when we arrested Tobias the first time. He calmly gave himself up and was compliant throughout the arrest. I tried to tell my superiors that something didn't feel right, but they told me 'everything will be fine'."

She looks down and kicks from foot to foot.

"After the police van was blocked in, Curtis O'Malley and an unknown male accomplice ran towards the police van. I was escorting the van at the time, so I got out and shot at Curtis. I winged him, but he proceeded to shoot a couple of rounds at us, before blowing the van's back door open. He injured a lot of officers. Captain Milligan was seriously hurt - he's now in ICU."

I take my time to process everything she's told me, but it's too much to digest and I feel like I could retch.

"So, he's gone?" I ask, now trembling.

She looks at me with her worried eyes.

"We found the big rig abandoned a few blocks away. It was in pretty bad shape. All prints have been wiped. We have no lead at the moment."

I gawk at her, shocked at Tobias's craziness, but more so that he has a brother, perhaps crazier than him.

"So, what happens now?" I ask.

She clears her throat and we both stare back at Trent, who is now slumped in a chair, looking pale and afraid. He looks up and catches us both staring at him. He tries to straighten himself up to look tougher, but is betrayed by his own shaking. Rachael turns back to me quickly.

"Mark. I hate to say this, but if you stay here, you are at risk."

I step back, surprised. "What are you saying?"

She steps closer to me and for a moment, I think she is going to arrest me, but she keeps her hands by her side and smiles encouragingly.

"I'm saying that Tobias may try and come after you. From what I heard, he was stewing violently while he was in jail. He told everyone that it was your fault he was in there. If you stay here, Trent may also be in danger," she explains carefully.

I look over at Trent who now has his head in his hands. I open my mouth to protest, but close it again.

"He doesn't know about Trent at the moment. We need to keep it that way," she continues softly.

It makes a lot of sense. I don't want any harm to come to Trent, but then a troubling thought dawns on me.

"Where will I live?" I ask.

She sucks in her lips and looks lost in thought briefly.

"Well, you could stay with me until we have caught them," she suggests.

Live with Rachael? The thought is appealing. That means I will be with her every day, but then a far more troubling thought bursts my bubble.

"But … if I live with you, and if Tobias is surely coming for me, *you* are in danger too. I can't let that happen, Rachael."

I now feel conflicted, but she smiles at me.

"I'm prepared for Tobias if he comes. I have a weapon, Trent doesn't. You're a lot safer with me and I'll be fine, I promise you," she says reassuringly.

I stand motionless, feeling numb, but she walks over to me and puts her arm around my shoulders.

"It's for your own safety."

I hug her weakly.

"Go and collect your things," she says.

I walk past her slowly, grabbing my rucksack along the way and retreat into the bathroom. I turn on the faucet at the sink and splash my face with cold water. *How could this happen?* I grab my toothbrush and stuff it into my rucksack. I turn slowly and re-enter the living room. I stoop down by the pull-out bed and pack the rest of my belongings, including the clothes Trent gave to me not so long ago. I look back at Trent and Rachael, but they're not looking at me. Quickly, I lift my pillow up and retrieve the small photo of Grandma. I pull my wallet out and stash it in there. Rachael glances over briefly, just as I put my wallet into my bag. She stares at me, her eyes full of questions, but she turns back to Trent after a couple of seconds. I feel terrible. I don't want to leave Trent behind. He took me in after my release when I had nowhere else to go. He took care of me and I have given him nothing in return. I slip my bag onto my back and take one final look around the apartment before I hear Trent weeping softly. I look in his direction, Rachael is standing over Trent with her hand on his back in a bid to comfort him.

"It'll be okay, Trent. I promise," Rachael soothes gently, but Trent keeps his head in his hands.

"I have missed him all this time, Rachael. I thought I would never see him again, now he's leaving again," he sobs.

I never realized how much Trent missed me, through all the years I was gone, through all the years I wasted with… *him. That monster.*

"I understand. I'm just trying to protect you both. You can still see him," she soothes calmly.

I walk closer and they both look at me. Trent stands and hugs me hard.

"You're like a brother to me, Mark. Please be safe." He continues to weep into my shoulder as I hug him back.

"I know, Trent. Thank you for everything."

He lets me go and wipes his eyes. I offer him a warm smile which he returns weakly.

"I *will* see you soon," I reassure him.

He nods as I turn back to Rachael.

"I'm ready," I say.

She takes my hand and leads me outside, followed swiftly by Trent. With one final look at him, I pat him on the back and climb into Rachael's police car. Rachael mutters something to Trent, but I can't make it out. He beams at her and takes me by surprise by giving her a swift hug. When Trent releases her, she joins me in the car, starts the engine and slowly, I'm driven away to start a new life with Rachael.

We arrive back at Rachael's apartment having barely breathed a word during the short ride. I am feeling troubled and scared knowing that Tobias is out there somewhere, but he isn't alone this time; he has a brother. I'm still trying to comprehend this information. Rachael parks up and climbs out the car and I follow her automatically. She takes my hand and leads me upstairs.

"The elevators are out of order. Can you manage the walk?" She smiles apologetically.

"Guess there's no other way," I respond solemnly.

We head towards the stairs and begin the fifteen-story climb. Once we get to the top, I am out of breath and huffing, but Rachael seems unaffected by it; she is obviously in better shape than me. She unlocks her door and we step inside, then she locks the door quickly behind us. She rushes to the window and glances out to the street below. I take my bag to her bedroom and toss it into the closet. Closing the door, I rest my back against it and pray to myself that Trent will be alright on his own, but I will still see him at work, so I have that to look forward to. I exit the room and Rachael is in the kitchen, rooting around in the freezer. She looks up.

"I've prepared a vegetable stew for dinner, if that's okay with you?" she asks.

"That's fine," I answer weakly.

She looks concerned, but then turns away and starts to defrost the stew on the stove. I make my way into the kitchen and look over her shoulder. The aroma of the stew is mouthwatering.

"Need a hand? I could do with a distraction," I offer.

She looks back at me and ponders for a moment.

"You could put the potatoes on to boil if you like," she says as she stirs the stew.

"Sure."

I go into the fridge and retrieve the baby potatoes. I look at the bag, furrowing my brow with confusion. *Do I need to peel them first?* I turn back to Rachael, about to ask, but she's already staring at me with amusement.

"Just put them straight into a pot of hot water," she explains, still grinning.

"Right." I smile back.

I fill a pot with warm water and place it on the stove, where it begins to boil. I rip the bag open and carefully pour the potatoes in. I like cooking with Rachael. It soothes my troubled soul, very therapeutic.

We continue to prepare dinner as a team as she places dumplings into the bubbling stew pot while I drain the potatoes. Finally, dinner is ready. I carry both plates and set them down at the breakfast bar. Rachael brings over two glasses of red wine and slides elegantly onto a barstool beside me. We both tuck in, savoring our meals, further soothing my soul.

"How are you going to find him?" I ask.

She looks at me mid-chew, then takes a sip of her wine.

"Do what we always do; roadblocks and wanted posters."

I blink at her. "Does that really work?"

She grins and giggles. "No. I'm teasing, Mark. I'm not sure how we'll catch him, but he will slip up eventually. When he does, we've got him."

I flush, feeling silly that I fell for her little joke so easily, but I'm not thinking straight. I can't stop worrying about Trent. I continue with my meal.

"This is amazing by the way," I compliment.

Her face lights up at my praise.

"Thank you. My dad has always disapproved of my vegetarianism. He always called it 'unnatural'," she murmurs.

I whip my face to hers. "Seriously?" I'm appalled.

She nods and smiles briefly.

"I think that's what it boils down to with him, he likes getting his own way. If someone's doing something different from him, it's not 'normal'."

She rolls her eyes, pushes her empty plate away and stands to clear the dishes.

"How does your mom put up with him?" I ask, stunned.

"She's a strong woman," she chuckles as she loads the dishes into the dishwasher.

I watch her and offer to help, but she refuses.

"How do you find time to do all of this?" I ask.

She closes the dishwasher and looks at me, puzzled.

"Time for what?"

I wave my hand around in the general direction of the apartment.

"Everything, really. Working long hours, keeping a nice clean home and cooking."

She folds her arms and leans against the kitchen counter.

"I just do. I like to keep myself busy."

"It's amazing," I smile.

She walks around the kitchen counter towards me and kisses me quickly. Not saying anything, we stare and admire each other. I'm the first to break my gaze away.

"What you doing tomorrow?" she asks.

I look back at her and think.

"I'm not working, so not a lot."

She smiles and straightens up, then turns and heads into her bedroom. When she returns, she's changed out of her uniform and into a pair of loose gray pants and a black tank top. I stare at her; even in loungewear, she is beautiful. She slumps onto the couch as I settle into one of the armchairs. She puts her feet up and rests her arm on the back of the couch.

"I was thinking, we could go out tomorrow, if you like." She looks at me expectantly.

"That would be nice. Where were you thinking?"

She shrugs. "Just see where we find ourselves. Do some exploring."

"Sure, that'll be fun."

She smiles and switches on the TV.

We watch TV together in comfortable silence. I am now sitting beside her on the couch as she rests her legs on my lap and I massage her feet softly. I glance at her from time to time; she is no longer interested in the TV; she's reading a romance novel. I continue to watch the TV, but like Rachael, I'm not really focusing. My mind is filled with dread and fear of Tobias' next move. Rachael starts yawning and rubs her eyes. She takes her feet off my lap and stands to switch the TV off.

"I'm going to bed," she says sleepily.

"Yeah, me too," I yawn.

We head into the bedroom together. She slips into bed as I get changed into a loose white shirt and a pair of boxer shorts. I slip in beside her and she rests her head against my chest. I reach over and switch off the bedside light.

"Good night, Mark."

I softly kiss the top of her head.

"Good night, Rachael."

She's quiet in moments, but my mind continues to whirl with unpleasant thoughts. *Will Trent be safe? What is Tobias' game?* But then a far more terrifying thought emerges. *What will happen to Rachael?* My eyes start to get heavy and I drift into a troubled sleep.

Chapter Thirteen

———∽∽∽∽∽———

L ight streams in through the curtains, waking me from my surprisingly dreamless sleep. I reach over across the bed, but Rachael is gone. I sit up, wondering where she is. An enticing aroma is coming from the kitchen. I crawl out of bed and slip on my navy robe. I enter the lounge as the smell draws me in. I see Rachael in the kitchen preparing breakfast, I slowly walk towards her.

"What smells so good?" I ask.

She whirls around and looks startled, armed with a spatula, but a slow smile spreads across her face when she sees me.

"I'm making poached egg and avocado on toast. Want some?"

I slide onto a barstool.

"Please," I respond gleefully, forgetting my fears from last night.

She turns away and continues with what she's doing, giving me a chance to observe her. She is wearing her silk dressing gown, revealing her bare, shapely legs. *How does a man like me get so lucky with a woman like her?* I'm distracted by my appealing thoughts that I don't notice Rachael sitting beside me and placing her hand softly on my arm as she sets the plate down. I snap out of my reverie and look down at my breakfast. I've never tried avocado or poached egg before, but it does look good. I take a small testing bite and as expected, I'm not disappointed.

"This is incredible," I say with a mouthful.

"Good. I've always liked it."

"I've never tried avocado before. I will definitely be eating it more often now though."

She turns to me and looks stunned.

"You have never tried avocado before? How have you avoided it for twenty-nine years?"

"I've always been more of a meat and two veg kind of guy," I chuckle.

She laughs and gives me a little jab in the ribs. I laugh and jab her back and soon we both can't stop laughing.

"What are we doing today?" I ask.

She sips her coffee, contemplating a response.

"I was thinking we could go for a walk, get some air."

"Great."

We both get up from the kitchen island and walk into the bedroom to get ready to go out. I pull on my denim jeans, simple black shirt and my leather jacket. Rachael, however, has made more of an effort, sporting tight jeans which shows off every curve excellently, a flowing white blouse and a pair of knee-high boots. We make our way to the door as she grabs her jacket on the way out.

We stroll hand in hand through Central Park. We are midway through November, and the trees have long ago lost their leaves. I peek over at Rachael as the wind blows through her hair, prompting her to comb it out of her eyes. She glances at me and smiles. We make our way to Bow Bridge where we met up after my release and take a seat on the same bench. We watch the pedestrians pass by and listen to the kids playing on the green nearby. I turn to face her.

"Tell me more about Officer Bailey," I say.

She looks at me suddenly and frowns a little.

"Why?"

"I just thought, you've met Trent, I would like to get to know *your* friend."

She looks away and goes quiet. I hope I haven't offended her. I'm about to apologize, but she finally answers.

"Her name, as you know, is Stephanie. We first met when we were just eight years old." She smiles at the memory.

"My father always took me to the precinct to meet his work colleagues. One day, Steph was there with her father and we hit it off immediately."

I listen closely, keen to learn this new information she is giving me. She continues.

"Steph always told me she was going to be a cop, just like her dad, but when she was fifteen, he was killed while on-duty. She became more determined to become a cop. My dad encouraged me to join her, so I did. We went through the academy together."

"Thank you for telling me. Would it be possible to meet her when she isn't on-duty? Maybe she will be more laid back with me."

Rachael frowns again.

"I'll try, but like my father, she is very stubborn when it comes to ex-offenders."

I furrow my brow, matching her expression.

"So I've seen."

I remember the unpleasant experiences I've had with her as Rachael scoffs.

We've been sitting for a while, making small talk and watching the world go by. She shivers a little, then stands up.

"I'm cold. Let's go home," Rachael says.

She offers me her hand and I take it without hesitation. We head over the bridge and make our way back to the apartment, but Rachael stops suddenly and pulls out her cell, checking the number. She looks perplexed, but answers.

"Steph?" she answers and listens intently.

I look at my surroundings and wait for her to wrap up her call, but I'm distracted when I see her put her hand to her chest in shock.

"What? You're sure?"

I look at her. Her expression suddenly changes from calm to mad and I start to worry, trying to listen.

"No, I understand. I'll be right there." She hangs up.

"What's wrong?" I ask, my anxiety blooming in my chest.

She turns to me slowly.

"Tobias has been sighted. He attacked a member of the public who recognized him from our police files. I'm sorry, I need to go."

"It's okay. Do what you need to do. Just be careful."

She nods at me and takes my hand hurriedly.

We arrive back at Rachael's apartment. She bursts through the door and rushes into her bedroom. I follow after her and watch as she throws off her casual clothes in double quick time and gets changed into her police uniform. She rushes back out the bedroom, giving me a quick kiss along the way while tying her hair quickly into a neat, tight bun, albeit with a couple of loose tendrils. She rushes to the front door and I trail after her.

"Be safe, Rachael," I call after her as she races down the corridor and summons an elevator.

She looks over her shoulder and smiles at me but doesn't respond. There's a loud ping and she dashes into the waiting elevator. I close the door and go to the window where I see a waiting police car at the entrance of the complex. Rachael races outside and jumps in, then it speeds away. I pace the room feeling restless. These are the days I hate the most, when she is chasing a lead on Tobias. He's dangerous. I try to reassure myself that Rachael won't be alone in this, she always has back-up at hand, but nothing soothes my aching terror of what Tobias is capable of.

Morning turns to afternoon and I've still heard nothing. I have tried to occupy myself, but nothing has worked. I don't really want to go out again, so I give Trent a call. It goes straight to answerphone; he must be at work. I try to call Rachael, but like Trent, it goes to answerphone. I'm driving myself crazy; the silence in the apartment is deafening. I rake my hands through my hair in frustration. I hate not knowing what's going on and I reluctantly resort to going outside as a last-ditch attempt to calm my nerves.

I walk the streets with no real destination yet again, hoping that I'll run into Rachael somewhere, but I highly doubt it.

I walk through the Rockefeller Centre to observe the newly decorated Christmas tree, then continue on to Bryant Park where tourists happily chatter loudly to each other. I keep moving, now finding myself in Times Square again. I'm only a few blocks away from Trent's place, but he won't be home. My nagging anxiety still gnaws at me, frustrating me further. I mentally slap myself. *Will you get a grip, Flint? She will be fine.* I hold my head up and continue through Times Square. I walk towards the NYPD station, hoping I will see her here like I did before. There are a lot of police officers standing outside who are watching pedestrians walk by, but I don't see her. I walk round and find more officers, mounted on horses. I approach slowly, trying to make out the faces which are obscured by their helmets.

"Mark," a voice calls.

I look around to detect the source of the voice, but I can't see anyone.

"Mark."

I look towards one of the officers sitting on a big brown horse and realize that the officer is Rachael. I approach quickly, but this makes the horse flinch back in terror. I stop and back away. Rachael takes off her helmet and pats the horse to calm it.

"Easy, boy. Easy," she soothes him.

"What are you doing here?" she asks.

Rachael dismounts the horse and grabs his reins, leading him slowly towards me. I stand still, not wanting to frighten the animal anymore.

"I was worried about you. Did you find him?"

She frowns. "No. He was long gone. I'm just finishing my shift now."

She calls to one of the other officers. "Stevens."

A tall, stocky man approaches.

"He's all yours," she says.

For a moment, I think she is referring to me. *No, she means the horse, stupid.*

Officer Stevens takes the reins from her and mounts the horse.

"Come on," she says to me as we begin to walk home together.

We arrive back home and she throws her keys onto the kitchen counter before undoing her hair, which falls in a stunning mahogany wave around her shoulders. She sits on the couch as I stand in the middle of the room, watching her. She draws out a large exhale, sounding frustrated.

"I'm sorry if I distracted you," I say.

She turns to face me but looks away again.

"It's not that," she says quietly, untying her shoes and taking them off one at a time.

"I *really* thought we had him this time."

I sit opposite her.

"He's sneaky and very cunning. You're doing your best, and as you said, he will slip up eventually," I try to reassure her, but she still doesn't smile.

"But surely, you know something that we don't. You could give us the lead we've been waiting for." She sounds hopeful.

I lean back in my seat, shaking my head slowly.

"I just don't know, Rachael. I'm sorry."

She sits back, disappointment evident on her face. Suddenly, she stands up and paces the room with her hands on her head.

"So that's it? You can't give me anything?" she half-shouts and I quail in shock.

"What do you want me to say?" I ask, stuck for words.

She sits down again.

"Anything. Why is he like this? How did you meet him? Why did he come out of hiding just to attack a member of the public? Anything that may give us a clue."

I think hard, wanting to give her something.

"I told you how I met him. He took me in when Grandma died. I was living in Chicago Union Station. He gave me food and shelter. He was good once."

She glares at me, wanting more.

"He can't be good. He tried to turn you into a criminal," she states firmly.

I flinch a little.

"I guess I didn't see it that way. Like I told you, I was young and desperate. He went mad and lost his way after the gang disbanded. He shot two of our guys dead for betrayal and I escaped with my life. That's all I have."

She rubs her face, before turning her attention back to me.

"That will have to do for now, then," she sighs.

"Where are your parents, Mark? Why didn't they raise you?" she continues, more softly.

I give her a hard stare.

"I don't know, and quite honestly, I don't want to talk about it. I don't care about that part of my life anymore."

She puts her hand on my knee. "You must care."

I jump out of my seat and pull at my hair angrily.

"I don't, Rachael. They abandoned me when I was six, and they never came back. Grandma took it on herself to raise me, but then she died; that's all I have to say. I don't want to discuss it anymore." It's my turn to half-shout.

She blinks at me.

"I just want to know you better. You need to stop letting your past beat you up."

"That part of me is dead and buried, and I want to keep it that way. Don't you understand?" I growl.

"I understand."

I slump onto the couch and pinch the bridge of my nose.

"But can I ask you one more question?" she continues.

I groan, annoyed.

"*What?*"

"Are your parents..." She can't even finish the sentence, but I understand what she is asking. "I don't know if they are dead or alive; probably dead. I don't care either way."

She gazes at me. "Then I won't ask anymore." She finally surrenders.

I return her gaze, feeling relieved, but guilty.

"I'm sorry. I don't mean to yell. I'm just not ready to discuss it," I explain.

She nods. "Then, don't."

I scoot closer to her on the couch and cup her face. We watch each other closely for a while before I attempt to comfort her.

"Back to the *real* matter at hand - you'll find Tobias and bring him to justice."

"I know I will."

She lifts her lips slowly to mine and we kiss each other gently, then it intensifies until we are lost in each other again.

I wake and glance over at the alarm clock on the nightstand; 5:15 am. It is still pitch black, but I struggle to get back to sleep. I reach out to find Rachael but again, she is absent. I feel a crumple on her pillow, like paper. I sit up and switch on the bedside lamp, causing me to squint. I rub my eyes and find a note on her pillow. I pick it up and scan it quickly.

> *Good morning, Mark. I have been called into work urgently; something came up. Please try not to worry today. I will be home as soon as I can. Rachael Xx.*

I take a deep breath and ruffle my hair. Rachael is dealing with another emergency at work. *Is it related to Tobias again?* I shake off the unwelcome thought and now, fully awake, I get out of bed and prepare for my morning shift at the hotel.

It's raining hard as I walk to work. I pull my coat over my head and run the rest of the way. I finally arrive and am soaked through. I shake myself off as best I can, then make my way into the lobby. I'm surprised to find that Melissa isn't standing and waiting for me like she usually does. I look around and see Trent sitting behind his desk, picking at his breakfast burrito. He looks up and beams when he sees me. I smile back and offer him a quick wave. He jumps up from his desk, discarding his half-eaten burrito, and runs towards me. He surprises me by folding me into a big bear hug. I return it as best as I can manage, but my arms are pinned to my side. He finally gives me the chance to breathe and releases me.

"How've you been?" he asks, grinning at me.

I think for a moment and shrug a little.

"I'm good, but…" I stop.

Trent's smile slips a fraction before his brow knits together.

"What?" he prompts.

I breathe out heavily.

"Rachael had a lead on Tobias yesterday. She had to rush to work, but she was too late when she arrived." I look back at Trent who is now scowling and scratching his head.

"He escaped again?"

I answer with a nod. He shakes his head and sniggers sarcastically.

"Slippery bastard, ain't he?"

I chuckle. "Sure."

Our conversation is unfortunately cut short by Trent spotting Mr. Levitt exiting the elevator.

"Catch you later," he says hurriedly before scrambling back to his desk.

I make my way to the stairs, en route to the staff room, when I hear my name being called.

"Flint," he states clearly.

I turn slowly and Mr. Levitt is glaring at me. He doesn't look pleased. I sigh before trailing towards him. I look up slowly and he regards me carefully through his specs.

"Yes, sir," I say, standing up straight.

"Join me in my office for a minute," he says coolly.

Christ. What have I done now?

Together, we head to the elevators and ride up in silence. I start to fidget with my fingers anxiously, wondering if I have done anything wrong, but I can't place anything. We arrive at his floor and make our way towards his office. He opens the door and steps in first. I trail after him. As we enter his office, I'm surprised to find Melissa sitting opposite the desk. The world falls away at my feet. She looks up and smirks at me arrogantly. I return with a scowl and pull my gaze away from her.

"Sit down." Mr. Levitt points at the vacant seat beside Melissa, I sit down begrudgingly.

I watch as Mr. Levitt sits at his desk and unbuttons his jacket. He then looks from me to her.

"Melissa told me that you threatened her a couple of days ago." Mr. Levitt looks in my direction expectantly.

Threatened her?

My mouth falls open in shock and I give Melissa a quick glance, but she is now looking at her feet, playing the role of the victim very well. I turn back to Mr. Levitt who has got his fingers steepled in front of him, waiting for my answer.

"That's ridiculous," I finally manage.

I hear Melissa sob a little beside me.

"He did, sir. He said if I didn't help him, he would get me fired," she whines.

I roll my eyes. Mr. Levitt glances at her and hands her a handkerchief, which she accepts.

"Can you excuse us for a moment please, Melissa?" Mr. Levitt asks.

She stands, then exits the room swiftly, closing the door softly behind her. Mr. Levitt turns back to me.

"I thought you would be a hard worker, Mark. I gave you a chance when no one else would. Trent trusted you, and so did I," Mr. Levitt begins, shaking his head disappointedly.

I hang my head and feel the anger boiling up inside me. I look back at him.

"I didn't threaten her," I say slowly.

He looks at me and removes his glasses.

"I have heard her side of the story. Why don't you explain yours?"

I take a breath and think of how to explain it properly, but without sounding like a whiny teenager.

"She seems to have had a problem with me since I mentioned that I have a girlfriend. She makes me do practically all of the work, without contributing much herself."

Mr. Levitt looks surprised briefly.

"Why did you tell her that you have a girlfriend? It's not really appropriate for the workplace," he says.

"She asked me, and I answered."

He puts his glasses back on and looks at me expectantly, so I continue.

"She expects me to carry everything. The vacuum, the mops, the bucket, everything. I've tried asking her for help, but she keeps walking away. I dropped the bucket by accident and spoiled the carpet. Yes, I did shout at her. I was angry, but I cleaned up the mess straight away."

I take a deep breath. Mr. Levitt nods his head slightly and looks away from me.

"Thank you, Mark. You may go now. Call Melissa in for me on your way out, please."

"Yes, sir."

I stand and dash out the door. Melissa is standing with her back to the wall outside the office when I exit. I fold my arms and walk past her as she starts to snigger childishly and mutters something under her breath. I whip round but control my temper.

"Mr. Levitt wants to talk to you now, snitch," I mutter.

She stops laughing at me and looks worried. She scowls angrily and scurries into the office. I walk down the corridor and make my way to the staff room to deposit my bag and coat into my locker before I get on with my job at last.

I polish the lobby floor with the buffer. Trent smiles at me every so often and I occasionally return it with a weak smile of my own. He has tried to talk to me, but he's busy with customers. I continue to polish the floor slowly as my mind drifts to Rachael. I hope she's okay and the emergency is under control. The ping of the elevator's arrival gets my attention. I look up and see Melissa and Mr. Levitt exit. She now seems a lot more upset, but I don't care and try to ignore them. Mr. Levitt stands next to me. I turn off the buffer and look up, not saying anything.

"You won't be working with Melissa anymore," he announces.

What does that mean? Am I fired?

"Why?"

He frowns and glances over at Melissa, who is collecting her things from the back room.

"She quit," Mr. Levitt says quietly.

I'm surprised but relieved and satisfied as well. Mr. Levitt gives me a long hard stare before he turns on his heel and heads back towards his office. A moment later, a defeated Melissa shunts past me on her way out without making any eye contact, causing me to drop the buffer. I decide not to give her the satisfaction of a response and ignore her. She doesn't work here, and I won't have to deal with her again.

My day is slow, but I work better on my own rather than with Melissa, who is no longer here to antagonize me. On my lunch break, I head out into the rain and dash to the nearby delI to buy myself and Trent a pastramI sandwich. I return to the hotel and head to the staff room. When I enter, Trent is reading his book. I stroll over happily and hand him one of the sandwiches.

"You're in a good mood all of a sudden. Is this for me?" Trent says, looking down at the sandwich.

I grin at him.

"Yes, I got you one as a thank you for everything. Also, Melissa quit today."

Trent smiles. "Finally."

I sit beside him and we eat our lunch, chatting animatedly to each other. I've missed him and his banter.

It's been a long day, but I've just finished cleaning the last guest bedroom of the day and am now preparing to clock off. During lunch, I agreed to walk home with Trent. I grab my things and meet up with him in the lobby, then we head out together. It's still raining hard, but thankfully, Trent is equipped with an umbrella. As we walk side by side, he demands to know more about the encounter I had with Mr. Levitt and Melissa today. I tell him everything as Trent laughs occasionally and explains that no one seemed to get on with her. It's a pleasant walk and I am enjoying the catch up with my friend, but we soon arrive at his apartment.

"Do you want to come in?" he offers.

I'm tempted but shake my head.

"Nah, sorry. I'd better get home and check on Rachael."

He briefly looks disappointed, but then smiles and pats me on the back.

"Maybe next time. Be safe," he says.

"Sure," I respond.

With one final glance and a thumbs up, he heads inside, and I continue to make my way home alone.

I'm nearing Rachael's apartment, but I begin to feel apprehensive. The feeling that I'm being watched is back, but worse than ever. I try to shake off my paranoia as ridiculous, but it doesn't shift. I stop and scan my surroundings; nothing seems out of place, just commuters and tourists walking around me and the heavy flow of traffic. I continue on my way but walk a little faster until I'm almost running. I arrive back at Rachael's and duck inside out of the rain. I nod a quick greeting towards Tom, then ride up to Rachael's floor in the elevator. I unlock the front door and hope that Rachael is home. I have missed her all day. I enter the lounge and she's sitting on the couch, already changed out of her uniform and huddled in a beige blanket. Sitting beside her is Officer Bailey; she is also out of her uniform, wearing a black polka dot blouse and denim jeans. They chat and laugh loudly to each other until they spot me, then they are both silent.

"Uh, hi," I greet, feeling slightly awkward.

Officer Bailey says nothing but eyes me suspiciously. I creep by them, feeling out of my comfort zone.

"I'll leave you girls to it."

I head for the bedroom, but then Rachael stands and puts her arm around my shoulders.

"Don't be silly. Sit down. Can I get you anything?" she asks.

I shake my head and slump into the nearest armchair. Officer Bailey continues to regard me, and I fidget uncomfortably.

"So, how was the emergency?" I ask, attempting to spark a conversation.

Rachael and Bailey glance at each other, then look back at me.

"Unresolved, I'm afraid." Rachael looks disappointed.

"What happened?" I ask.

Rachael is about to answer, but Bailey cuts in.

"That's classified, Mr. Flint."

I sit back and look at Rachael, despondent. She jabs Officer Bailey.

"Steph. His name is Mark," she scolds, insistent.

I smile at her gratefully. Bailey frowns at first, but then regains her composure and offers me a quick smile.

"Sorry. Mark," she resigns.

I don't know what to say to Bailey to make her warm to me a little, but I take a stab at it.

"That's okay. Steph."

There. Hopefully, that worked.

"Rachael tells me you met when you were both eight," I say, trying to keep her talking.

Bailey looks at Rachael in surprise and then back at me.

"We did, yes. Our fathers introduced us to each other."

"That's right. She told me that too."

Bailey finally grins at me for the first time. I think I may be winning her round, like Rachael did Trent.

"Can I ask you something, Mark?" Bailey asks, leaning forward in her seat.

"Anything."

"Of all the women you must have met while working for Tobias, what made you so infatuated with Rachael?"

I blink at her, gobsmacked to be asked such a personal question. I peek at Rachael, who is gaping at Bailey.

"Stephanie," she hisses, but I hold my hand up.

"It's okay, Rae," I assure, and face Bailey again.

"It's an easy answer, really. You're right, Stephanie. I *did* meet a lot of women when I was with Tobias. He used to have service girls that worked for him, but the thing is, none of them appealed to me, in fact, they revolted me. They had sex for money, and only money. They wouldn't have loved me at all, nor would I. Even though this sounds crazy to a lot of people, the day she arrested me, I knew she had a kind and gentle spirit, and she knocked some sense into me, literally."

Rachael sniggers at the memory and I turn to smile at her briefly before turning back to face Bailey who also chuckles.

"I've never been in love before. I didn't know the first thing about love until I met Rachael. She's helping me through a difficult time; she's taught me a great deal and, as my best friend put it, I've really landed on my feet."

Bailey looks from me to Rachael quickly.

"That's it?" she asks.

I smirk.

"That's all there is to it."

Rachael smiles warmly at me.

"Good. Just don't hurt her," Bailey continues.

I smile reassuringly.

"I wouldn't dare."

Rachael is now sitting on the arm of my chair, still draped in her blanket.

"I'm putting an end to this now. That's enough, Stephanie," she demands.

Bailey holds her hands up in a defensive gesture.

"Just advising," she says quietly.

Rachael sighs and takes my hand.

"You and my father both, but I wish you would both just stop. Can't you just be happy for me?"

Bailey stands and walks towards her, takes both her hands and pulls her up into a hug.

"I *am* happy for you," she breathes.

Rachael softens and returns her hug.

"I'd better get home. It's getting late," Bailey continues, releasing Rachael and collecting her purse.

Rachael follows her to the door, and they chat quietly. Moments later, Rachael re-enters the lounge.

"Sorry about her," she says.

"I understand. It felt good telling her. Hopefully, she'll understand now."

"I didn't realize you felt so strongly for me. No one ever did before."

She looks down solemnly. *That will never do.*

"Come here," I say, opening my arms to her.

She walks over slowly and sits on my lap. She wraps her arms around the back of my neck, and we stare longingly at each other until our lips lock. We are soon enthralled in passion once again.

We lie in a post-coital glow on the couch, Rachael resting her head on my naked chest, her hair spread across us in waves.

"I should get dinner started," she says, sitting up and attempting to pull the blanket out from under me to cover herself.

I smile and pull her back down.

"Don't go," I croon softly.

She laughs and playfully grabs the cushion from under my head and hits me with it.

"You sure like knocking some sense into me with things, don't you?" I laugh.

"It puts you in your place," she laughs back.

She gets up quickly before I have a chance to grab her and she struts arrogantly into the kitchen, draped in the blanket. I struggle up onto my elbows and admire her as she hunts around in the kitchen cupboards. She frowns and turns her hazel stare at me.

"I haven't gone shopping. We don't have anything."

"Yes, we do, we have each other," I chuckle.

She turns bright red and turns her back to me to shield her bashful look.

"Stop it," she chuckles back.

"We could order Chinese," I suggest.

She looks back at me and smiles.

"Chinese it is."

We eat our Chinese takeout straight from the boxes that it came in and drink cheap white wine. These are the sort of evenings I have always craved for; cheap wine, crap TV, but most desirable of all, my Rachael. She puts down her empty takeout box and re-fills her wine glass.

"What do you want for dessert?" she asks.

I twist my mouth playfully and glance at her suggestively.

"Not me!" Rachael laughs and slaps me on the shoulder.

I pout jokingly.

"Then, I don't mind."

She stands, heads into the kitchen and opens the freezer.

"I have mint ice cream," she calls, showing me the tub.

"Sounds good to me."

She scoops out two generous portions and hands me a bowl.

"Are you trying to fatten me up?" I laugh, showing her the mountain of ice cream in my bowl.

"You need more meat on your bones, so… yeah, I suppose I am."

We laugh together and I take a spoonful. I hope evenings like this one continue. I couldn't be happier. I just hope nothing will get in our way and ruin this happiness.

Chapter Fourteen

~~~

The last couple of days have been rejuvenating. Rachael and I both had a much-needed day off work, giving us an opportunity to rest at home and get to know each other a little more. She has learnt that I'm terrified of heights and that my birthday is in May. I have learnt that her favorite color is purple, she adores animals and hates selfishness. Trent and Rex have been a breath of fresh air, showing me more of what the Neapolitan has to offer. They showed me the rooftop bar after my shift and we enjoyed drinks together. We laughed and joked, and I envisioned taking Rachael up there with me. We are well into the latter half of November and it's getting colder. New York is looking more magical with Christmas decorations on every street corner and in every shop window. I feel a pang of annoyance; the light-up ceremony is just over a week away and I still haven't asked Rachael if she wants to go with me. I aim to ask her tonight.

It's early evening and I had an exhausting day at work, but it was a lot more enjoyable since Melissa's departure. I've been able to work at my own pace and not in someone else's shadow. I sit in Rachael's living room, playing on the PlayStation 4 while she rushes around, getting ready for her late shift. We exchange occasional glances and smiles at each other, but otherwise, we are very quiet, just doing our own things. Rachael continues to rush around, tying her shoes quickly and grabbing a banana before she flies out the door.

"Bye," she calls quickly.

"Bye," I call back and return to the game that I'm playing.

The light-up ceremony comes to my mind. I jump up off the couch, forgetting to drop the PlayStation remote that's still in my hand, and rush after her, forgetting to put shoes on.

"Rachael," I call. No answer.

I rush to the elevators; luckily there is one already on our floor. I dash inside and continuously stab the button for the underground garage. The doors slide shut and I'm descended painfully slowly. Eventually, it arrives in the garage and I dash out, the tarmac cold and rough against my bare feet. Luckily, she's still here, about to climb into her car.

"Rachael."

She stops and faces me. I stand in front of her, out of breath.

"I'm late for work. Can it wait?"

"Just a quick question," I rasp.

She raises her eyebrows in amusement.

"Would you like to go to the Rockefeller Christmas tree light-up ceremony with me? It's on the thirtieth."

"The thirtieth?" she says, more to herself.

She looks deep in thought, then smiles, kisses me and climbs into the car. She rolls down her window.

"I'd love to," she responds, then speeds away.

I feel ten feet tall. I'm overjoyed that I've finally asked, and she said yes. I clap my hands together, forgetting I still have the

PlayStation remote in my hand, which drops to the floor with a loud clatter. *Crap.* I stoop down quickly to pick it up and turn it over to examine it. It's got a few scratches, but otherwise, it looks okay. I make my way back upstairs and shut the front door behind me. I put the PlayStation remote back on its dock and switch off the console. I sit in the quiet apartment and ponder to myself. In this moment, my life has never felt so full. I have a good job, a lovely home, a best friend and an amazing girlfriend. A thought hits me like a bolt of lightning, I want Rachael to be more than my girlfriend, I want her as my wife. It's probably a bit too soon. After all, we've only been dating for a couple of weeks, but I've never been so in love or so sure of anything. I decide to go out and think about it a little more. I slip on my chucks and leather jacket, then make my way out. It's five-forty in the evening, but the streets are fully lit and it's freezing. I zip up my leather jacket and look for a quiet place to sit and think. Central Park is too busy, so I make my way towards the Columbus Circle Subway Station.

After a reasonably short ride, I get off at 125th Street and walk a couple of minutes until I find myself at Marcus Garvey Park. It looks relatively quiet in there, so I head in. I observe my surroundings; they're pleasant and I'm surprised just how quiet it is here. I find a vacant bench and take a seat. In the corner of my eye, I see a man holding a newspaper, dressed in a beige trench coat and a smart pinstripe suit. He strolls over and sits beside me. I shift across the bench a little so that we both have some space. The stranger opens his newspaper and starts to read.

"Don't you just love this time of year?" the stranger speaks, presumably to me.

I glance at him, confused. "Quite stunning."

He puts his newspaper down and turns to face me.

"Mark, right? Mark Flint?" he asks.

I whip my face round to look at him. He is now staring at me with his bright green eyes and grinning in a way that intimidates me. *It can't be.*

"How do you know me? Who are you?"

The sense of fear grows within me.

"Oh, you know. I've seen you around, with a policewoman, I believe," he smirks.

I stand to walk away, but he follows closely behind. I stop and confront him.

"Who are you?" I demand.

He smiles.

"That doesn't matter."

I turn to walk away again, but he grabs my arm, spins me round and pushes me up against a tree, pinning me to it. My blood rushes to my head and alarm bells start sounding. *What does this man want with me? How does he know about Rachael?*

"Tobias O'Malley wants you to call your girlfriend off his tail," he hisses.

I widen my eyes and suddenly recognize him.

"You're his brother, aren't you? You're Curtis."

He laughs and I feel his piercing green eyes go right through me, just like his older brother used to.

"Toby said you were a smart lad. Glad to see it for myself. Call off your girlfriend."

"And if I don't?"

I begin to feel foolishly brave as a look of anger flashes across his face.

"If you don't?" he repeats, before pulling a blade out of his coat and showing it to me.

My heart is in my throat as I eye the blade.

"Then we will not be held responsible for what we do to her," he sneers.

I'm filled with rage.

"Don't you dare touch her," I hiss.

"Or what?"

He suddenly lunges the blade at me, I scrunch my eyes shut and wait for the impact, but it doesn't come. I hear a loud chip of wood and open my eyes. Looking to my left, I see the knife dug into the bark of the tree, a couple of inches from my face. He smirks and finally lets me go, he pulls his knife out of the tree before he walks away.

"You're an idiot. You and your brother will lose," I gloat angrily.

He looks over his shoulder, then charges back at me and punches me hard in the stomach. I cough and double over on the ground in pain. He kicks me hard in the ribs causing me to roll onto my back as he stares down at me.

"This is your only warning, boy," he sneers again.

Curtis turns and walks discreetly towards the exit of the park, leaving me on the ground as I clutch my ribs and groan in pain. A man walking his schnauzer spots me as I struggle to get to my feet. He rushes over.

"You alright, sir? What happened?"

He helps me up, pulling me by the arm. As I try to straighten myself up, I cough furiously.

"I was attacked."

The stranger gasps and looks around for the attacker.

"Shall I call the police?"

"No. I just want to go home. My girlfriend will help me."

I stagger out of the park, assisted by the kindly stranger, who hails a cab and helps me inside when it arrives.

"Thank you so much," I manage, offering him twenty dollars from my wallet.

He looks at the money and shakes his head.

"Just one human being helping another. I hope you get better soon and catch your attacker."

I thank him again and instruct the taxI driver to take me home. I sit in the comfort of the cab, but my ribs are hurting worse now.

When we arrive, I tip the driver and head to the entrance of Rachael's apartment building. Tom opens the door, but looks at me with concern as I stagger in.

"Mark? Are you okay?" he asks, narrowing his eyes.

I collapse to the floor, exhausted. Tom gasps and kneels down beside me. I clutch my ribs in agony and Tom starts yelling for someone to help. Another man, who is smartly dressed rushes out from a side door and helps Tom get me to my feet. They both lead me to the elevators and ride up with me to Rachael's floor. They help me to the front door where I hand them the key from my pocket. Tom unlocks the door and takes me inside. The two men place me on the couch and eye me, looking unsure of what else to do. The unknown man kneels beside the couch and smiles gently.

"My name is Mr. Jenkins. I look after the apartments here. What happened?"

I shake my head, not wanting to tell him, I just need Rachael.

"Could you call my girlfriend, please?" I wheeze.

Mr. Jenkins frowns, then gets to his feet and whispers something to Tom who proceeds to rush out. Mr. Jenkins comes and sits next to me again.

"Tom will deal with it," he says, placing his hand on my shoulder.

Sooner than I'd expected, Rachael bursts through the open door. She is followed in by a paramedic, Officer Bailey and her father, Chief Clarke. Mr. Jenkins stands up to give us all some space. Rachael rushes to my side and examines me closely, stroking my head soothingly.

"Mark, what happened?" she says hastily, her eyes wide with worry.

I cough and attempt to explain.

"I went out for a walk. Curtis found me and he attacked me."

Rachael's eyes widen in anger, then she glances at Bailey and her father.

"Steph. Get some ice," she instructs.

Bailey rushes into the kitchen and collects a bag of ice from the freezer. She hands it over to Rachael who then lifts my shirt. I'm shocked to find a large bruise covering my stomach. Rachael places her hand to her mouth, but she proceeds to apply the ice pack to my bruised area. I wince in pain. The medic bends down next to Rachael and checks my bruise. I flinch as he pokes and prods me.

"Nothing major. Just a little bruising. I will prescribe you some pills to help with the pain, but if they don't help, you need to get to ER urgently for further tests." he instructs while handing Rachael a piece of paper.

"Thank you. I'll keep an eye on him," she says.

He nods, stands up and leaves the apartment. Rachael covers my naked torso with a blanket before taking a seat beside me. Officer Bailey and Chief Clarke sit in the armchairs opposite and Mr. Jenkins turns to leave.

"Thank you, Mr. Jenkins," Rachael calls.

He turns, then smiles at Rachael and shuts the front door behind him.

"Tell me everything that happened, Mr. Flint," Chief Clarke says, leaning forward with his fingers steepled.

I look at Rachael, who smiles reassuringly.

"It's okay, Mark," she soothes.

I look at Officer Bailey who is ready to take notes of everything I say. I begin to tell them everything about how I went out for some air and stopped at the park for a break. Officer Bailey scribbles furiously.

"What happened next?" Chief Clarke asks.

"Curtis O'Malley arrived. He was wearing a beige trench coat and a suit, he sat beside me. We talked for a bit, then he asked me to call Rachael off Tobias, but I refused," I explain.

I feel rather than see Rachael flinch. I look over and take her hand. Chief Clarke looks at me intensely before sitting back in his seat and talking into his radio.

"Be on the lookout for Curtis O'Malley, last spotted at-."

He puts his hand over his radio. "What park were you in?"

"Marcus Garvey Park."

He nods and returns to his radio. "Last spotted at Marcus Garvey Park in Harlem."

He stands up. "We'll check it out."

He looks down at Rachael who quickly gets to her feet, but her father shakes his head.

"You stay, Rachael," he orders.

She sinks slowly back down as his eyes shine with love at her before he returns his gaze to me.

"Thank you for the information, Mr. Flint," he says and starts to walk away.

"Dad?" Rachael hisses.

He stops in his tracks and sighs heavily.

"Thank you, Mark."

I blink at him, surprised. He leaves the apartment, followed closely by Officer Bailey. I look at Rachael, amazed to hear her father call me by my first name for the first time. *What changed his tone?*

"I spoke to him about it on the ride over," she answers my unspoken question.

I grin and lean up, eager to touch her, but drop back down in pain, my ribs and stomach seizing me.

"Just take it easy. I'm going to run down to the pharmacy, grab you these pills," she informs, holding up the piece of paper the paramedic just gave to her.

"Don't be long," I beg as she slips on her coat.

"I won't."

She walks out the front door and closes it softly behind her. I pull the blanket higher over myself and without realizing, drift off to sleep.

I'm awoken by an enticing aroma. I look towards the source of the smell and see Rachael in the kitchen cooking something. I look over as best I can, still feeling dazed. *What time is it?*

"What you doing?" I whisper.

She turns and smiles when she sees me awake.

"Ah, you're up. The pills are on the table next to you. Just take them when you're ready. I'm preparing you some soup for dinner," she says and resumes what she's doing.

After a while, she sits beside me and hands me my soup. I shuffle up, trying to ignore the throbbing pain and dig in eagerly, suddenly famished, though not for long.

"This is delicious. What is it?" I ask.

She peeks over at me.

"It's potato and leek, one of my favorites."

We both enjoy the delicious soup that she's lovingly prepared.

"What time is it?" I ask.

She glances at her phone. "It's eight-fifty."

"Really? How long was I asleep for?"

"Not long. We'll go to bed after our soup. You need some rest."

After finishing my last spoonful of soup, I pick up the pillbox from the table, pop one out and down it with a glug of water. I settle back down onto the couch.

"Thank you."

Rachael smiles.

"It was nothing," she says.

She collects my empty bowl and heads into the kitchen to place it into the dishwasher. My thoughts resume to my earlier planning, from before the Curtis debacle. I know that in my heart and soul, I want Rachael to be my wife. But when to do it?

"When's your birthday?" I ask.

She sits back down and looks at me.

"December 1st. I'll be twenty-eight this year," she states.

"Not long then. I will need to think of something special for you."

"Don't push yourself."

"It won't be a problem."

I smile as I start to hatch a plan.

Chapter Fifteen

I wake early. I still have a slight ache in my ribs where Curtis gave me a swift kick, but I feel considerably better, thanks to my painkillers. Rachael was concerned to leave me on my own as she left for work earlier this morning, but I insisted I would be fine.

Rachael called Mr. Levitt on my behalf and explained what happened, so I have the day off. I've spent the last few hours mulling over what to do for Rachael's birthday, but I'm struggling to think of anything. Event planning has never been my specialty. I contemplate calling Trent for advice. I climb out of bed and grab my cell. He answers almost immediately.

"Mark, how are you feeling? Rachael told me everything."

"Hey, Trent. I'm getting better, I'm taking medication. How are you?"

"I'm good," he responds.

"Good. I need to talk to you about something important. Are you free today?"

He's silent for a moment, then he answers.

"I'm working at the moment, but I'll be free in about an hour."

"Great. Where can I meet you?"

"Central Park? Near the Bethesda Fountain?"

217

"Cool. See you there." I hang up.

I'm looking forward to spending some quality time with Trent. I hadn't realized just how much I miss his company. I hope he doesn't object to my plan to propose to Rachael, but I'll have to wait and see.

I'm on my way out the door just as Rachael emerges from the elevator. She looks exhausted. She spots me and smiles.

"Hi, Mark. Feeling better?"

"Much better. You're home early."

"I couldn't stop worrying about you. I was let out sooner than expected," she explains.

"That's sweet," I smile.

She smiles back, then eyes me suspiciously.

"Where are you off to? Shouldn't you be resting?"

"I'm just going to spend some time with Trent."

"Can't he meet you here?"

I scramble for an excuse.

"I need some air. Don't worry, he'll look out for me."

She looks reluctant and appears to be contemplating whether to question me further, but thankfully, she smiles widely.

"Have a good time and be careful."

She leans in, kisses me swiftly, then walks past me into the apartment. I continue to the elevators, press the call button and wait for its arrival.

I walk briskly through Central Park on this chilly day, casually striding past Bow Bridge where I stop momentarily. I have fond memories of this place. I glance over at the bench where Rachael and I once sat and marvel at how far the two of us have come. I reluctantly tear my gaze away and walk on. I find Trent sitting on the wall by the Bethesda Fountain. I take a seat beside him as he looks across at me.

"Hey. How you doing?" he asks.

I respond with a wide grin and look ahead, taking a deep breath. I can feel Trent continuing to stare at me, so I glance back.

"What's up?" he asks.

I turn to face him and cut to the point quickly.

"I'm planning to ask Rachael to marry me," I state proudly.

Trent briefly looks stricken. He stares at me wide-eyed with his mouth open. I cock my head at him as he gapes at me.

"Well?" I prompt.

He shakes his head and sits up straight, then he leans in closer to me.

"Are you sure?" he whispers.

"Of course. Why?"

He links his fingers together in front of him and fidgets uncomfortably.

"Bit soon, don't you think?"

I knew someone would ask me that and it makes me feel a little bitter.

"Maybe, but I love her, Trent. I know that I want her for the rest of my life."

We sit for a moment, watching the other people walk around us, then Trent finally turns back to me.

"If that's how you feel, Mark, go for it, buddy."

He takes me by surprise, I blink at him and give him a face-splitting grin.

"Really?" I ask.

He answers simply with a quick nod.

"Is that what you wanted to talk to me about?" he asks.

"Mm, hmm."

"Mark, you're a grown man. You don't need to ask my permission. If a woman came along that I wanted to marry, I wouldn't ask you."

He looks at me squarely in the eye.

"If she is the woman for you, grab her with both hands and don't let her go," he continues.

I look down at the floor, feeling touched and so cherished by my friend.

"There's something I need to show you. Come with me," Trent says suddenly.

He gets to his feet and waits for me to follow.

"What is it?" I ask, nonplussed.

He cocks his head to the side and grins.

"You'll see."

I get to my feet, my curiosity taking over, and I walk with Trent back to his apartment.

As we get closer, Trent turns to me quickly.

"Oh, I forgot to mention. My mom is here from Buffalo; she'll be thrilled to see you again."

"Is that what you wanted to show me?"

He laughs. "No, no. Just thought I would let you know."

We make our way inside, up the stairs and to Trent's front door. He pushes it open and gestures for me to enter first, just like the first time he bought me here. I have fond memories of this place. A short lady with a blonde bob cut is sitting on the couch. She looks towards us; first at Trent, then at me. She grabs the arm of the couch in shock.

"Mark. It can't be," she says quietly.

"Hello again, Mrs. Wilkinson."

She gets up slowly and steps closer towards us. She examines my face as I stand still, smiling at her. Trent breaks the silence.

"Mom."

She looks at Trent and beams.

"You never told me Mark was back."

Trent shrugs. "I wanted to surprise you."

She's standing up close to me now and places her hand gently on my face.

"You look just like her. Your grandma. Jeni."

I look away from her and can feel the tears brimming. She places her hand to her mouth and steps back, guiltily.

"I'm sorry. I know it still must be hard for you. I can't believe she's gone."

"It's okay. It's good to see you again, Mrs. Wilkinson."

"Alison. Please, call me Alison."

Trent frowns and pulls my arm. He leads me to the couch where I sit down. He turns his attention to his mom.

"Mom, we need to show him... you know," Trent hisses.

Alison nods once and retreats into Trent's bedroom. *Show me what?*

Seconds later, she returns, carrying an envelope and a cardboard box. She places it at my feet and hands me the envelope.

"Your grandma left this with strict instructions to give it to you when the time was right. I think it's long overdue," Trent says gently.

I examine the envelope. In Grandma's neat handwriting is inscribed: *Mark*. I rip it open and pull out a piece of paper which is folded neatly. I unfold it and read aloud.

My dearest Mark,

From the second you were born I knew you would be special. Rest assured, your parents did love you. I think you are old enough to know that your father got in deep with some very bad people. He owed them a lot of money and they threatened to harm you. Your parents weren't the bad people you thought they were. I'm so sorry I didn't tell you this sooner. I was left heartbroken, as were you when your parents left us, but know this; the years that you lived with me, the years I took care of you, they were the best. You were a breath of fresh air in my life after your grandpa left us. I have been saving for you so that you can have a bright future. I have left you some money that Alison, Trent's mother will give to you when you next see her. Keep it safe and spend it on whatever will make you happy. Also, I have left a package with Alison. It contains a lot of items that are very dear to me; they're now yours. Please take care of them. Know that I will always be with you and I will always love you. I've always been proud of you. Don't grieve over me, live your life and find love, like I found in your grandpa and in you.

Love always,
Grandma.

I fold up the letter and hang my head. Trent places his hand on my back as Alison sits beside me.

"You alright?" he asks gently.

I look up at him and offer a weak smile, then I turn to Alison. She smiles warmly and takes my hand, then she stands again and heads back into Trent's room. When she comes back, she is carrying a silver metal box. She places it on my lap, and I look down at it. Slowly I open the lid and gasp in disbelief. There's a lot of money in here! It takes me a while to count it all up, but she's left me twenty-five thousand dollars. I have never seen so much cash! I've only had one hundred dollars in cash at one time. Trent looks over my shoulder and whistles.

"She really wanted a bright future for you. You can afford those engagement plans now."

Alison whips her shocked expression at us both.

"Engagement plans?"

Trent sits back in his seat. "Oops."

She looks at me and I smile at her.

"I've been seeing someone recently. Her name is Rachael," I explain.

"Well, I must meet her," she says, clapping her hands excitedly.

"I'll make sure you do."

We all eye the cardboard box that was dropped at my feet.

"What's in there?" Trent asks, pointing with his chin.

I bend down and open it up. Inside, I find a leather biker jacket and a few photos. I examine each one fully. One photo is of my grandpa wearing the jacket and sitting proudly on his Harley Davidson motorcycle. Another is my mom and dad's wedding and the last one is my parents smiling gleefully, and sitting between them, a baby; it's me. I stroke the photo delicately. *We all look so happy. What happened to you all?* I drop everything back into the box. I have so much to process and I need some air. I stand quickly as do Trent and Alison, as I head for the door.

"You're leaving?" Alison asks.

I turn back to face them both.

"I just need a walk. It's been wonderful to see you again, Alison."

"Will I see you again?" she asks.

"Soon," I promise.

Trent grabs the metal box where I accidentally left it on the couch.

"We should put this money in the bank, then go ring shopping for Rachael. What do ya say?"

I blink at him a couple of times. I've been given so much to think about, but I remember Grandma's advice on the letter; *'Don't grieve over me, live your life and find love.'* Grandma wants that for me, so I'll get it. My motivation to propose to Rachael resurfaces immediately.

"Let's do it."

The bank visit was a nightmare. I had no ID and no proof of address, so I couldn't open an account. Trent argued with the teller for a good while until he suggested depositing the cash into his account for safekeeping. I was reluctant, but he assured me that he wouldn't touch a cent. We deposited all but three thousand dollars of Grandma's money, which we keep pocketed for the ring shopping.

It was an exhausting search, but I settled on a white gold ring with a solitary diamond in the middle and smaller diamonds surrounding it. It's stunning and perfect for Rachael. I told Trent I wasn't going to propose until near her birthday, but he insisted I should purchase it now so that it's ready. I spent two and a half grand on the ring and gave Trent five hundred for my contribution to the time I was living with him. He initially refused, but I insisted that he take it. Trent and I exit the store.

"I need to run. Me and Mom are going out for a meal soon," Trent explains.

I hug him hard. "Thank you, Trent."

He puts his hand on my shoulder, then turns to walk away. I watch him until he disappears into the crowd. I walk in the opposite direction and make my way back to Rachael. I have the ring, now I need a time and place.

On the way back, I mentally ask myself an important question. *Where should I hide the ring?* The last thing I want is Rachael discovering it. I head inside quickly and hope that Rachael is still asleep after her shift. I walk in, close the door as softly as I can manage and tip-toe to the bedroom. Rachael is, indeed, tucked up in bed, fast asleep. I close the bedroom door slowly so as not to disturb her and try to hide the ring box somewhere in the lounge. Nowhere seems appropriate. I can't hide it in the drawers or cupboards as she may find it. Suddenly, the sound of her footsteps gets my attention. I stuff it into my rucksack just in time as she enters the lounge. She sees me and smiles sweetly.

"You're back. Did you boys have a good time?" she yawns.

"It was great," I answer, trying not to sound flustered, which I seem to get away with.

"Good."

She breezes past me into the kitchen and begins preparing lunch.

"Do you want me to do that?" I offer, but she shakes her head and laughs.

"Last time you made me a meal you nearly burnt the apartment down."

I frown, trying to remember. "What are you talking about?"

She raises an eyebrow at me, then I remember the omelet fiasco. I flush, embarrassed and turn my heated face away from her.

"It wasn't my best day." I laugh at myself.

She giggles, then starts busying herself with some tofu dogs. I've never really eaten vegetarian food until recently. I must admit, it's starting to grow on me. The smell of the tofu isn't great, but I'm willing to try it. She hands me a plate while she tucks in eagerly. I stare down at it suspiciously.

"Go on, try it," she prompts, her mouth still half full.

I pick it up and take a bite. It's nicer than I expected. She looks at me, pleased.

"See?"

I smile at her gratefully.

"How was your shift?" I ask, prompting a conversation.

She rolls her eyes and puffs out. "Busy."

We continue with our tofu dogs in comfortable silence. She finishes hers before me. She slides off the barstool elegantly and sits on the couch, crossing her legs.

"What were you and Trent up to?" she quizzes.

I peek at her briefly and turn away.

"Nothing much," I lie.

She chuckles.

"You are a hopeless liar. C'mon, tell me."

I desperately try to think of something. *How I am going to get out of this one?* I am stuck for an answer, so I shrug my shoulders. She is about to say something else when the phone rings. She looks at the number and answers it.

"Hi, Mom," she says.

I take a breath; saved by the phone call. I finish eating and sit beside her. She continues to listen carefully, then her eyebrows shoot up in shock.

"What?"

I look at her and instantly recognize this expression. I've seen it before, and I don't like it. My gut tightens uncomfortably. She looks down and places her head in her hand.

"I'll be there immediately. Thanks for letting me know."

She drops the phone to the floor with a loud clatter. I'm about to ask what's happened, but she starts to cry softly. I pull her to me and stroke her hair.

"What's wrong?" I ask, as she sobs softly into my chest.

"I need to catch the bastard."

Her face shifts from grief to anger.

I have an idea who she is referring to but ask anyway. "Who?"

She looks up at me with her tear-stained face and I wipe her eyes.

"Tobias, Curtis, or both," she snarls.

"Rachael, what is it?"

"My father. He's been shot."

She flops back onto the couch, causing me to jump up and I stare down at her stunned.

"Is he…?"

"No, he's still alive. I need to see him."

I offer my hand.

"Let's get to the hospital."

She continues to lie on the couch, staring up at the ceiling.

"Rachael, come on."

I grab her hand and pull her up. She stands slowly and I lead her quickly towards the door as she grabs the keys on our way out.

Rachael drives a lot more aggressively than I'm used to. She weaves through the heavy traffic, occasionally cursing under her breath whenever we're caught up. We finally arrive at Lenox Hill Hospital; she finds a space to park and leaps out the car, bolting towards the main entrance. I dash after her. We rush through the automatic double doors and towards the polished reception desk. A young, blonde woman sits behind it, drawn to her computer screen. As we approach, she looks up and gives us a welcoming smile.

"Can I help you?" the kindly receptionist greets.

Rachael steps forward.

"My father was recently admitted here." She's flustered.

The woman looks down at her screen.

"Name, please."

"Colin Clarke," Rachael responds hastily.

The lady taps on her keyboard, then looks up at us again.

"He's on the second floor. The elevators are just through these doors and on your left."

She points at another set of double doors.

"Thank you so much," Rachael says, before dashing off again.

I trail quickly after her, catching up at the elevators. She punches the call button, then shifts from foot to foot nervously. I risk a quick glance at her, but she doesn't return it. She looks down at her hands and picks at her fingernails. The elevator arrives, we step in and I press for the second floor. The doors close smoothly and we start to ascend. I look at her again, but she continues to look down. I take her hand in mine, and this gets her attention. She looks at me out the corner of her eye and smiles meekly.

"It'll be okay," I say, trying to reassure her, but I don't believe my own words.

Her smile fades as she withdraws her hand.

We arrive on the second floor and step out of the elevator. We make a left and head for the trauma ward. We push through another set of sterile doors, then we arrive at another desk, which I assume is the nurses' station. Rachael begins talking to a nurse. I give her some space but watch her. The nurse frowns a little before making her way out from behind the desk and gesturing for Rachael to follow her. She does so quickly but stops and turns to me.

"Come on," she calls to me, and I follow after her.

The nurse leads us down the corridor and stops outside a door.

"He's in here. Room six. Call me if you need anything."

The nurse smiles sympathetically at Rachael before turning and heading back down the corridor. Rachael looks at me momentarily, then knocks on the door softly. No one answers, so we enter the room quietly. Colin is in bed, covered in bloody bandages wrapped around his chest and seemingly unconscious. He has a mask over his face as he breathes softly into it. Rachael places her hand to her mouth and begins to pale.

"Oh, Dad."

She rushes to his bedside and sits on the edge. She takes his hand, but he doesn't respond. She begins to sob softly and I can bear it no more. I walk over and stand by her side, placing my arm around her. She releases her dad's hand and hugs me hard. We say nothing, we just hold each other as I rock her gently. She pushes me away and holds her father's hand again. I stand back to give her some room and sit on a chair in the corner. I look at Mr. Clarke who remains asleep.

"Would you like me to leave you alone for a minute?" I whisper.

She looks at me and sniffs, then nods slightly. I stand and make my way to the door, open it and take one final glance at her, then leave.

I pace the corridor, wondering what to do with myself. I decide to get a coffee, so I head for the vending machines. I turn a corner and see Louise and Mrs. Clarke who are seated in some chairs, holding onto each other, looking down at the polished floor. I approach them and Louise looks up. She smiles and stands to greet me.

"Hello, Mark."

I nod at her and sit beside them.

"Hello, Louise, Mrs. Clarke," I greet them both.

Mrs. Clarke looks up at me, her eyes red-rimmed. She takes my hand.

"I'm so happy to see you again. Where's Rachael?" she asks, looking around expectantly.

"She's with your husband."

Mrs. Clarke smiles slightly and looks down.

"Good," she says more to herself.

Louise sits back down next to her mother.

"What do you know about the man who did this?" Louise asks, looking at me seriously.

Mrs. Clarke's head whips up and she gives her daughter a seething look.

"Louise," she hisses.

"It's okay. I'm willing to help any way I can."

They both look at me expectantly as I think about what to tell them. I take a breath and lean forward.

"I know that Tobias is an evil, uncompromising psychopath. He will do anything to get his way. His brother, I'm not sure."

They look at each other, then at me.

"How do we catch him?" Mrs. Clarke whispers.

I sit back in my seat and shake my head.

"I'm sorry. I don't know. He knows how to evade capture when he wants to."

They both look disappointed before Mrs. Clarke stands up.

"Try to find a way, or Rachael could be next," she warns, then she walks down the corridor, her heels clicking against the polished floor. I watch after her, then turn to Louise.

"Mom's right, you know. If this man is as bad as you say, it *could* be her next."

I blink at her at a total loss for words. She glares at me for a moment, before she also stands and follows after her mother. I sit alone with my head in my hands. Rachael's safety has always been a concern, but what can I do? I just don't know how to face it. If the unimaginable happens, I will blame myself for all eternity. I know what they say is true, but I just don't know how to stop him. I run my hands through my hair down to the base of my neck, feeling hopeless.

I don't know how long I've been sitting in the corridor, but Rachael's cracked voice catches my attention.

"There you are."

I look up and she's standing in front of me. I stand.

"How is he?" I ask, but her face falls.

"It's okay. Don't worry," I reassure.

She smiles at me gratefully, before she offers me her hand and we walk back to Mr. Clarke's room together. When we enter, there is a nurse examining Mr. Clarke's wound with Mrs. Clarke firing a barrage of questions at her. We sit on the opposite side of the room and watch as the nurse cleans the wound and applies a new dressing. She turns around and sees Rachael's horrified expression, but the nurse smiles.

"Everyone need not worry. The wound isn't as bad as we originally feared."

This seems to lighten up Mrs. Clarke. "Really?"

The nurse turns to her.

"No, Mrs. Clarke. The doctors have run their tests. The bullet hit the top of your husband's sternum, but it didn't penetrate deep enough to cause life-threatening injuries. We had to put him into a medically-induced coma, just in case, but if all continues to go well, we will wake him soon."

Mrs. Clarke beams and looks at us all.

"That's great news, isn't it, guys?" She sounds uplifted.

We all smile at her, but then a dark thought crosses my mind as I look at Mr. Clarke. I recognize this type of injury. I have seen Tobias do this on a number of occasions to threaten his enemies. He wasn't intending to kill Mr. Clarke; this is a warning shot; this is to say he is getting close. I realize he is after me, this is his warning to me, which means Mrs. Clarke and Louise were right, Rachael is his next target.

Chapter Sixteen

We say our quick goodbyes to everyone. It's getting late and we have been here for a few hours. Mr. Clarke still hasn't woken up, but we have been assured that everything is fine and he will be taken out of his coma soon. We leave the hospital and make our way back home.

"Good news about Dad," Rachael beams, sounding a lot more optimistic, but I have a tight knot in my gut.

The traffic is now moderately light, so it doesn't take long to get home. We head into the parking lot and she parks in her designated space. I'm first out of the car. I'm struggling to cope with my dark thoughts. She follows behind as we walk to the elevator.

"You alright?" she asks.

I shake my head, batting away my troubled thoughts and respond with a grunt. She unlocks the door and we head in. I slump onto the couch and feel increasingly sick.

"Would you like a drink?" she offers.

I shake my head and stare blankly at the opposite wall. I feel Rachael's concerned eyes on me, but I don't look at her. It sounds like she is in the kitchen, but within moments, she is sitting beside me.

"Mark, what's wrong?" she presses, but I continue to say nothing.

She places something down on the table and grabs my face in both her hands, forcing me to look at her.

"Please talk to me."

I gently prize her hands from my face and stand up, putting my hands on my head. She stands with me, but remains where she is, making no attempt to touch me. I pace the room, occasionally glancing at her and notice her getting increasingly upset and desperate. I sigh, not wanting to be responsible for that look.

"It's my fault," I finally manage.

She blinks rapidly.

"What is?"

"Your father, getting shot."

I glance towards her. She looks at me with her mouth open in complete surprise, before she makes her way towards me, but I step back.

"Mark, this isn't your fault. How can you say that?"

I turn away from her and rub my face.

"Tobias never misses."

I hear her gasp. "What?"

I turn my attention back to her.

"He never misses," I repeat.

She gapes at me but doesn't respond.

"What he did to your father, it's a warning. To me."

I step towards her as she continues to stare at me, but this time, she takes a step back.

"He's after me, and he is going to get to me through you," I explain.

A lump is now forming in my throat.

"How do you know that?" she whispers.

I sigh and look down at my feet.

"I've seen him do it before."

She steps back further. I try to follow, but she holds her hands up as a warning not to come any closer. I freeze and watch her cautiously.

"You *knew* about this?" she breathes quietly.

"I had a feeling, but I didn't think he would do this to your dad."

Rachael's face turns from stunned to furious.

"You've seen him do this before? You held vital information about this bastard from the cops. From me?"

Her voice is beginning to rise.

"Rachael, I didn't know-" I start, but she holds her hands up again and I go quiet immediately. She turns and opens a drawer. She removes something, but I don't know what it is. Then I notice, she is holding handcuffs.

"I should arrest you," she hisses.

I stare at the handcuffs fearfully and try to think of something to say that will defuse this situation.

"I'm sorry," I attempt, but it doesn't work.

She walks over and snaps the cuffs on my wrists. I look up at her, but she remains vehement.

"Rachael, I swear, I didn't know he would go after your father. I'm sorry that he did."

"It's obvious he would go after my father. He's the goddamn Chief of Police. The father of your girlfriend and you didn't know he would target him?" she bellows.

I'm stunned; I've never seen her so irate. I lower my head, ashamed.

"You can lock me back up if you want, but I want you to know that if I had known about this, I would have done anything to stop it."

She looks down briefly, then returns her gaze. She looks torn on what to do next as she continues to hold onto the cuffs around my wrists.

"I need to make sure he doesn't get to you, Rachael. Maybe you should just let him find me, use me as bait if you have to."

She scoffs.

"That's the stupidest thing I have ever heard. We are not using you as bait. We'll find him another way."

She removes the handcuffs and I rub my wrists.

"But he could hurt you or-."

She stops me. "Let him try."

I smile at her and attempt to hug her, but she pushes me off.

"Now, I have something I need to tell you," she says, looking guilty herself.

"Maybe you should sit down first," she continues.

I furrow my brow, confused, but sit anyway. She joins me and takes my hand.

"I know you wanted to leave it, but I just couldn't," she starts.

I stare at her seriously.

"What did you do?"

She looks away, then stands up and heads to the chest of drawers again. She opens a drawer and pulls out a folder.

"My father has some friends in the Chicago Police Department. We did some digging and…" she stops suddenly, takes a deep breath and continues.

"Mark, I don't know how to say this… Your parents were both found dead in 1993. They died from gunshot wounds. I'm so sorry."

I stare at her, wide-eyed with shock, then I'm struck with such anger I have never felt before. I leap off the couch and glower at her.

"How could you? I told you, that part of me is dead and buried. I wanted to keep it that way. You went behind my back!?" I shout.

She stares at me and attempts to approach me, but I back out of her reach.

"The truth had to be known. I did this for you, so that it would be easier for you to move on," she tries to explain calmly.

I'm horrified and begin to pull and twist at my shirt angrily.

"I don't want to face this. That was my choice to make, not yours."

"I'm sorry. I know this must be hard," she whispers, tears now streaming down her face.

"You wouldn't know the first thing about what I went through," I seethe, before turning on my heel, grabbing my jacket and slamming the door on my way out.

I roam the dark streets, furious with what I have just heard. I told her that I didn't want to know about my parents, but she looked them up anyway. *Why has she done this to me?*

It's a freezing night and I cough as the bitter wind bites into me. I have lost track of how long I have been out here. I'm not ready to go back to Rachael's place, so I head towards Trent's.

I press the intercom button for Trent desperately and wait. No answer. I try again and wait a couple of minutes, but still no answer. I try to call him, but it goes straight through to answerphone. *Oh yeah, he's out with his mother.* I sit on the cold concrete of the sidewalk and wait for a while. After a short time, I'm so cold that I have no choice, I need to go back home. With that depressing thought, I stand up and start heading for Rachael's.

I stand outside and think of what to say to her when I get inside. Nothing is coming to me. My mind is swimming with negative thoughts, and I feel so depressed. I head inside begrudgingly, but Rachael isn't in the living room. Her bedroom door is closed, so I assume she's in bed. I walk to the door and listen. I can hear what sounds like soft weeping inside, Rachael is crying. I feel like I want to rush to her and comfort her, but I can't, I'm still too angry. I huff, annoyed and grab a spare pillow and quilt from the linen closet in the hall, place it on the couch and lie down, still fully dressed. I rub my eyes and desperately try to sleep, but for most of the night, I lie awake, tossing and turning. I groan and get back up and pull my wallet from my bag. I take the photo of Grandma out of my wallet and look at it closely.

"Why didn't you just tell me the truth? You could have spared me so much pain. Why did you lie to me?"

Tears trickle down my cheeks, but I dash the tears away furiously and, without thinking, I drop the photo to the ground and lie back on the couch. I finally manage to get to sleep, but my dreams are haunted by the last time I saw my mother alive.

I wake suddenly and sit bolt upright. For a moment, I thought I heard my mother's voice, pleading me to help her, but I was obviously dreaming. I shake my head, trying to eradicate the sound of my mother's voice still ringing in my ears. I throw the spare duvet off myself and get up. Rachael's bedroom door is open, so I step inside. Rachael is getting dressed in her police uniform. She turns and sees me standing in her bedroom doorway. She scowls at me and turns her back to me. I walk further into the room, wanting to apologize for my despicable behavior last night, but before I get the chance, she whirls round and storms past me. I go after her.

"Look, I'm sorry," I shout.

She turns around and leans against the wall.

"You have a lot to be sorry for," she seethes.

I hang my head and walk closer to her and extend my hand, desperate to touch her, but she backs away.

"Don't you dare come near me or so help me you will wind up behind bars again."

I drop my hand and stare at her helplessly.

"I really want to understand you, but you just won't let your guard down. You're being stubborn and selfish. I'm going to work; get your shit together, now," she screams.

Her look of fury continues to bore into me, then she turns and walks out the door, slamming it shut behind her. My mouth drops open in shock as I stare at the closed door. *So that's how being stormed out on feels. She didn't accept my apology.* I rush to the window and wait for her to emerge.

I see her white Mercedes as she pulls out of the parking lot and speeds down the street. I feel utterly deflated. I sit on the couch and look down at my feet. I notice the photo of Grandma that I discarded yesterday. I pick it up and, without looking at it, I stuff it back into my bag. I check my watch; it's nearly six in the morning. I sigh to myself sadly and start to get ready for a grueling day at work with no positive thoughts to guide me through it.

I walk through the bustling streets on my way to work, but I can't shake the misery I'm feeling today. I feel a familiar chill in my bones, and it isn't the winter breeze that blows softly past my ears. I pull my jacket over myself and start to rush; I'm late for work. After jogging five blocks, I arrive at the hotel, breathless. I'm ten minutes late, so I hope Mr. Levitt doesn't notice. I enter through the double doors and my heart sinks more, Mr. Levitt is standing in the lobby with his arms folded, looking straight at me. I groan inwardly and approach him slowly.

"Where have you been?" he snarls.

I shrug slightly. "Sorry. Rough day."

He unfolds his arms and sighs.

"Try harder, Mark," he says softly and walks away.

I look at him, surprised. I really thought I was going to get fired, but he seems to be giving me the benefit of the doubt. I turn on my heel and head to the staff room to remove my jacket and start my day.

I exit the janitor closet and walk into Rex and Trent who are talking excitedly about a new video game they are looking forward to. They stop when they see me, and Trent smiles warmly.

"Hey, man."

His enthusiastic voice annoys me further.

"Where were *you* last night?" I ask Trent suddenly.

He looks stricken at my tone.

"I was out for dinner with Mom. Don't you remember?"

I nod, remembering him mentioning it after we left the jewelers. The memory of purchasing Rachael's engagement ring depresses me further and I try to walk past them, but they follow after me quickly.

"What's up?" Trent calls.

I turn. "Forget it."

I walk faster to get away from them. I should have called in sick today, I just want to be alone.

I'm cleaning the guest bedrooms, getting ready for more over-excited tourists to arrive when Trent and Rex enter, surprising me. *It must be their lunch break.*

"How are things with you and that cop girlfriend of yours?" Rex asks.

I look at him and scowl slightly. Trent kicks him a little, which makes him wince.

"Her name is Rachael." Trent corrects him curtly.

Rex holds up his hand humbly and smiles pleasantly.

"Sorry. How are you and Rachael getting on?" He corrects himself.

I look down at the floor, then back at them. Trent's smile fades when he sees my expression.

"Have you proposed yet?" Trent asks quickly.

I shake my head as he frowns at me.

"Her father was shot by Tobias yesterday. We had an argument last night, if you must know," I snap at them both.

"I'd better get back to work," Rex says awkwardly and darts away from us.

I watch Rex rush off and turn my attention back to Trent, who is scowling after him.

"Don't mind him, he hates conflicting subjects," he explains.

I try to walk round Trent to get back to work myself, but he grabs my shoulders and stares at me, his eyes crinkling with concern.

"You will fix this. I know you will," he reassures me before finally leaving me standing in the cleaned bedroom.

I watch after him, then collect my supplies and make my way to the next room.

I collect my jacket from the staff room and head down to the lobby. Trent is leaning against the wall when I emerge from the elevator.

"Want to walk home together?" he smiles.

I'm tempted to refuse but feel like I could do with the company.

"That'd be nice."

He grins and we make our way to the exit. I open the door for us both to leave, but something catches my attention in the lobby. I look over and there is a man in an oversized black coat standing with his back to us, with his head lowered. I try to ignore him, but an uneasy feeling grips me. I look around the lobby, but no one seems bothered by his presence. I turn to Trent, who is also looking towards the man.

"I should check it out," I say.

I close the door and start to approach the man cautiously. I tap him on the shoulder.

"Do you need help, sir?" I offer.

"Yes, I think I do," the stranger responds in a smooth voice with his back still facing me.

Oh no. It can't be. I try to remain calm and consider that it may just be my imagination.

"What can I help you with?" I ask, feeling increasingly unsure of the situation I find myself in.

"I'm looking for someone," he says quietly.

I step back and look over at Trent, who is now on his way over. The stranger turns round and takes off his hood. I gasp and step back further. My fears are confirmed. It's Tobias. I stand with my mouth open; Trent stands by my side, scowling furiously, but Tobias continues to grin an evil twisted smile.

"I'm going to have to ask you to leave," Trent orders.

"Or what, boy?" he threatens, before looking back at me.

"Mark, it's so good to see you again. I would like to apologize for my brother's unruly behavior the other day," he continues.

I don't believe a word as I glower at him.

"I can't say I'm feeling as enthusiastic to see you again," I say bluntly.

He laughs loudly.

"That's no way to greet an old friend. What about the person I need help identifying?" he snarls, looking at me, then at Trent.

"I will never help you," I snarl back, feeling brave.

Tobias displays an all-tooth grin and opens his coat revealing his revolver. I look at it, stunned and watch him carefully.

"It will only take a minute of your time, then you can get back to... *this*."

He waves his gloved hand in the general direction of the hotel lobby, then reaches into his jacket. Trent steps forward, placing himself between me and Tobias. Tobias stops and frowns at Trent.

"Relax, boy. I have no quarrel with you."

Tobias sounds calm but sinister. Trent stands where he is, refusing to move.

"Trent, don't," I plead, but he ignores me.

Tobias reaches into his jacket again and pulls out a piece of paper. He unfolds it slowly and shows it to me. I step closer to get a better look, then blanch in horror. It's a photo of Chief Clarke, with a big red cross scrawled over the image. Below that, there is a photo of Rachael. I am suddenly washed over by anger. I lunge at him, but Trent grabs me, holding me back as Tobias cackles evilly.

"So, you know who she is? Well, me too."

He looks at the image admiringly.

"Pretty girl. Quite a life you have built for yourself. Not bad for a ratty little orphan. Call her off my tail, or she will end up like her daddy, but in a far worse condition," he warns.

I look at him furiously as I try to wrestle Trent off, but he holds on firmly. Tobias continues to smirk at me.

"Do we have a deal?"

"Go to hell," I whisper angrily.

He folds the photo back up and places it in his pocket, shrugging at me, mocking me.

"I tried," he says quietly, as he starts to button his coat back up then he walks casually out the hotel and out of sight.

Trent finally releases me and stares at me with concern.

"You're above that asshole," Trent growls.

I shrug him off and make for the door.

"Mr. Flint?" Mr. Levitt calls, stopping me in my tracks again.

I am really not in the mood for any more today. I close my eyes and purse my lips tightly in frustration, but I count to ten, then look over to find Mr. Levitt standing by the elevator, so I rush over.

"Yes, sir?" I say.

He grabs my arm and pulls me quickly into the backroom, Trent follows after us.

"What happened just there?" Mr. Levitt asks, visibly concerned.

"I don't know what you mean, sir," I deny, but Trent shakes his head at me slowly.

"I saw it on the CCTV footage, Mark. What is going on?" Mr. Levitt asks me again, so I give in.

"He was my old boss. He's threatening my girlfriend," I explain.

Mr. Levitt steps back in surprise.

"Why?"

I shake my head.

"My girlfriend is a cop. My old boss, well, he's a criminal."

I'm looking at the floor as I explain, but when I look up, Mr. Levitt looks at me with warmth and understanding.

"Take a couple of days off, Mark. I think you're stressed."

I open my mouth to protest, but he shakes his head and points towards the door. I sigh and turn away, then walk out through the door to start making my way home. My mind is in overdrive; I can't stop thinking about my conflict with Tobias. If what he says is true, Rachael is not safe. I forget about our argument from last night and this morning, and before I realize what I'm doing, I dash home as fast as I can. I need to speak to Rachael urgently.

I burst through the door, desperate to speak to Rachael, desperate to hold her, desperate to protect her, desperate to apologize for how I've acted. I look around the apartment, but she isn't here.

"Rachael?" I call, feeling bile rising in my throat.

What if Tobias got here before me? Has he taken her?

"Rachael?" I call again, a little louder this time.

To my relief, she walks out of the bedroom in her dressing gown, looking a little confused and tired. She scowls slightly at me and leans against the door frame.

"Oh, you're home early."

She glances down at her wristwatch and looks back at me expectantly.

"You didn't get fired, did you?"

I say nothing but stalk towards her. She glares at me and backs away, but I'm determined to hold her. I reach her and wrap her in my warm embrace, kissing her desperately, grateful that she's safe and well. She attempts to push me off, but she gradually relaxes, returning my kiss with a passion of her own. She pulls away and stares at me with wary concern, erasing her prior scorn.

"Mark, what is it? What's going on?" she breathes softly, cupping my face gently.

I stare longingly at her, but then gently push her away. I can't bring myself to tell her what happened at work today, I know how angry she will be. I groan inwardly and walk to the window with my hands on my head.

"Mark?"

I glance over my shoulder but say nothing. She still stands by the bedroom door, looking at me.

"What's wrong?"

I look away again and stare out the window, resting my forehead against the cool glass. I can hear her footsteps as she walks towards me. I turn slowly and stare at her. She places her hands on my arms and looks up at me, her hazel eyes rimmed with worry.

"Please speak to me," she begs.

I take her hand and lead her to the couch. We both sit and she continues to stare at me. I brace myself to tell her but feel too cowardly to do it.

"I can't," I whisper.

Her mouth drops open in horror, but then she displays a more determined look.

"Mark," she warns.

I quail at her menacing tone and relent.

"What I'm about to tell you could be dangerous to your safety."

"For Christ's sake. I can look after myself. Have you forgotten what my job is? I face danger every day," she states frustratingly.

"Tobias came to my workplace today."

Rachael stares at me in alarm and jumps up, taking me by surprise.

"What? What did he say?" she blasts.

I hang my head, anxious how she'll react next.

"He told me to tell you to back off or he'll…" My voice trails off, I just can't say it.

"Or he'll what?"

"I can't."

"Tell me."

I rub my face.

"Or you'll end up like your daddy, but worse."

I quote Tobias' words, still looking down. She doesn't react immediately like I'd expected, so I peek up at her. She's staring down at me, looking full of wrath. She is radiating tension and her whole body starts to shake.

"Anything else?" she whispers eerily.

"No."

With a steely expression, she turns and stalks into the bedroom away from me, angrily slamming the door behind her. I shudder, feeling cold. I think about going after her, but I don't dare move. Soon, she re-emerges in her uniform.

"You've only just been to work," I query.

"*And*?" she hisses at me.

I approach her, but she puts her hand up. I stop quickly.

"Just stay away," she growls.

I sink slowly back onto the couch and before I can attempt to stop her, she is out the door. I'm shocked by Rachael's reaction. I can't tell if she's mad at me or she's simply desperate to have Tobias and his brother off the streets. I get up off the couch, feeling more restless than ever. I try to call Rachael, but it goes straight to voice mail.

I spend most of the afternoon feeling remorseful for everything. I desperately want her to come back home, but hours tick by, and there is still no word from her. I try calling her again, no luck, so I leave her a message.

"Hey, it's only me. Please come home or at least let me know that you're okay."

I hang up and put my cell down.

I wait a few agonizing minutes, then my cell rings. I jump at it frantically, but it's only Trent. I groan and answer.

"Hey," I breathe grumpily.

"Hey man. I just wanted to know if you're okay."

His voice is laced with anxiety.

I breathe out silently. "I'm fine."

"Have you spoken to Rachael?"

My mind is racing, and I don't want to talk long.

"Yeah. She's gone to work."

He's silent.

"Listen, Trent. I appreciate the concern, but I'm waiting for an important phone call."

I hear him sigh deeply before he responds.

"Sure. I'm here for you. You know that, right?"

"Right," I answer, then hang up and throw the phone down beside me.

I try to find something to do to distract myself from the nagging depression that threatens to grip me. I eye my rucksack by the front door and unpack everything from it. I remove my lunch box, the contents barely touched, and place it on the kitchen counter. I hang up my leather jacket and check to see if there is anything else inside the bag, but there doesn't seem to be. I take it to the storage cupboard and throw it inside, but I hear a loud rattle as it lands. I take the bag back out and rummage around inside, locating the source of the noise. I pull out a small box and examine it carefully, then I remember; Rachael's engagement ring. I sigh and feel my heart sink. I desperately want to give her this, but with the threat of Tobias, and our relationship on the rocks, it just doesn't seem possible at the moment. I put it back gently and slink slowly into the bedroom. I lie on the bed, hoping that Rachael is on her way home now.

A sudden noise wakes me. I hadn't realized I had fallen asleep. I switch on the bedside light and check the alarm clock; it's just past three in the morning. I get off the bed and make my way into the living room. Rachael has returned and is sitting on the couch looking at her phone. She glances up at me. I smile, but she doesn't return it. She returns her attention to her phone as my smile fades. I sit in the armchair opposite her.

"Have you only just come in?" I ask.

She looks up again and places her phone down beside her.

"Yes," she says curtly.

I flinch at her cold tone and wonder why she's so mad at me.

"Look. If you're upset about last night, I'm sorry. It was a shock to hear about my parents. I've ran from it for so long, I wasn't ready to face it, but I am now. Thank you for telling me. I wish I said that to begin with."

She finally offers me a small smile.

"Okay. Don't ever run out on me again. I already had that once."

Her smile is replaced by her serious expression.

"I know. I'm sorry."

I feel terrible for making her feel this way, but I vow to myself never to act so childish again. I hold her hand and am keen to change the subject.

"How's Captain Milligan getting on?" I continue.

Rachael frowns.

"Sorry. You don't need to answer that," I say quickly.

"No, it's okay. He's not good. Curtis' attack was bad; he almost killed him. He has a couple of gunshot wounds to the chest. He's lucky to be alive - he was wearing a bullet-proof vest."

I put my hand to my mouth and am about to offer my sympathy, but she continues.

"But we made some progress today. We think we know where they are."

I glance up and suck in my bottom lip.

"Rachael, you can't go after him. He nearly killed Milligan, he put your father in hospital and he has already threatened your safety. Tell me where he is. I will force him to surrender to the police," I plead.

I know I probably sound like a whiny child right now, begging to have something that's beyond my reach, but I don't care.

"Mark, we have been over this. I have to go after him, it's my job. You can't seriously believe that you'll be able to convince him to turn himself in." She chuckles at this clearly ludicrous suggestion.

"I could try," I say, feeling hurt, but determined.

"No, that's the end of the discussion. I don't want you to be a hero, I want you safe. I'm going with Officer Bailey on Friday to stake out the location of his suspected hiding place."

She stands.

"But for now, I'm going to bed. I've had a long day and I'm tired."

She walks into the bedroom without another word. I stand to follow her, thinking desperately of how to talk her out of this, but it's going to be impossible. I watch her discard her police uniform and climb into bed in her bra and panties.

"Well? Are you joining me?" she says suggestively.

She's obviously trying to distract me. *I thought she said she was tired.* Her distraction works, like it always does. I strip out of my own clothes in double quick time and leap into bed. She giggles keenly.

"Eager, Mr. Flint?"

She winks and I smirk at her.

"With you, Rachael Clarke, always."

Saying nothing more, we kiss, and once again, our passion takes over, totally obliterating the memories of our earlier scuffle.

Chapter Seventeen

The sun beams through the small opening in the curtains. My eyes flutter open, I stretch and look over, but Rachael is gone. I sit up and can hear the shower running. I smirk to myself and lie on my back reminiscing on what happened last night. If that's how we're going to make up after an abysmal confrontation, I'll take it any day. I climb out of bed and sneak into the bathroom. Rachael is holding her face up, welcoming the warm water cascading over her face and down her bare, slim figure. As quietly as I can, I slide the cubicle door open and step in behind her. I gently stroke her naked back which makes her jump and swing round, looking alarmed.

"I didn't mean to startle you," I croon.

She smiles and pulls me under the heated water with her. She pushes me against the wall, the cold tiles against my warm back makes me shudder, but I gradually embrace it.

"Good morning," she breathes, her mouth close to mine.

I look into her eyes.

"Good morning," I return.

Soon, her lips are on mine.

I feel refreshed, and it wasn't the shower that helped. The stress of Tobias has melted away, and now that Rachael has a lead on him, she seems a lot happier and laid back. However, I'm still dreading Friday when she goes on her stakeout with Officer Bailey and her team.

"What are you thinking?" Rachael asks, pulling me out of my thoughts.

I glance at her as she smiles and pushes her plate of half-eaten blueberry pancakes away.

"Just the stakeout on Friday. I really don't want you to do it, Rachael."

It feels good saying it, but her smile diminishes.

"Mark, please. We talked about this again and again."

She glances at me from across the table.

"Well, we didn't really. You kind of distracted me," I chuckle.

Her smile returns more broadly and she looks to be reminiscing.

"You're right, but I don't want to talk about it now either. I'm a cop, it's my job to take criminals off the streets. Trust me, I'll be fine."

She takes both my hands in hers. I grin and nod reluctantly, then stand and clear our plates away.

"Anyway, to change the subject, Dad is finally awake and is coming out of hospital later this afternoon. I promised to visit him at home. You're welcome to come along."

I turn away from the dishwasher and she catches my uncertain look.

"Your father doesn't really approve of me. Maybe I will just stay here."

She frowns, but then a thought crosses my mind. If I go to see her father, I could ask for her hand. *Christ knows how that will go down.* I dread to think. I let out a silent groan, but Rachael wraps her arms around my neck and kisses my shoulder.

"*Please,*" she begs playfully, batting her eyelashes innocently.

"On second thoughts, I would love to come."

"You're sure?" she asks.

I nod. "Absolutely."

It's three in the afternoon and the sun is beginning to sink behind the New York skyline, turning the sky a bright shade of orange. The traffic is heavy as Rachael drives through the tunnel towards Brooklyn. Frank Sinatra croons softly in the background, something about 'strangers in the night'. I have barely breathed a word. I'm nervous about asking Mr. Clarke for his daughter's hand and I think I already know what the answer is going to be. The thought saddens me. Rachael reaches over and squeezes my knee reassuringly.

"You'll be fine."

She seems to answer my unspoken thoughts. *Has she figured out what I'm planning? I hope not.* I respond with a smile. We drive down Marlborough Road and she pulls up smoothly into the driveway outside the Clarkes' house. I jump out quickly to open the driver's side door. She giggles and elegantly steps out.

"A gentleman all of a sudden."

I take her hand and we walk together to the front door. Mrs. Clarke answers the door and greets Rachael warmly.

"Great to see you, darling," she gushes, holding her close.

Mrs. Clarke then turns and hugs me.

"Mark, so lovely to see you again."

Rachael pulls me away and I drape an arm around her waist. Mrs. Clarke smiles kindly at us for a moment, then leads us to the living room.

"How's Dad?" Rachael asks as we make our way further inside.

Mrs. Clarke rolls her eyes.

"He's stubborn, as ever. He's been holed up in his study ever since we got back. He insists on returning to work as soon as possible."

Rachael sniggers.

"Typical Dad. I have some news for him. May I see him?"

I sit on the couch, as does Mrs. Clarke.

"Of course you can, darling."

I reluctantly let go of Rachael as she makes her way out of the living room and towards the study to see her father. I stare at the doorway where she just exited through, waiting to see if she comes back.

"So, how've you been?" Mrs. Clarke asks me.

I turn my attention to her and smile.

"Not too bad. Work is good at the hotel. How are things for you, Mrs. Clarke?"

She frowns disapprovingly.

"Please, call me Sara. Not bad, I suppose. Great to have Colin home at last, but I worry about his return to work. Colin and Rachael have such demanding and dangerous jobs," she grimaces.

I nod and offer a reassuring smile. *I know how that feels.* Every day, I worry for Rachael's safety, but know that I can't stop her either. I wonder if I should tell her about the stakeout on Friday, but I decide it's best not to; she's had enough to worry about recently. I change the subject instead.

"I was wondering if I could speak to your husband when Rachael is done with him?" I whisper, leaning forward.

She arches her brow at me.

"Sure. Do you mind me asking what it's about?"

I look over my shoulder to make sure Rachael isn't coming back and lean in closer.

"I would like to ask for Rachael's hand."

Sara sits back and her mouth falls open.

"Are you sure it's not too soon?"

I frown to myself.

"Maybe it is, but I love her so much. I will lay my world at your daughter's feet."

Sara is silent for a moment, then she beams at me.

"Then I don't see a reason why not," she smiles.

I beam within. I clearly have Sara's approval, but the hard part lies in wait, Colin Clarke.

Rachael re-enters the room with a big smile on her face. She comes and sits beside me, taking my hand, then she starts chatting to her mother.

"Dad is still being his usual self. He tells me he *insisted* to the doctors that they let him out early," Rachael laughs.

Sara rolls her eyes playfully.

"Yes, he did. He insisted that he had been shot enough times in his career, it was almost second nature."

Sara laughs with Rachael as they continue their conversation happily, then I stand. Rachael stops talking and looks at me curiously.

"Just need to use the restroom," I lie.

Rachael looks at me suspiciously but returns to her conversation with her mother. I walk into the hall and realize that I don't know where Mr. Clarke's study is. I start knocking and checking in different doors down the hallway.

"What are you doing?" Mr. Clarke booms behind me.

I whirl round to find Mr. Clarke standing with support from a walking stick, scrutinizing me. I swallow nervously.

"Mr. Clarke. I'm sorry. Um, I was looking for your study. I was hoping to have a word with you... if you don't mind, sir," I ramble.

He arches his brow at me before heading back down the hallway. I follow eagerly.

"How's the wound?" I ask.

He peeks down at me briefly, then looks straight ahead.

"Stings a little, but I'm used to it."

He doesn't display any emotion and I choose to keep quiet. He leads me upstairs and through a door on the right. I step into his study. A large oak desk is the biggest thing in the room; it has two green leather chairs on one side and a singular leather chair on the other; that must be Mr. Clarke's seat. A MacBook lays closed on the desk. I look around at the walls, they are decorated with police academy certificates, medals for honor and bravery, and at the back of the room, behind his desk is a large photo of Mr. Clarke in uniform, holding one of the medals proudly. Mr. Clarke walks past me, rests his walking stick against the wall and settles into his seat behind his desk, his fingers steepled in front of him.

"Quite a career you've had, sir," I acknowledge.

He looks around the room quickly and for the first time, he smiles at me.

"I have been on the force for thirty-two years. I followed in my father's footsteps, but we didn't come here to discuss my career. What did you want to talk to me about?"

He points his hand towards one of the green leather chairs. I sit down and am suddenly struck with nerves. I straighten my back and square my shoulders, then face Mr. Clarke.

"I wanted to ask you…" I stop.

He continues to watch me carefully. I try again.

"I just wanted to ask about Rachael."

He leans forward in his seat.

"What did you want to ask me about my daughter, Mr. Flint?"

He looks at me sharply through his specs, and I can feel myself sweating. I wipe my forehead with the back of my hand and continue.

"I wanted to ask your permission for-"

I'm interrupted by the sound of the door opening. I spin round in my chair, hoping that it isn't Rachael, but it's Mrs. Clarke who breezes in and stands by her husband's side. I look at her briefly, she winks at me.

"Louise is keeping Rachael company," she explains.

I smile gratefully.

"You were saying?" Mr. Clarke prompts.

I look back at him.

"I would like your permission for your daughter's hand… in marriage."

He slumps back into his chair and takes off his specs, throwing them onto the desk in front of him. He rubs his face, seemingly aggravated. When he looks back at me, he looks angry.

"Mr. Flint," he booms.

I sit back in my chair and await his obvious 'no', but he is silent. I risk a look in his direction and Mrs. Clarke has her hand on his shoulder. They are glaring at each other with some sort of unspoken words. In a way, it is uncomfortable to watch. Finally, Mrs. Clarke speaks.

"Colin, think of Rachael."

He continues to stare at his wife, at a loss for words.

"I *am* thinking of her. Do I let my daughter marry this man? He's-" he starts, but is cut off by Sara.

"A good man, and Rachael loves him, and he loves her. You can't deny them that. Give him a chance, and let Rachael make the decision on her own."

Mr. Clarke looks from me to his wife and back again. After what feels like an eternity, he taps her hand softly.

"Darling, would you leave me alone with him for a minute?" he asks.

She nods once, gives me a long stare, then exits.

"Mr. Flint."

I look back towards him, and he stops and clears his throat.

"Mark. Do you love my daughter?"

I smile. "With all my heart."

He stands, collects his walking stick and slowly walks around his desk until he is standing in front of me.

"You better not hurt her. I could have murdered the last boy that did," he warns.

I swallow, my mind drifting back to her scumbag ex-fiancé that she mentioned earlier.

"I wouldn't dream of it."

He goes back around his desk and sits back down.

"Rachael is old enough to decide what she wants, and I wouldn't dream of getting in my little girl's way," he says, while looking at the framed photos on his desk.

He looks up.

"Mark, you have my blessing to propose to Rachael."

I feel such a warmth of happiness, I beam and leap up from my seat. I stretch across the desk and shake his hand gleefully, surprising him.

"Thank you. Thank you so much. You have made me the happiest man."

I rush to the door, opening it wide.

"Mark," Mr. Clarke calls.

I look over my shoulder at him.

"Make it good for her, she deserves it."

I respond with a nod and close the door softly behind me. I rush downstairs and find Rachael in the hallway saying her goodbyes to her mother and sister. She spots me coming down the stairs.

"There you are. We're going home now," she says.

I stand by her side.

"Tell Dad to get well soon from me," Rachael says to her mother.

"Of course. Thank you for coming, both of you."

I hug Mrs. Clarke and surprise her by giving her a kiss on each cheek.

"Thank you," I whisper so only she can hear.

Rachael and I turn and head for the front door, but Rachael turns when Louise squeals happily.

"Oh, we're having the family over for Thanksgiving tomorrow. Please tell me you're both coming?"

Louise looks over eagerly, clasping her hands together and bouncing on the spot while Sara glances at us expectantly, then scolds Louise gently to stop bouncing around. Rachael grins and laughs at her sister's exuberance.

"I look forward to it."

Thanksgiving. Of course, it's tomorrow. I can't remember the last time I celebrated it properly. I'm looking forward to that. I grin at Louise and Sara, then take Rachael's hand and walk down the driveway towards the car.

On the drive home, Rachael doesn't suspect a thing. The important conversation I had with her father less than ten minutes ago is still unknown to her. I am buzzing inside. I can't believe he agreed. Now, I need to keep my promise to Mr. Clarke and make the proposal unforgettable. The journey back is relatively quiet. Rachael hums along happily to Sinatra as I sit quietly, planning, until I can bear the silence between us no more.

"How was your father?" I ask.

I already know, but I want Rachael to believe that I didn't see him in the short time we were there. She looks in my direction, then focuses on the road, smiling fondly.

"His usual self, always a good sign."

She chuckles to herself slightly as we return to Manhattan.

We arrive back home and Rachael heads straight for the kitchen.

"I'm going to make myself a coffee. You want one?" she asks.

"Yes please."

I sit on the couch and remove my shoes. My good mood is soured slightly when I remember the stakeout on Tobias on Friday.

"What time do you leave on Friday?" I call over to her.

She turns away from the kettle and leans against the breakfast bar.

"Early. Why?"

"Just wondering."

She returns to making our coffee, then sits beside me and hands me my cup. I take a sip and look down at the dark liquid, feeling troubled and desperately hoping that Rachael won't go, but she can't be swayed, and I know no matter what, she will go through with it.

"Hey." She touches my arm lightly.

I glance at her as she smiles sweetly.

"I understand your concern."

I look back down at my mug and respond with a sniff. I hear her put her mug on the table, then she crawls into my lap. I put my mug beside hers and wrap her in my arms.

"I'll be fine. There will be quite a lot of us going," she says, trying to reassure me.

"Can I at least know where it is?"

Her mouth forms a thin line.

"I'm sorry. I can't. It's for your own safety."

I look down at her and kiss her lightly.

"Send him my regards, and be careful."

"I'll be back home in time for tea."

We both laugh and kiss again, but this time, we don't stop.

Chapter Eighteen

I t's Thanksgiving. I have fond memories of celebrating it with Grandma. She always went over the top with food preparation and I was always stuffed afterwards. Rachael and I had a lie-in together this morning, which was a welcome treat.

"What do you want for breakfast?" Rachael calls into the bedroom while I'm getting dressed.

"I don't really fancy anything. I'll save room for dinner later," I call back, remembering that we have dinner with the Clarkes later today.

She comes into the bedroom and watches me get dressed, smirking cheekily.

"Stop staring, it's rude," I joke, throwing my shirt at her.

She laughs and catches it, then walks over so we are standing nose to nose.

"What do you want to do before dinner?" she asks suggestively.

"I would like to do a number of things with you at home, but I promised to meet Trent at the Thanksgiving parade when we had drinks the other day."

She pouts and looks disappointed.

"You're welcome to come along," I offer.

She smiles and claps her hands excitedly.

"I'd love to. I'm normally on shift this time of year, so it'll be a nice change," she enthuses.

Later, we have a quick bite to eat and then get ready to go out to meet Trent at the parade. On the way out she grabs her car keys but then grimaces.

"I think we'll walk. The streets are *undrivable* this time of year."

She places her keys back on the hook, then we're out the door.

It's a freezing day, but we are wrapped up warm. Rachael looks beautiful in her long, black coat, red woolly hat and scarf. We walk hand in hand towards Macy's on 6th Avenue. We round the bend leading to Macy's and the streets are lined with excited people awaiting the parade. We blend in with the crowd, and Rachael starts chatting to me happily.

"I've always loved the Christmas season."

I look at her out of the corner of my eye and grin at her.

"Me too. It was the only time my family came together properly."

Her smile wavers and I feel instantly guilty for spoiling her good mood.

"Sorry. I don't mean to be so negative," I apologize.

She envelopes me in her arms and we snuggle close in an attempt to keep warm. I bask in the bliss as we hold each other close, but we are soon interrupted by the sound of Trent's voice.

"Hey, Mark, Rachael," he greets loudly.

We both groan in unison, letting each other go as the ball of energy that is Trent bounds over to hug Rachael, then he gives me a hard slap on the back, slightly making me wince due to my bruising.

"Oh, sorry. I forgot." He sucks his lips in and holds his hands up.

I pat him on the arm in way of forgiveness and smile crookedly.

"Hi, Trent. Nice to see you again," Rachael grins.

He gives her a warm smile, then turns to look at his mother standing beside him.

"Rachael, this is my mom, Alison. Mom, this is Rachael, Mark's girlfriend."

Alison steps forward eagerly and beams at Rachael.

"Hello, I'm so pleased to meet the lady that captured Mark's heart, and so pretty."

Alison hugs her, taking Rachael by surprise.

"Mom don't embarrass her," Trent scolds lightly.

Alison steps away and flushes.

"Pleased to meet you, Mrs. Wilkinson," Rachael greets.

Alison turns to me and gives me a gentle hug, which I return.

"The parade will be starting in a couple of minutes," Trent says, seemingly eager to end the awkwardness.

After a few minutes of waiting, we hear music as the parade begins to march up the street. The crowd starts cheering joyfully as the various floats, dance performers and giant balloons pass us. Marching bands from different schools perform as Rachael watches with childlike delight. A Sesame Street float grinds to a halt in front of us. I have vague memories of watching this on the TV as a kid, but as the puppets start singing, I roll my eyes. Rachael laughs and

Trent elbows me in the ribs, making me wince again. This time, I brush him off.

"Hey, it's something you'll need to get used to if you want kids," Trent whispers jokingly.

I blink at him. *Me, with kids.* I never considered the possibility before, but with Rachael, the thought is appealing. *One step at a time, Mark.*

Thankfully, the Sesame Street float passes, and I try to stay focused. More giant balloons start arriving, one of which is Thomas the Tank Engine and behind that, Ronald McDonald. I hate clowns. I attempt to leave through the crowd until it passes, but Rachael grabs my arm.

"Where are you going?" she whispers.

I eye the giant clown and look back at her.

"I hate clowns," I hiss.

She looks towards the balloon and giggles softly.

"It's not real, Mark."

"I know that, but I always had nightmares of them when I was a kid."

She holds onto my arm reassuringly and I decide to stay. I wish I hadn't, as unseen to us, underneath the Ronald McDonald balloon, there stands an actor dressed as the creepy clown in a giant red shoe car. I look away, not wanting to watch, but Trent laughs at me mockingly.

"Shut up," I hiss.

He twists his mouth to stem his laughter, but can't hold it long. Alison slaps him round the back of the head.

"Ow. *Mom.*"

It's my turn to laugh at him as he scowls and sticks his tongue out at me. Rachael grabs me joyfully, distracting me from my boastfulness.

"Here comes the NYPD marching band."

I look down the road, and sure enough, I see men and women dressed in their NYPD finery. I look at Rachael, but she watches as they march by and play their instruments in perfect tune. A giant inflatable policeman follows behind them. I chuckle to myself.

"What's funny?" Rachael asks.

"Nothing."

"This is my dad's favorite bit," Rachael says.

"He couldn't make it today?"

"Nah. Mom insisted he stay home to rest."

My feet are starting to get sore. We have been standing up, watching the parade for nearly two hours. We have seen so many acts including dancers, various singers and plenty of floats and balloons. Everyone around us is buzzing with excitement and I assume Santa Claus is next. We wait a couple of minutes, but the big man finally arrives in his giant sleigh, pulled by his eight reindeer. Standing beside him is Mrs. Claus and his elves. Children scream for him as he waves in all directions. I feel like a kid again as a ridiculous smile spreads across my face.

"This is amazing. I've never enjoyed something so much in my life," I say turning to face Rachael.

A wide grin spreads across her face.

"I'm glad to hear it, but we should get going. We have dinner at my parents' house in an hour."

We both turn to Trent and Alison, who are also grinning widely.

"We need to go. It was nice seeing you both," I inform Trent.

He gives me a quick one-armed hug, then does the same to Rachael.

"It was wonderful meeting you, Rachael," Alison says.

"Yes, and you."

We say our goodbyes, then depart back towards Rachael's apartment to prepare for the Thanksgiving banquet with the Clarkes.

We arrive at Rachael's parents' house. She glides smoothly out the car and we walk hand in hand to the front porch. This time, she doesn't knock, she simply opens the door and heads inside. I trail after her, but as I step inside, I'm taken aback at how many people stand in the Clarkes' living room. Rachael strolls in confidently, but I hang back and scan the room quickly. I recognize Mr. and Mrs. Clarke and Louise who are all standing by the fireplace, dressed in their finery, chatting to a few people I've never seen before. Louise bounds over to me and grabs my hand.

"Come and meet the family," she gushes, pulling me in the direction of the elderly guests.

I look around for Rachael, desperate to be rescued from her over-enthusiastic sister, but there is no sign of her. Louise taps an unknown gentleman on the shoulder.

"Grandpa, have you met Mark, Rachael's boyfriend?"

He turns slowly and smiles, extending his hand. I shake warmly and note that he looks like Mr. Clarke, but older. This must be his father.

"No, but I have now," he jokes and chuckles.

"Nice to meet you. Rachael has spoken very fondly of you. I'm Derrick, Colin's dad. My wife is dying to meet you. Where is she anyway?"

He looks around for his wife and I find myself copying him, which is stupid. *I don't know what she looks like!*

"Ah, there she is. Darling," he calls to a woman in a sparkly black dress standing in the dining room.

She looks over her shoulder, then joins her husband.

"This is Mark, Rachael's boyfriend." He points at me.

"Aha, hello. I'm Katherine."

I shake her hand appreciatively, then she begins to bombard me with questions: *How did Rachael and I meet? Where? When?* I'm overcome and attempt to answer her, but Rachael is soon at my side.

"Gran, Grandpa. Being nice to Mark?" she jokes.

"Always, dear. Lovely man," Grandpa Clarke says.

She pulls me away quickly before her gran has a chance to start on me again.

"Thank you," I mouth.

"It looked like you were having some trouble, so I thought I would help out."

"I'll need to answer your gran's questions sometime," I chuckle.

A ghost of a smile plays on her lips.

"Another time," she responds.

I'm led into the kitchen where Mr. and Mrs. Clarke are preparing Thanksgiving dinner. We don't talk long, as they are occupied with steaming the vegetables, but I greet them quickly and make my way back to the living room with Rachael. We sit on the couch, furthest away from the loud chatter coming from her grandparents. Our peace doesn't last long, as we are soon joined by another elderly couple sitting in between us.

"I don't believe we've met. Rachael, are you not going to introduce us?" the lady eyes Rachael.

"Of course. Nana, Gramps. This is Mark, my boyfriend."

They both look in my direction and grin.

"At last," the lady gushes.

But her husband elbows her.

"Evelyn," he warns.

Rachael flushes and stands, walking back towards the kitchen, leaving me to face her maternal grandparents, I assume. I turn back to the couple and offer my best smile.

"Sorry about Evelyn. She thinks that because of her age, she can say whatever she wants. We are very pleased to meet you. I'm Royce Walker, Sara's father. You've already met my wife." His glasses shine from the fireplace and I shake his and Evelyn's hands.

"It's nice to meet you," I say, quietly.

"How did you and Rachael meet?" Evelyn asks.

Oh, God. I groan inwardly and have no idea how to answer.

"It's complicated."

"I like complicated." Evelyn leans in.

I shift my eyes and suck in my bottom lip.

"It's okay, you don't have to mention it. Right, Evelyn?" Royce says, facing his wife.

She frowns, but then regains her smile.

"Of course."

Rachael returns and looks at her grandparents.

"Dinner is ready," she informs.

"Finally! I'm starving." Royce rubs his hands in anticipation.

I stand and link my arm through Rachael's as we make our way to the dining room. Everyone takes their seats, Rachael to my left and Louise to my right. Mrs. Clarke emerges from the kitchen, carrying the biggest turkey I've ever seen. She sets it down on the table and begins to carve a portion for everyone. Mr. Clarke emerges behind her, wearing a ridiculous Christmas sweater and carrying several bowls that he sets down in front of us. There is an assortment of dishes containing potatoes, vegetables, stuffing and of course, gravy. My mouth waters and I hadn't noticed just how hungry I am.

"Please everyone, help yourselves," Mrs. Clarke announces.

It's a free-for-all as everyone starts to dig into the various dishes on the table. I hang back and wait for my chance, hoping it's not all gone by the time I get to it. Mrs. Clarke places a vegetarian wellington in front of Rachael.

"That's yours, dear," she says.

"Thanks, Mom," Rachael smiles.

I finally see my opportunity at the food and take it. Mrs. Clarke sits at the bottom of the table and raises her glass.

"Happy Thanksgiving, everyone."

We all raise our glasses and chorus in unison.

I place my fork down on my empty plate after consuming Mrs. Clarke's delicious pumpkin pie. I sit back in my chair, totally stuffed and drink my red wine as I listen to the banter between Rachael and Louise about who's the best poker player. The atmosphere in the room is filled with life, and for a while, my worries of Rachael's stakeout tomorrow are forgotten.

"How are you feeling, honey?" Mrs. Walker asks Mr. Clarke.

He beams at her and pats his hair awkwardly into place.

"I'm okay thank you, Evelyn. It's more annoying than anything now."

Mrs. Clarke rests her hand on Mr. Clarke's arm and smiles fondly at him.

"We all had quite a scare when we heard you had been shot. How did it happen?" Mrs. Walker continues.

I listen intently and dread Tobias being brought up. I look across the table nervously. Mr. Clarke takes a sip of his brandy and eyes me discreetly.

"I was chasing a lead on one of our most wanted felons. I caught up with him in a park in Manhattan, but he was waiting for me. I ordered him to surrender, but he shot me," Mr. Clarke explains.

I pale as Mrs. Walker puts her hand to her mouth in terror.

"Oh, Colin. That's awful, isn't it, Royce?" She darts a startled look at her husband.

"Mm hmm," he mumbles, his mouth still full of food.

Katherine, who is sitting to Colin's left, places her hand tenderly on his.

"Well, at least you're okay."

The serious conversation has now got Rachael's attention. She grimaces and shakes her head before getting to her feet and clapping her hands together.

"Right. Who's up for a game of poker?" she announces.

Rachael has beaten poor Louise four times at poker, but her sister still refuses to give up.

"One more game," Louise whines.

Rachael checks her watch, prompting me to glance over. It is nearing eleven o'clock.

"Sorry, I should get home. I have a big day tomorrow," Rachael says.

Louise pouts begrudgingly.

"We'll play again soon," Rachael promises.

"C'mon, Mark."

I stand from the couch and wrap my arm around her waist, then we quickly wish everyone well. We walk to the door with everyone following closely behind. Rachael slips her coat on and hugs her parents and grandparents.

"You be careful tomorrow, you hear me?" her dad whispers.

"I will," she smiles reassuringly.

"You will call the minute you get home, right?" her mom begs.

"The second," she promises.

I say my farewells to everyone, then lead Rachael to the car. She climbs into the driver's seat as I climb into the passenger side. She starts the engine and glides smoothly out of the Clarkes' driveway.

"That was a nice day," she says, smiling across at me.

I smile with her, but feel sick and wish tomorrow wouldn't come. Rachael has a dangerous task ahead of her tomorrow. She will come face to face with the man I once considered to be my father figure, now he is nothing but a deranged lunatic. An idea springs to mind.

"I want to come with you tomorrow," I blurt out.

She shoots me a disapproving look, then returns her attention to the road ahead.

"Out of the question."

"Please," I whisper.

She sighs and places her hand briefly on my thigh.

"I know you are scared for me, but the answer is no."

I sit back in my seat, stewing for the rest of the journey home. Neither Rachael nor I dare to breathe a word. I look at her occasionally, but she seems to be stewing in her own thoughts. I know there is no way to stop her. My gut twists with agonizing thoughts of what Tobias could do. My old life has come back to haunt me in ways I never thought possible. My new life is at risk, and there's nothing I can do to protect it.

Chapter Nineteen

———∿∿———

The sound of a gunshot and a woman screaming startles me awake. I sit bolt upright, breathing hard and sweating. I rub my face, trying to calm myself down. Rachael enters the room, already in her uniform.

"You alright?" she asks.

"Bad dream," I say quietly.

She sits on the edge of the bed next to me and combs my floppy hair away from my face, then she kisses me.

"I'll be off soon," she says.

She stares at the dread on my face and smiles.

"I'll be fine."

I stare at her and long for her to come back to bed. I'm about to offer, but her cell starts ringing in the living room, so she stands and rushes out to answer it. I get up and start to get dressed when I hear Rachael shouting.

"Don't you dare hurt her!" she screams.

I rush out of the bedroom, wearing only my boxers to see what is going on. Rachael is pacing the room with her hand over her face.

"Please don't," she begs into the phone before she bursts into tears.

I'm filled with rage. I grab the phone off of her, shocking her further.

"Who is this?" I bark.

"*My.* It is nice to hear your voice again."

I know who this is immediately.

"Tobias? How do you have Rachael's number?" I say furiously.

He chuckles.

"That doesn't matter. Listen, I will tell you what I have just told her. She was coming to stake me out today, I have told her not to bother. She's to come alone to my hideout without her posse."

I swallow, bile rising in my throat.

"She won't be doing that. I won't let her."

I look over at Rachael, who is weeping on the couch.

"Oh, she will. You see, I have her baby sister."

My world falls away at my feet and I collapse into the nearby armchair.

"Louise? She's innocent in all this. Let her go," I demand.

"I disagree. She is affiliated with you and Rachael, so that makes her leverage. Your girlfriend has an hour, and don't bother trying to call her or anyone else. There is a bomb rigged to blow beside her. If you or your girlfriend do anything stupid, she gets blown to bits."

I feel nauseated.

"How do we know you have her?" I ask, then the line goes dead.

I drop the phone in shock and glance at Rachael.

"You need to call them off," I whisper.

She looks at me with her tear-stained face.

"Are you crazy? We can't do that."

I look back at her and shake my head.

"Rachael, you have to. He will kill her if you don't. We will go and get her ourselves," I say, getting to my feet.

She stands but seems unsteady on her feet.

"We?"

"Yes, 'we'. You can't face him alone. I won't let you. Just call Steph, tell her it's off."

She bends down slowly and picks up her phone where I dropped it. She punches in a number and waits for an answer.

"Steph, it's me. No time to explain, but the stakeout is off. I will be coming shortly to collect one of the police cars for my regular patrol. Have the keys ready for me outside."

She listens, then pinches the bridge of her nose.

"I don't have time. I will explain later. Please just get me the keys."

Without another word, she hangs up. I rush into the bedroom and grab a shirt and my jacket.

"Let's go," Rachael shouts.

I rush back out of the bedroom while pulling on my jeans and shirt and head for the door. Rachael grabs the keys and we run together to her Mercedes.

We pull up outside the 17th precinct. Stephanie is standing in the doorway, looking perplexed. Rachael looks at her and waves quickly, then glances at me.

"Stay in the car."

Before I can argue, she jumps out and runs over to Steph. They chat hurriedly and look to be arguing. Rachael throws her hands up in the air and says something else. Bailey nods and hands her the keys to one of the police cars. She takes them and signals for me to follow her. I rush out and head to the cruiser that Rachael is already in.

She drives at speed with the sirens blaring.

"First time I've ridden in a police car upfront," I joke, trying to lighten the mood, but it doesn't work. Rachael remains silent with a look of fury on her face.

"He will pay for this," she mutters.

I sink into my seat and say no more.

We arrive at a dilapidated building somewhere in Brooklyn. Rachael switches off the engine and steps out the car. I do the same and rush to her side; she sighs heavily.

"The old grain terminal. It's been abandoned for decades. He was here all this time."

I take her hand.

"Let's go," I whisper.

We walk along the docks and round the building; piles of rubble litter the ground. Curtis is patrolling, holding a sub-machine gun. I quail as I eye the gun. He turns to face us, grinning wickedly. Rachael looks at me out the corner of her eye.

"I have my pistol in my holster. If something goes wrong, use it," she mouths at me.

I nod my understanding.

Rachael draws her gun from her holster and walks towards Curtis slowly. He smirks and glances down at his watch.

"Holster your weapon, officer. Your sister is in there," he says, pointing with his firearm to a rusted door.

"I'm not finished with you," Rachael hisses, before holstering her gun and shunting past him to make her way towards the door.

I follow closely and push the door open. It creaks loudly as we both step inside. It is a rundown warehouse; old empty boxes litter the room, rusting pipes stick up out of the ground in different areas, burnt-out fuse boxes and graffitI sprayed on several beams. We see a woman tied to a chair with a bag over her head at the other side of the room.

"Louise," Rachael calls and rushes over.

"Wait," I call and attempt to grab her, but miss.

I race after her as Rachael reaches Louise.

"Louise. I'm here," Rachael says, then removes the bag.

I'm horrified, as is Rachael. It's not Louise at all, but Melissa. She sneers in my direction.

"Surprise. Heads up," she crows.

We turn, and the last thing I see is Tobias with a crowbar. He strikes me hard over the head, knocking me out cold.

I wake with a blinding headache. I blink in the light, but my head is killing me. I attempt to move, but an unknown force stops me. As I become more conscious and alert, I notice that my hands are bound behind me and I realize that I'm tied to a chair. I struggle against my restraints desperately.

"Uh-uh. I wouldn't do that if I were you."

I lift my head to look straight ahead, Tobias is crouched down on the ground, facing me.

"Where's Rachael?" I demand.

He grins slightly and points to his left. I look over and am horrified to see Rachael, who also has her hands bound, by her own handcuffs, but she's not in a chair like me. Curtis is clutching her with his gun to her head. I widen my eyes in terror and stare back at Tobias.

"Please, don't hurt her."

He hoots with laughter, then stands and walks towards Rachael. I watch helplessly as he reaches her, stares at her for a moment, then touches her face softly.

"Tobias, please," I beg.

He ignores me completely. Rachael says nothing, but jerks her face angrily out of Tobias' touch. He looks down at her police badge, then suddenly rips it with force from her uniform and throws it the ground. He returns his gaze to her.

"Officer Rachael Clarke. 17th precinct. Am I right?"

She looks at him with an anger I have never seen before, albeit betrayed by a touch of fear.

"You never had Louise, did you?" she whispers.

"You think I wanted that stupid brat? She's worthless to me, but the perfect lure to bring you to me." He stops and looks over at me, grinning happily.

"I was only expecting your girlfriend, but as usual, you can't do as you're told. Still, I got two for the price of one. The cop who refuses to stop chasing my tail and the traitor who went behind my back."

I hang my head, but Tobias pulls my hair painfully so that I'm forced to look at him. I grunt in pain.

"That hurt, you know, Mark. After everything I did for you, and you send the dogs after me."

I blink at him.

"You got me arrested. You set me up," I say.

"*No.* I didn't get you arrested, she did." He points to someone behind me.

I turn as best as I can to see who he's referring to. Tobias finally releases my hair as I see Melissa standing in the corner, looking glum. I furrow my brow and look back at Tobias.

"Why?" I ask, not understanding.

He crows with laughter again and looks towards Melissa.

"She's my spy. I order her to do something, and unlike you, she follows through. Isn't that right, Melissa?"

I turn to face her again and scowl angrily; she hangs her head and picks at her fingernails. *Her nervous habit. It makes sense now. Something isn't right here.*

"Now you are in love with the officer that arrested you?"

He sniggers and twists his mouth arrogantly.

"What was it, Mark? Hmm?"

He looks at Rachael again, then back to me.

"*Oh,* I get it. The uniform. You've always been a sucker for a girl in uniform."

My face heats up with fury. I spit on Tobias' face. He flinches away for a second and wipes his face with the back of his hand, then without warning, he hits me hard around the cheek with the barrel of his revolver. I spit blood to the floor and cough violently.

"Stop this, now!" Rachael screams.

"Shut it!" Curtis shouts back at her.

I look up to face him again.

"That was a foolish mistake, Mark. Now, your lady is in trouble," he tuts, enjoying himself.

"You were bad news the second she laid eyes on you. I thought I taught you how to treat a lady," he sneers.

"I know more than you," I spit back.

He turns his back to me and starts pacing the room slowly.

"In fact, I know *much* more than you think. You see, I was a married man once, to a beautiful woman, just like your Rachael. Then my world crumbled at my feet. She left me and ran off with my youngest brother. You know what I did next?"

He turns his piercing green eyes on me as they shine with mirth.

"No, but I'm sure it couldn't have *possibly* been as bad as what I've been doing." I opt for sarcasm and he grins.

"I tracked them down. I shot him, then let my wife grovel a bit, then I shot her too."

I look at him with disgust.

"You're an evil, twisted man," I say.

He stares at me with wrath, then shrugs mockingly and walks back towards Rachael. He takes her head in both hands, then, without warning, back-hands her once across the face. She grunts in pain as she falls to the floor and doesn't move. Curtis cackles with laughter as Tobias stands over her. I struggle hard against my restraints.

"Stop it, you bastard! Leave her alone!" I scream.

Curtis pulls Rachael back to her feet as Tobias treads slowly back to me. He stares down at me, then kicks my chair backwards so that I'm now lying on the dirty floor.

"I will be taking your lady friend with me as compensation for the trouble you've caused me."

He peeks over at Melissa who looks terrified. Tobias smirks.

"Blackmail is a wonderful thing," he gloats.

I look at Rachael.

"I'm so sorry," I whisper as tears start to roll down her face.

"You two, so in love. You're tugging at my heartstrings," Tobias says sarcastically, before looking at Curtis.

"Don't kill him. I want the pleasure of that myself. Let him grovel for a while over the woman he failed to save," he says darkly.

He then snatches Rachael from Curtis' grasp and heads towards a rusted door, dragging Rachael with him. She continues to pull and struggle against her cuffs, then he slings her over his shoulder as she screams, and they disappear from my sight. I stare blankly at the door that Tobias took Rachael through. I feel helpless and guilty, just like he wanted.

"I'm so sorry, Rachael," I whisper again, hoping that she heard me.

Curtis cackles with laughter, his loud footsteps thundering in his military-style boots, and the sound of the safety being taken off his gun. I see him in my eyesight as I lay on the floor.

"Tobias didn't want me to kill you, but I'll save him the trouble by doing it now. He will understand when I tell him. I'm going to enjoy this," he sneers, pointing the gun down at me.

"How can you enjoy this? He killed your brother," I ask, disgusted and terrified.

He laughs and lowers his weapon slightly.

"The idiot deserved it. He won't be missed, and neither will you."

He draws the gun back at me and presses it against my forehead. I squeeze my eyes shut and wait for the gunshot. I hear a loud bang and flinch, waiting for the pain to arrive, but it doesn't come. I open one eye to see what has happened. Melissa is standing over me holding a crowbar. She looks at me deadpan, then glances at the floor. I find myself mirroring her and see Curtis slumped at her feet, unconscious. I blink up at her, befuddled. She offers me a small apologetic smile.

"No time to explain," she says quickly.

She pulls the chair up and cuts me free from my restraints. I stand and look at her, suddenly furious.

"You've got a lot of nerve," I start coldly.

She plays with her hands.

"You're welcome," she half-jokes.

"Tobias got to Rachael because of *you*, you led him to me. Rachael is *gone,* because of you," I shout.

She lowers her head and sniffs.

"I had no choice."

"What are you talking about? I haven't got time for this. I need to find Rachael."

I go to make my exit, but she shouts after me.

"'Blackmail is a wonderful thing'. Tobias just said so."

I look over my shoulder at her, now curious at what she wants to say.

"He threatened to kill my family. He kidnapped my brother, held him hostage. This was the only way to get him back alive."

I turn so that I'm facing her and place my hands on my hips.

"There are easier ways," I say angrily.

"I know that now."

Curtis groans slightly and in the periphery of my vision, I see him struggling to his feet. He grabs the gun that lays on the floor and points it at Melissa.

"Watch out," I warn.

I run towards her and throw her to the floor just as the sound of a gunshot rings through the empty room. I feel a sharp burn on my arm. I scream in sudden pain and look down at my shoulder. Blood draws from the wound. I place my hand over it, but feel weak. I fall to the floor and see Curtis' feet strolling towards me.

"There's no way out, Mark."

He points the gun down at me. There is a loud bang at the door, followed by another. As one, we all look towards the door and within seconds, several police and S.W.A.T. officers are storming the room, fully kitted in bulletproof bodysuits and holding automatic rifles. Curtis looks horrified.

"Police. Nobody move! O'Malley, drop your weapon," they all shout.

Curtis looks to be considering his options, but after a few agonizing seconds, he wisely drops the gun to the ground with a loud clatter. Melissa gets to her feet, looking wide-eyed with alarm as they continue to charge in. I dare not move as they surround us. The last to enter is Officer Bailey followed swiftly by Chief Clarke. They both stop and look around the room until their angry eyes rest on me. They rush over quickly.

"Where's my little girl?" Chief Clarke demands.

"Tobias took her that way. Through that door."

I point to the old rusted door and Chief Clarke looks in my direction. He then turns to his S.W.A.T. team.

"All of you, follow me. Now," he commands, pushing past me, along with his S.W.A.T. team as they race through the door.

Officer Bailey watches as they disappear, then returns her serious gaze at me. I think she is going to berate me or arrest me, but she glances at Melissa and Curtis who are being detained by other officers.

"Sanchez, Randall," she calls loudly at the two officers making the arrest.

They look towards Bailey.

"Take those two downstairs," she says, pointing towards Melissa and Curtis.

"Yes, ma'am," a Latin-American officer responds. *I assume that's Sanchez.*

She cuffs Melissa and leads her out the door. Officer Randall attempts to follow Sanchez out, but Curtis elbows Randall in the stomach. Randall falls to the ground and Curtis kicks him in the face, then he turns to run out the door. Officer Bailey is hot in pursuit.

"Freeze!" she shouts, pulling her pistol from her holster.

He doesn't stop, and as quickly as it started, there is a gunshot. Curtis collapses to the ground, blood pouring from his leg. He bellows and curses in pain. I watch, stunned and approach Randall who is still on the ground.

"Are you okay?" I ask.

"Yeah. I'm fine."

Randall wipes the corner of his mouth. I grab his arm and help him to his feet.

"Thank you," he says, before bending down to collect his police cap and helping Officer Bailey remove Curtis.

I'm standing alone in the empty grain terminal, still feeling the blood streaming from my shoulder. I place my hand over the wound to compress it but am distracted by raised voices coming from above. I turn quickly just as Bailey re-enters the room, carrying a first aid kit.

"Mark, that wound needs treatment," she calls to me, placing the bag at her feet.

I look at the door and slowly step towards it.

"Mark, I know what you're thinking. Don't do it," she warns, pointing at me.

"Rachael's up there. I need to go."

Bailey steps towards me, but I dash away from her and race through the door and up some rusted stairs, taking two at a time. *That jogging practice came in handy.* Bailey is hot on my heels, as she pursues me in an attempt to stop me. She doesn't catch up in time, as I burst through another door at the top. I'm standing on the roof, the wind whipping around me and the bitterness stinging my gunshot wound. I ignore it and look towards Chief Clarke and the S.W.A.T. unit all standing together with their rifles pointed at Tobias.

"Lower your weapons," Chief Clarke commands to the S.W.A.T. team.

They all obey, lowering their rifles. I push my way through them so I can join Chief Clarke at the front to get a better look at what's going on. Chief Clarke looks down at me when I'm standing by his side. He furrows his brows angrily and attempts to push me away.

"Uh-uh. I wouldn't do that if I were you, Chief," Tobias threatens.

To my horror, Tobias is standing at the edge of the roof, holding Rachael at gunpoint. She still has her hands tied. He spots me and sneers in my direction, full of hate.

"Did you think I was bluffing, Mark? I said no cops. I *will* kill her," he yells.

I look at Chief Clarke who looks as helpless as I am.

"I didn't call them," I say desperately and truthfully.

"I should have killed you when I had the chance," he snarls.

"Maybe you should have asked your brother to do it. Not that he's any good to you anymore."

Tobias thinks for a moment, then smiles wickedly.

"Jail is the best place for him. As long as I'm free."

He looks at Rachael, as do I. She looks terrified and is tear-stained, but is trying to hold firm. I step forward slightly.

"You take one more step, and she's dead," he shouts, pulling Rachael closer to the edge.

I freeze on the spot and hold my hands up.

"You can have me, Tobias. Just let her go," I plead.

"Why would I want you?"

"Your brother is gone. I'll come back to you. Back to my old life. All I ask is for Rachael to be spared."

I'm bluffing, but this is the only way.

"Mark, what are you doing?" Rachael's horrified.

Chief Clarke attempts to grab me, but I shrug him off. Tobias frowns at me.

"You must think I'm an idiot. I would prefer to kill this one and let you live with the pain for the rest of your days," he shouts, quickly deducing my bluff.

"We will shoot!" Chief Clarke shouts.

I look back at him and give a slight shake of my head as a warning.

"You wouldn't, Chief. By the time you shoot, I will move your little girl into your line of fire," Tobias jeers.

I try to step a little closer again, but Tobias turns the gun away from Rachael and points it at me.

"You're a fool. You thought you could outwit me, and you have lost. Now, I'm going to have to kill your pretty lady," he says, continuing to point the gun at me.

He walks Rachael back further, then he stops and smiles once more.

"But first, I will kill you. Goodbye, Mark."

Rachael suddenly kicks her foot backwards into Tobias' shin. He screams out in pain, releasing Rachael from his grasp. I rush forward and grab her, pushing her behind me towards Chief Clarke. Tobias grabs his weapon, gets to his feet and points it at Rachael.

"I'll kill you for that!"

I lunge furiously at Tobias, shoving him hard. He wobbles on the edge, then reaches out and grabs hold of my shirt, before falling back and taking me with him. The last thing I hear is Rachael screaming my name in despair as I hit the grimy river below. I struggle desperately against the current, trying to swim up to the surface, but I feel a force holding me back. I look down as best I can. Tobias is wrestling with me, holding me under before plunging a knife into my thigh. I scream out, but all I hear is the water sloshing around me as I ingest a lungful of the revolting, contaminated water. Instinctively, I pull the knife out of my thigh and without looking, I slash at Tobias blindly with it. He releases me and

I continue to swim towards the surface. I'm becoming weak from blood loss, my wounds stinging. I feel faint, but will myself to swim faster. The darkness is closing in and I can't swim anymore. I hear a splash above me as the water ripples. An unknown force grabs me by my shirt. I don't know what is going on, but soon I'm pulled above the surface. I feel the cool air against my face and inhale a lungful. I see a lot of commotion and hear a lot of distorted shouting, then I'm lifted out of the water completely. I feel a hard slap on the back and I cough up the foul water as dry heaves rack my body. I lie on the gravel and look up, grateful to the person who just saved my life. It's Rachael. She's dripping wet and smiling down at me. I reach up.

"*Rachael*?" I whisper.

She hugs me hard and starts weeping into my shoulder.

"That's my shower for the day," I joke weakly.

She weeps harder and clings to me.

"Thank God you're alright," she cries.

I pat her back deftly, then look down at my thigh. It's bleeding heavily and I become delirious. I fall back against the gravel, falling away from Rachael's embrace.

"No, Mark. Please, stay with me," she panics.

I close my eyes and as hard as I try to fight it, I begin to welcome the darkness.

Chapter Twenty

———❦———

It's dark outside. I look around, oblivious to where I am. I feel stabs of pain from my leg, shoulder and face. I'm in a sterile room, wearing a white gown with a mask over my face and a florescent light beam is shining through my door. I hear a rhythm of beeps to my right. I check my arms - various wires are coming from them. I look to my left to find Rachael sitting in a recliner beside my bed, reading a book and looking forlorn.

"Hey," I rasp.

Rachael puts her book down and looks at me. She instantly gets to her feet when she sees me awake. She leans over me and strokes my face tenderly which makes me wince. I notice a big bruise on her face. I slowly raise my hand in a vain attempt to stroke it better, but she takes my hand and grins at me.

"It's okay. It's not that bad," she assures.

"*Where?*" I breathe.

"Just relax. You passed out. You're in the hospital," she explains calmly.

"I'm sorry," I choke back tears, the memories all flooding back.

She frowns at me.

"What are you sorry for?"

"For what happened to you, with Tobias."

"You have nothing to be sorry for. Tobias is gone; you saved me. That's all that matters now."

I take her hand.

"You saved *me*," I answer back.

She smiles and kisses me sweetly, then presses her forehead against mine.

"Tobias is gone?" I ask.

She looks back and shrugs.

"He never resurfaced. We're searching, but we've had no luck."

My mouth drops open in shock as I continue to regard her carefully. I now remember the bruise on her cheek was inflicted by Tobias' swift hand. *Bastard.* I'm about to ask her if she's okay, but there's a knock at the door. Trent pokes his head round.

"Hey. Can I come in?" he asks.

"Of course. Sit down," Rachael smiles, shifting over to give him some room.

He walks in and shakes his head at me.

"What were you thinking?" he chides.

I manage to explain the event to him in full. When I am done, Trent is speechless until he finally answers.

"At least you're both alright."

Then an unsettling thought springs to mind.

"Louise?"

Rachael looks at me.

"Tobias never had her. I checked on her; she's fine," she clarifies.

Trent glances at Rachael. "No more Tobias?"

"Nope. He's finished. But the search for his body continues."

I yawn a little and they both glance at me before Trent stands.

"I'll let you get some rest. I'll visit again soon. Mom wishes you well," he says.

He gives my good shoulder a slight squeeze, then walks to the door.

Rachael fluffs my pillow and lays me back down. Soon, I drift off again.

The nurse checks my leg and shoulder as Rachael watches. The nurse looks at me and smiles.

"You are a very lucky man, Mr. Flint. The knife missed your femoral artery by a few centimeters. Your shoulder is healing nicely too. How are you feeling?"

I test my leg and rotate my shoulder, but I wince a little. My shoulder doesn't hurt too much, but my leg is still very sore.

"You'll feel better in a few days. You're welcome to go home," the nurse smiles, then she turns to Rachael.

"Make sure he gets plenty of rest. Nothing too strenuous."

Rachael nods, listening carefully.

"Of course," she says.

The nurse continues to smile at us, then leaves the room.

"Let's get you up and dressed," Rachael says.

After some effort and a bit of struggling, I am sitting on the edge of my hospital bed as Rachael dresses me slowly, occasionally stopping to check that she isn't hurting me.

I struggle myself up onto my feet, but collapse back down. Rachael frowns and leaves the room momentarily. I wonder where she's going, but soon she's back, followed by a doctor.

"This isn't necessary," I insist, trying to get to my feet again.

The doctor watches on, but to my annoyance, I collapse again.

"I'm Dr. Tucker. Please may I check your leg?" he asks kindly.

I sigh but resign. I unzip my pants and pull them down slightly with Rachael's assistance. Dr. Tucker steps closer and takes a quick look.

"Maybe a crutch will help you for the time being. We don't want your wound to reopen," he suggests, looking at Rachael, who agrees with him.

Dr. Tucker walks out, then shortly re-emerges with a single crutch and hands it to me.

"Try again with that," he says.

I put my pants back on, then struggle to my feet once more, holding onto the crutch this time. It still hurts, but I don't fall back. Dr. Tucker smiles.

"Good to know it helps. See you next week so we can check you over."

He opens the door for us and again with Rachael's help, I wobble my way out of the hospital and towards her waiting car.

I've been back home for a couple of days and am so relieved to be here. I smile to myself as I remember our struggle when Rachael undressed me and put me to bed. She is refusing to let me leave the bedroom with an exception for bathroom breaks. She insists I eat in bed, which I've always hated doing. Rachael is off work for a while. Her father almost insisted on it, much to Rachael's protest and dismay, but she is busy looking after me. My thoughts are distracted by Rachael walking in, holding her cell.

"Mr. Levitt wants a word," she says, handing me her phone.

I look at her nervously as she shrugs apologetically, then leaves me alone. I place the phone to my ear.

"Morning, sir."

"Good morning, Mark. Rachael called and told me everything. I'm so sorry I didn't believe you. I really did think you were stressed when you mentioned him," he says wholeheartedly.

"You have no reason to be sorry, Mr. Levitt. You're right, I was under a lot of stress, but it was because of him. You had no way of knowing."

He sighs deeply then continues.

"Well, I hope you get well soon."

"Thank you, sir. I'm sorry I can't come into work anytime soon."

He scoffs slightly.

"Don't be silly. Take your time and get better soon."

I smile gratefully.

"Did you hear about Melissa?" I ask curiously.

He sighs again.

"Yes, I did. Such a shame. She seemed trustworthy when I first met her. At least she's trying to make amends for her actions."

I furrow my brow.

"What?"

"Didn't Rachael tell you? She's in witness protection. But I'll let her fill you in on the details," he laughs.

Rachael walks back into the room, followed by a nurse.

"Thank you for your call, sir. I'd better go."

"Take care, my boy."

I drop the phone on the bed beside me and look up at Rachael and the nurse.

"Hello, Mark. I'm Nurse Crowe. How are you feeling?" she asks.

She drops her bag by the bed and kneels on the floor beside me as Rachael perches on the edge of the bed.

"Much better, thank you."

Nurse Crowe grins. "Well then, let's take a look."

I pull the duvet back and she leans in a little. She pokes at me and I grunt slightly. My leg barely hurts at all now.

"It's healing very well," Nurse Crowe says, looking at Rachael who grins happily.

"We'll remove your stitches soon," she continues, now getting to her feet.

"He can get out of bed now. Fresh air might do him good," she says to Rachael.

"Does that mean I can still go to the light-up ceremony?" I ask like an over-excited child.

Nurse Crowe turns to look at me and chuckles.

"Definitely."

Rachael shows Nurse Crowe out. I'm thrilled. I was getting worried. The light-up ceremony is tomorrow, and I thought the nurse would forbid me from going. I was planning on proposing to Rachael there, but then I remember, her birthday is soon. I need to start planning, but I'll need some help. I reach for my cell and am about to call Trent, but Rachael comes back in.

"I'm going to make some lunch. Would you like it in here or at the table?" she smiles.

"I would prefer a change of pace. At the table, I think."

She giggles. "It won't be long."

She turns and exits the room again. I wait a couple of seconds, then call Trent, who answers almost immediately.

"How are you feeling?" he asks.

"Better. The nurse is allowing me to go out."

"That is good news."

"It is. Listen, I need to talk to about… you know what."

Trent is silent for a moment, but then it seems to click.

"Ooh, that. What do you want to discuss?"

"I need you to do a couple of things for me."

I end my call with Trent; it went well. Hopefully, he can get the preparations done in time. Rachael calls from the living room that lunch is ready. I grab my crutch from the floor and hobble my way out. Rachael is sitting at the dining room table, but when she sees me, she jumps up and rushes over.

"It's okay. I'm fine," I insist.

She walks by my side, occasionally grabbing my arm when I wobble, and I take a seat at the dining table. I look at the bowl in front of me; it smells delicious.

"Tomato and pesto pasta," Rachael explains.

"It smells fantastic," I say, grabbing my fork.

She grins at my compliment and we tuck in.

After lunch, we go out for a stroll. Rachael walks beside me, her arm linked through mine. We walk slowly through Central Park, over Bow Bridge and towards Bethesda Fountain. We sit on the wall as I catch my breath. She glances at me anxiously. I turn and smile at her which she returns fondly. I catch a quick peek from her in the direction of my injured leg.

"It doesn't hurt," I promise her.

She smiles but looks like she doesn't believe me.

"Would you like to go back home?" she asks.

"No. I'm enjoying this."

She looks over towards a café.

"Let's go and get a drink," she offers.

I stand carefully, taking my weight on the crutch and we walk to the Loeb Boathouse.

I sit at a table overlooking the frozen lake. Rachael stands in line, waiting to be served. I ponder to myself about the events that took place a few days ago between me and Tobias. He threatened everything I cared about that day, and I nearly lost it all. Tobias paid the ultimate price at the end though; he's gone. He won't come after me, or anyone else anymore.

"What are you thinking?" Rachael returns, placing the tray she is carrying onto the table.

"Nothing," I smile.

She eyes me suspiciously.

"Withholding information again, Mr. Flint?"

I laugh loudly. "From you, never."

She picks up her latte and takes a sip. I do the same. I can't help feeling nervous about the proposal I'm planning on her birthday. *Is it too soon? Will she say 'no'? Christ, I hope she doesn't, that would be torture.* I need a clue, but I need to keep it discreet.

"What do you want for your birthday?"

She looks across at me, and thinks, then she smiles broadly and reaches out for my hand.

"I have it already," she answers simply.

I look at her puzzled and she laughs. "I have you. That's all I want."

I grin. This statement gives me the confidence boost I needed. Now, I'm sure, but then a barrage of questions strikes me.

"How did the cops show up?"

It's her turn to look momentarily confused, but she catches on quickly.

"It's simple, really. Our police cars are all equipped with a tracker. I explained to Steph subtly what was going on. I told her to keep an eye on where my police car went, give it half an hour, then follow."

I gape at her.

"That's sneaky."

She shrugs. "I know."

"What happened to Curtis?" I continue.

"He's going nowhere. After being treated at the prison hospital, he was transferred upstate and thrown into Sing Sing."

"And Melissa? Mr. Levitt mentioned she went into witness protection?" I ask.

"Yes, she did. Sorry I didn't mention it earlier. She applied for the witness protection program for herself and her brother. All she had to do was sing like a canary."

"How did Melissa get involved with Tobias to begin with?"

"Well, from what she told us, she needed to borrow money and went to Tobias. She couldn't afford to pay him back, so he took her brother as leverage and forced her to do favors for him. Her brother was even cajoled into assisting with the prison van break."

I remember her mentioning an unknown male accomplice before. That was *him*.

"At least they're safe now. That's good to know."

Rachael checks her watch.

"We should get back."

She stands and helps me to my feet. We walk out of the café and head for home.

We arrive at Rachael's floor, but quickly notice that her front door is open. She draws her off-duty firearm from her holster and slowly approaches the door. She looks back at me and puts her finger to her lips, silently shushing me, I nod compliantly and place my back up against the wall. *It can't be.* She pushes the door open and rushes inside. Everything is silent, and I pray Rachael is okay.

"Surprise!" a group of people shout, disrupting the silence.

Moments later, Rachael emerges back out of the door, her weapon now holstered.

"It's alright, Mark. False alarm."

I make my way inside to find Mr. and Mrs. Clarke, Louise, Officer Bailey and Trent all standing in the living room.

"Guys, you could have let me know you were visiting. I could have shot you," Rachael scolds.

Her father steps forward with the biggest grin I have ever seen plastered on his face. He hugs Rachael, then steps towards me. He shakes my hand so enthusiastically I feel he is going to rip it off.

"Glad to know you're alright, Mark," he beams, then he turns to everyone else in the room.

"Let's give this brave duo a hand, guys."

I'm deafened as everyone erupts into applause for us both and Trent whistles a few times. Mr. Clarke stands back in front of Rachael who is flushing violently.

"*Dad*," she hisses.

"But that's not the reason we are here. Rachael, I have always been proud of you, but what you did the other day was dangerous and stupid." Mr. Clarke is serious now.

Rachael lowers her head "I know Dad, but-."

Mr. Clarke raises his hand, silencing her. *That's where she gets it from.*

"I'm not finished. Due to your bravery and courage, the police force have all agreed that you will no longer be Officer Rachael Clarke. From now on, you will be known as Sergeant Rachael Clarke." He hands her a brand-new police badge.

My mouth falls open. She's receiving a promotion. Rachael stares at the badge in disbelief, then gapes at her father.

"I can't believe this. I haven't seen the rank of detective yet. I haven't even taken the test to become sergeant," she rasps astounded.

"I know that. It's the rank you deserve after what you did. But, if you're not ready, you can say no," Mr. Clarke continues.

She stares again at the badge, smiles and pins it to her jacket. Mr. Clarke smiles happily and everyone rushes in to congratulate her. I join everyone, but Trent pulls me aside.

"Are you sure you want to marry a sergeant? I mean, if she was intense before..." he whistles through his teeth. "Imagine what she will be like now," he jokes.

I look at Rachael, who smiles and laughs with Officer Bailey. I smile at her and face Trent.

"I'm sure."

Trent smirks, then produces a more serious expression.

"You forgot the box that your grandma left you. It's in the bedroom closet. Show it to Rachael, she deserves to know."

"I will. Thank you."

He smiles, then walks into the kitchen and starts chatting to Louise. Mr. Clarke pulls himself away from Rachael and strides over to me.

"We haven't forgotten you, Mr. Flint."

I look at him, worried about what he's implying. He reaches into his jacket and I half expect a pair of handcuffs, but he produces a shiny bronze medallion.

"This is for you, courtesy of the mayor," he says, placing it round my neck.

I examine it and look back at him.

"It's for bravery. You know, when I first met you, I didn't like you. I wondered what my daughter was thinking, being in love with an ex-felon. Now, I understand. You are a good man. You were willing to sacrifice yourself for her. I hope soon, you will pop the question. I look forward to calling you my son."

I smile.

"All the people in this room, sir, they're already my family. Thank you for the medal."

"Wear it with pride."

He clutches my shoulder kindly.

Rachael comes to join us, then she eyes my medal and beams at me.

"Looks like we both got something."

"We sure did. Congratulations by the way... Sergeant Clarke."

She laughs and grabs my hand.

"Louise has started making her famous margaritas. Be careful, they're lethal."

I laugh and watch Trent. He looks to be chatting Louise up.

"I think she has an admirer," I point with my chin.

Rachael stares at them both and rolls her eyes.

"If he hurts her, he'll wind up behind bars," she jokes.

"Don't let him hear you say that."

We laugh together as the celebrations get into full swing.

Everyone starts to leave. Mrs. Clarke kisses Rachael on both cheeks.

"Congratulations, darling."

"Thanks, Mom."

"Drop by soon, won't you?"

Rachael smiles. "Soon."

Mr. and Mrs. Clarke leave, then Steph hugs Rachael and rushes out after the Clarkes. Trent is last to go, accompanied by Louise. He stops in the doorway and offers me a crooked smile. I wink at him and he sticks his tongue out playfully, then he hugs Rachael goodbye.

"Cute sister, by the way."

Louise giggles like a two-year-old and slaps his chest.

"T, stop it."

He smiles down at her as they stagger out the door. *They must be drunk.* Rachael shakes her head at them, but she shuts the door and joins me on the couch.

"Well, that was nice. Trent and Louise seem to be getting along," I nudge her.

"M, stop it." She misquotes her sister's words, laughs and mockingly slaps me on the chest, the way Louise did to Trent.

We are soon in fits of laughter and can't control ourselves. At last, she composes herself and stands up.

"So, now what?" she asks suggestively.

I smirk at her and stand, grabbing her. I press her against me and we stare longingly at each other.

"Are you sure? You're not in pain?"

I shake my head.

"This is what I need."

She grins widely, then we kiss with a fiery ardor. It alights my body, so I pick her up as she wraps her legs around my hips. Ignoring the slight sting in my leg, I carry her to the bedroom, our tongues entwined. I throw her onto the bed and unzip my pants. She watches closely.

"Be gentle," she begs mockingly.

"Not a chance," I respond and jump onto the bed beside her.

We kiss fiercely again, our breath mingling as we remove each other's clothes. We lay on the mattress in our underwear. Rachael laughs wickedly and pulls the quilt over us, covering us.

Chapter Twenty-One

⁓

Tonight, we head to the light-up ceremony, and tomorrow it's Rachael's birthday. I've organized to take us ice-skating in the park, followed by the proposal. I've been practicing my engagement speech for hours while Rachael is down at the precinct. She insisted on going this morning after I assured her that I would be fine. She isn't on-call today; she said she's missing her friends and wants to visit, but it has given me some alone time. I want to make her birthday special and am stuck on what else to add to my engagement speech. I grab my phone and call Trent. He answers.

"Did you have a good night with Louise?" I mock jokingly.

"Screw you. What do you want?" he laughs.

"I need your help."

He pauses for a moment.

"Tobias isn't back, is he?"

I laugh loudly.

"I sure hope not. I'm going to propose to Rachael tomorrow. I can't think of what to else to say. My speech is too short at the moment."

I hear a deep intake of breath, then he responds.

"Don't obsess over what's written on a piece of paper, Mark. Just tell her how you feel deep inside," he suggests.

I think hard, then I'm struck with the perfect speech.

"Thanks. I'd better go," I say happily.

"Later, man," he says.

I recite my speech for what feels like the hundredth time when I hear the front door open. I grab the sheet of paper from the table and stuff it into my pocket just as she enters the lounge. She furrows her brow at my nervous expression.

"What are you up to?" she asks suspiciously.

"Nothing," I say as calmly as I can manage.

She giggles.

"You're a hopeless liar."

She sits beside me.

"How was everyone down at the precinct?" I ask, trying to change the subject.

She smiles to herself.

"Everyone is good. They're all thrilled at my promotion and they wish you well. We're hoping for Milligan to be back at work in a couple of days."

"That is good news."

She slips her shoes off and lays her head across my lap. I look down at her fondly and deftly stroke her hair. She leans up and kisses me gently, then sits up suddenly.

"Oh, yeah. There's something I need to ask you."

I think hard and shift my eyes nervously.

"What?"

She stands up and grabs my hand then leads me into the bedroom. *Where's this going?* I sit on the foot of the bed as she opens the closet. She pulls out a cardboard box, the same box Trent returned yesterday. I look down at it, then peek up at her. She twists her mouth and gently kicks it towards me.

"What is this? It has your name on it."

I pat the bed beside me, and she sits down. I bend to pick up the box and place it in between us.

"It's a lot for me to process. I was going to show you," I explain.

She grimaces at my sad expression and strokes my arm softly.

"If you're not ready-."

"No. It's fine. You want to understand me? This is a start."

I take the lid off the box and take a nervous sigh, then reach in and remove the leather biker jacket and the photos. I hold it all to my chest, then pass her the jacket. She looks down at it and raises her eyebrows, not really understanding. I hand her the photo of my grandpa. She looks at it and recognizes the jacket.

"Who's this?" she asks.

"That's my grandpa. He died when I was very young, so I don't remember him."

I hand her the next photo of my parents' wedding. Again, she examines it, then peeks up at me. I dread the last photo the most, but I reluctantly hand it over. It takes her a couple of seconds to realize who the people are in the photo, but then she points at the baby.

"Is that?" she gasps.

I nod.

"Yep. It's me… and my parents."

She looks down at the photo again then back up at me.

"You all look so happy."

"I know, I don't know why they changed, but they did."

She nods sadly and places everything back in the box gently, then stands and kisses me.

"Thank you for showing me this."

I smile, then remember something else.

"There's more."

I get up off the bed and head into the living room to retrieve my wallet. She follows me out and we sit on the couch. I take the photo of Grandma and the letter she wrote out and hand them to her. She scans the letter quickly, then stares at the photo.

"This is her, isn't it? This is your grandma."

I nod and swallow the lump that is forming in my throat. She re-reads the letter and looks back at me.

"She says she left you money. What did you do with it?"

I shrug meekly and explain.

"I tried to open a bank account to cash it, but I couldn't. Trent's holding onto it for safekeeping."

"I can help you with the bank. We'll sort it later this week," she offers.

I smile gratefully and take the photo and letter from her, then stand and head for the bedroom where I stash everything together. I put the lid back on the box and place it back in the closet. Rachael stands in the bedroom doorway and grins widely.

"She would be very proud of you... I am."

I walk over to her and pull her against me.

"Hopefully, you know me a little better now."

She smiles and kisses me deeply, then hugs me hard. She glances across at the alarm clock on the nightstand.

"It's five o'clock. Do you still want to go?" she asks.

I nod my answer. She lets me go and starts to get changed. I stand for a minute and watch her. There's so much more I want to tell her, but I want to understand it myself first, about everything that happened to my parents. Once I know more, I will tell her.

"Hey, sleepyhead. You getting ready?" Rachael lightly jabs me, pulling me from my thoughts.

"Oh, yeah. Of course."

I have changed into a simple blue shirt and black jeans to accompany my leather jacket. Rachael looks radiant in her slim-fitted jeans and red, sparkly sweater. Lastly, she slips her coat on and takes my hand.

"Let's go," she says, opening the door.

We stroll hand in hand down the busy street towards a nearby restaurant. It has started to rain hard, so we duck inside and into warmer surroundings. We choose a table near the window and order a spinach and goat's cheese flatbread to share. We laugh and joke during our meal, and I am overcome with happiness.

"What are you thinking?" she asks, glancing at me from across the table.

I look at her and smile.

"You're beautiful."

She looks down modestly. I reach across the table and take her hands in mine.

"The *most* beautiful," I breathe softly.

She grins and looks away, blushing. Rachael has been a lot happier since Curtis was put behind bars, but Tobias' whereabouts are still unknown.

"Do you ever wonder what happened to him?" I ask out of the blue.

"Who?" she asks, furrowing her brow in thought.

"Tobias," I clarify.

She shakes her head almost immediately, taking me by surprise.

"He's dead, Mark. He was never found."

I nod, not sure how to respond and regret bringing up this subject, but I am assured by the fact that he will never bother us again.

"We should get going," I say, summoning the waiter.

"Check, please."

He scurries away but returns with the check promptly. I hand him the cash, then stand, as does Rachael. We walk out of the restaurant, hand in hand, towards the Rockefeller Plaza.

It's still raining hard, but there's a lot of people braving the weather. Rachael wisely brought an umbrella. She opens it out and I take it from her, shielding us both from the rain. It's busy around the plaza and we stand at the back of the crowd. I observe and admire my surroundings. Beyond us, there is a row of brightly lit angels playing trumpets, and the magnificent tree stands proudly at the center of the plaza waiting to be lit. The crowd around us chatter eagerly and I can hear, but not see, Dolly Parton singing on stage in front of us as people sing along out of tune.

"It's beautiful around here this time of year," Rachael gushes.

I glance in her direction, but she is fixated with her surroundings, staring at them in awe. After a few minutes of waiting, the music stops and everyone goes quiet. The MC makes an announcement, but we can't really hear what he's saying. I strain my ears in an attempt to listen, but the crowd starts jeering loudly, making it harder for me to know what's going on. Everyone begins to count down from ten. Rachael and I join in enthusiastically, then the tree in front of us comes to life. Rachael gasps in amazement as thousands of lights and the beautiful crystal star at the top shine brightly. Christmas music starts to play over the stereo system as everyone cheers and claps. The atmosphere is breathtaking; the spirit of Christmas is alive.

"That was wonderful. Thank you for inviting me, Mark. I can't believe I've never been before," Rachael enthuses.

I smile and grab her, pulling her up against me.

"You're welcome."

She kisses me quickly and turns back to the tree.

"It's beautiful," she whispers.

"Quite stunning," I say smoothly.

When she looks at me, she smiles, realizing that I wasn't talking about the tree, I was talking about her.

"Let's get closer," she says, grasping my hand.

We push our way through the crowd and walk past the ice rink. Rachael stops and admires the skaters.

"I have never been able to do that," she says as she watches several people pirouette on the ice.

"Rachael Clarke, something you can't do that I can," I laugh.

She whips her shocked expression at me.

"You can skate?"

"Sure. I'll teach you tomorrow. I still know a few tricks."

She pales. "I don't think so."

"Oh, c'mon. It's easy."

She giggles and gives me a playful push with her shoulder.

"If you insist."

We continue our way to the tree. She looks up at it, awed. I look with her, but my mind drifts to tomorrow, Rachael's birthday. Teaching her to ice skate followed by my proposal. I'm excited for her answer, but at the same time, I feel apprehensive about her possible rejection.

I yawn and turn onto my side. Rachael is still asleep, curled around me like a vine. Her sweet rose scent fills my nostrils. I peel myself away from her as subtly as I can, not wanting to disturb her. She murmurs something unintelligible in her sleep. I stifle a laugh and tiptoe out of the bedroom. *Time to make her breakfast in bed. Let's hope I don't screw it up this time.* I head into the kitchen and look in the fridge. I opt to make her egg on toast. *I can't burn that, surely.* I place a frying pan on the stove and heat a little oil. I place a slice of bread in the toaster, then crack a couple of eggs into the now hot pan. The egg spits and hisses violently, I turn down the heat and start on her coffee. I smell smoke coming from behind me. *Oh, not again.* I swing round and see smoke coming from the toaster. I pop the toast, but it's black. I sigh and try again. Finally, after my third attempt, I have succeeded to make toast. I place it on a plate and put the egg on top. I put her breakfast on a tray with her coffee and walk back into the bedroom. She is still asleep, and I feel bad about waking her. I sit on the edge beside her and gently comb her hair out of her face. She stirs and opens her bright hazel eyes. She smiles sleepily up at me.

"Happy Birthday, Rachael. I've made you breakfast."

She sits up, yawning as I place the tray on her lap. She looks down at it and giggles.

"You managed not to burn the apartment down."

My smile fades and my face heats, embarrassed. She strokes my face tenderly and kisses me on the forehead.

"Thank you," she whispers.

I grin, satisfied as she starts on her breakfast eagerly. I drink my mug of coffee, but don't feel like eating; my stomach is a ball of nerves.

After breakfast, we get ready to head out. I have changed into my charcoal suit and the ring is tucked safely into my inside pocket. It's strange that only a few weeks ago, I wore this same suit to court to beg for my freedom, now I'm wearing it for a much happier occasion. Rachael looks amazing in her tight black jeans, white chucks and a flowing blue blouse.

"Ready?" I ask.

She nods excitedly. I take her hand and leave the apartment, locking the front door behind us.

It's a bright but chilly day as we walk through Central Park, heading for Wollman Rink. We arrive and are handed our skates. I sit on the bench beside Rachael, pull on my skates and lace them up. Rachael already has hers on, but she looks towards the ice nervously. I touch her hand, which encourages her to look at me.

"You'll be fine."

She smiles but still looks unsure. I stand first and offer her my hand. She looks at it, then after some hesitation, she takes it. We slowly wobble to the ice. I step onto the ice and start to skate in a circuit. Rachael stands on the sidelines watching cautiously. I skate back to her quickly.

"It'll be okay. C'mon," I reassure.

She takes both my hands, and ever so carefully steps onto the ice with me. She wobbles and falls slightly, but I catch her and lead her to the edge where she can hold on for support. She clutches the edge and refuses to let go. I skate backwards, away from her.

"See, nothing to it," I call.

She smiles and rolls her eyes.

"You're showing off now."

I skate back over and offer both my hands again. She remains hesitant, but then slowly accepts them. I gently pull her away from the edge and into the middle of the rink. She looks back towards the safety of the edge, but I try to steady her nerves.

"It's all about balance on the blades," I explain.

She looks down at her skates, and back at me with a puzzled look.

"How am I supposed to balance on them? Look how thin they are." She points down at her boots.

"Don't think about it. Pretend you're walking."

She gives it a go, but again, falls slightly.

"I can't do this," she says.

"Of course, you can. Keep trying," I encourage.

She tries several more times, but is still struggling. I lead her back to the edge, where she clings.

"Watch me," I say and glide with ease around the circuit again.

She continues to watch me closely from the edge, then she ever so slowly attempts to move her feet. I go back and she grabs hold of my jacket. Slowly, I pull her away from the edge and this time, she moves her feet in a walking motion.

"You got it," I say as I take her hands.

She smiles proudly and has the confidence to let go of me. Now, she's skating on her own. I stay alongside her, just in case. She beams.

"When did you learn to skate?" she asks, suddenly curious.

"I played with my school hockey team. Best young years I had."

She tries to pick up speed, getting too cocky for her own good. She slips and falls backwards. I attempt to save her, but she grabs my jacket and pulls me down with her. We land with a loud bang on the ice.

"Tuck your fingers in," I instruct quickly.

We both clench our hands into fists to avoid the blades from the other skaters around us. I carefully get to my feet and pull her up with me. I examine her.

"Are you okay?" I ask.

She nods, then bursts into fits of laughter. I try to keep a straight face, but it's infectious. Soon, I can't help myself.

After struggling back onto dry land, we are both cold and a bit wet. I take my skates off, then help Rachael with hers. We put our normal shoes back on and leave Wollman Rink.

"What's next?" she asks.

"I have an idea. Follow me."

She takes my outstretched hand and we walk towards Bow Bridge. I hope Trent has set up my arrangements in time.

We are on our final stretch that leads to the bridge. I take a nervous breath, then stop to regain my composure. Rachael stands at my side and stares at me with concern.

"You alright? You're awfully pale."

She touches my face.

"I'm fine. Let's go."

We keep walking and round the last corner. Trent is standing, waiting for us.

"Trent, hey." Rachael rushes over and hugs him happily.

"What are you doing here?" she continues.

He looks at me, and I shake my head subtly, silently gesturing for him not to spill the beans. He grins cheekily back at Rachael.

"Just wanted to wish you a happy birthday. Um... Happy Birthday."

I palm my face and scowl in Trent's direction.

"Idiot," I mouth at him silently so Rachael doesn't hear.

She looks back at me and Trent shrugs.

"What are you boys up to?" she says, eyeing me suspiciously. "Follow me."

I gesture with my hand and lead her towards Bow Bridge. I'm the first to see it. Trent has done well. The bridge is decorated with fairy lights and flowers. There are tea lights in small vases on the ground leading to it. Rex stands at the other end, controlling the interested crowd. Rachael notices and looks from me to Trent, then to the bridge.

"Oh my god. What is this?" she gasps in astonishment.

I lead her onto the bridge, and she admires the flowers.

"Mark. This is beautiful."

She's lost for words as she delicately strokes and smells the flowers. *This is it. No turning back.* With one final nervous breath, I clutch Rachael's hand tightly and sink down onto one knee. Her hand flies to her mouth as her eyes brim with tears. The crowd Rex is patrolling are now peeking over with interest, murmuring in disbelief.

"Rachael, from the moment I saw you, I was in love. Your kindness, wisdom and beauty are above anything I could have wished for."

I pull the diamond ring from my pocket and hold it up to her. She's now weeping incessantly, muffled by her hands.

"I can't imagine life without you. Please be mine, always. I love you. Marry me."

Tears start rolling down her face as she continues to look at me. My heart is beating faster than it ever has before as I wait for her answer.

"Yes… I will," she finally whispers.

I slide the ring onto her finger, then she joins me on the floor, kissing me hard. We are deafened by a round of applause. I stand her up and press her hard against me as we continue to embrace each other with a loving, fierce passion. The crowd around us, including Trent and Rex, continue to cheer and clap. She examines her ring and laughs loudly.

"I knew you were up to something."

I smile and laugh.

"Just don't arrest me," I joke.

She laughs loudly, her head thrown back then she kisses me hard again. In this moment of pure bliss, I don't know how I got so lucky. This woman, Rachael Clarke, has loved me like no one else has and I love her so much. My sweet girl, my Rachael, my arresting officer, now my soon-to-be wife.

Lightning Source UK Ltd.
Milton Keynes UK
UKHW010727011220
374435UK00001B/256